Knowing You

SAMANTHA TONGE

KNOWING YOU

CANELO

First published in the United Kingdom in 2019 by Canelo

Canelo Digital Publishing Limited
57 Shepherds Lane
Beaconsfield, Bucks HP9 2DU
United Kingdom

A CIP catalogue record for this book is available from the British Library.

Print ISBN 978 1 78863 515 8
Ebook ISBN 978 1 78863 221 8

Look for more great books at www.canelo.co

For Martin,
the best friend anyone could have

Chapter 1

'Starting a new fashion?' says a tall man in a cap. He's wearing sunglasses even though it's winter and is squashed against me on the busy train.

I look down. This crowded space is sweltering, so I took off my coat and accidentally revealed that my jumper is on inside out. I blush but the man raises one eyebrow and makes me laugh.

'Hey, it doesn't matter, your hair is a great distraction – the curls are fantastic.'

We both grin. Clearly he's being polite. They are wilder than usual. Brushing them wasn't a priority when faced with being late to work because I wanted to spend as much of Valentine's Day as possible with Lenny.

Humming, I emerge from the musty depths of the London underground and make my way to Thoth Publishing. Thoth was the Ancient Egyptian god of writing. It was the unusual name that had first attracted me to the company. Historical words sound so solid and reliable. I push through the rotating doors and head to the silver lift. It slides open. I enter and press number three. Moments later, I reach the editorial floor just one minute after nine o'clock. I go into the staff kitchen, fill a miniature watering can and, before anything else, revive my desk plant.

'You must be desperate for your mid-week drink,' I say to the wilting flower heads.

'They can't understand, you know,' says my senior editor in an affectionate tone, putting two cups of tea on the desks.

'For a children's fiction editor, Irfan, you don't half lack imagination.'

I change out of my rain-splashed trainers and into smarter flat shoes. As a child, I used to share my secrets with a favourite cactus and Tinker the cat. I'd also chat with teddies and felt pangs of guilt when Mum eventually disposed of them at the charity shop.

After taking off my aubergine-coloured duffle coat and my bobble hat, I sit down. The office is open plan and I'm opposite Irfan. My space is organised and neat, with a pen tidy, a tub of multi-coloured paper clips, a photo of me and Lenny, a jar of cookies and a packet of keyboard cleaner wipes. Irfan teases me for using them every night.

I stare at the photo and think back to this morning. Lenny mumbled something about me being a great person. I teased him that he was only saying it because I cooked him egg and chips last night. He loves home comfort food. When eating out, Lenny only pretends to prefer high-end dishes. I wrapped my arms around his neck and moved in for a kiss, soaking up the intimacy that had been missing of late. In recent weeks he's seemed so stressed, working into the night and coming in with just enough energy to brush his teeth before bed.

It's Wednesday, my day for tackling submissions. I feel like a Gold Rush miner with a pan in his hand. I'm so lucky to be a junior editor working alongside Irfan after being promoted from publishing assistant. Lenny is trying to push his career forwards. He's still learning the ropes at a literary agency, and running its social media platforms has become a favourite part of his job. He's always attending some blogger get-together or book launch. No canapés go unsnapped for Instagram. No snippet of book news swerves his Twitter feed.

I pick a manuscript off the top of my pile. He keeps telling me to photograph our cat Flossie posed next to my authors' books in order to raise my profile but I don't require lots of followers or likes, because I reckon I have everything I need – although a new car that doesn't stall quite so often would be appreciated, along with a boiler that hasn't got a mind of its own. I have Lenny, a job I love and Flossie. Warmth radiates through my chest as I think back to this morning and how things felt like they had when we first got together. Lenny and I are celebrating Valentine's properly tonight but a rare spontaneous thought jumps into my mind. I know he said he'd be busy today, but everyone needs to eat – at lunch I'll pop over to his offices to surprise him.

At midday sharp, I wrap up well again. I head downstairs and into the reception. From his curved white desk, Hugo catches my eye. A gym fanatic, he looks strong enough to flick the desk across the building. Hugo's a people person and prides himself on knowing agents, authors and publishers on sight from memorising so many profile pictures. He shoots me his usual smile, which is warmer than his efficient one for senior editors but less flirtatious than that reserved for the young female interns.

I hurry to the nearby Euston underground station. An icy wind cuts across my face and I hitch up my scarf to cover my mouth. The earlier rain has morphed into small flakes of snow. My body rocks from side to side as I try to keep my balance in the stuffy train.

I climb up steps into the fresh air and spot the waffle house where we had our first date. We'd almost walked past, but a whiff of something toasty stopped my feet. Its door had creaked a welcome, which was seconded by the gurgle of a coffee machine. Soft jazz played and tangerine flames licked the top of the fireplace. Sweet and savoury smells jostled for our attention. We'd talked about our favourite authors and mutual obsession with Harry Potter. The conversation felt easy as we finished each other's sentences.

I'm just about to turn away when I see – is that Lenny in the window? I cross the road and push open the waffle house's door, my anticipation rewarded by the familiar creak. Despite not having been here for a while, it hasn't changed one bit apart from the vases of red roses for Valentine's Day. I walk in and warmth massages my shoulders. This February is so cold I'm wearing eighty denier tights under my trousers, which was my neighbour Kath's tip.

Lenny is sitting opposite a woman and his whole body spells enjoyment, from his gesticulating hands to his spread-eagled thighs. She must be a size eight and wears a stylish tailored trouser suit. Her ash blonde bob has been dip-dyed in pink and—

Oh my goodness. It's Beatrix Bingham. I can't believe it.

Along with my boss Felicity, she's one of the most respected science fiction editors in the industry. I've followed her career since my first internship and seen her at a couple of work functions. She edited the well-known *Earth Gazer* series. Felicity has never really got over missing out on that acquisition. The books charted high all over the world and the film adaptation of the second book is currently being screened. Science fiction isn't my favourite genre, but Beatrix's career is such an inspiration. She's razor sharp and one of London's publishing darlings. She's achieved so much and only just turned thirty. My pulse quickens.

I hold back for a second, take off my gloves and wipe my nose with a tissue. I pull off my hat and attempt to smooth down my hair. It hangs way past my shoulders but due to the curls looks much shorter. It's strange that Lenny didn't mention their meeting. He knows that I always read her blog. She replied to one of my comments once and I screenshot it. He'd teased me about how excited I was.

Her laugh flutters across the room like a butterfly. This is a dream come true. I cross the room and squeeze his shoulder.

Lenny looks up. 'Violet. What are you doing here?'

'I thought I'd surprise you, but should have realised you might have a lunchtime meeting.'

His cheeks flush. 'Yes. Sorry. I can't just—'

'Don't worry. I needed some fresh air anyway.' Lenny must be truly surprised because he doesn't introduce me to Beatrix. I hold out my hand. To my embarrassment, it shakes. Beatrix is such an influencer. She oozes the professional confidence I hope to acquire one day. 'It's fantastic to meet you. I've followed your career for years. Watching your progress has encouraged me no end. I'm Violet Vaughan from Thoth Publishing.'

After pausing, Beatrix takes my fingers. Hers feel limp.

'Can I just say,' she says in a cool voice, 'what an unusual coat. How very brave of you to wear it.'

Is it?

'Trixie – Beatrix – is heading up a new imprint called *Out There Stories*,' says Lenny quickly.

Trixie? Imagine being on such familiar terms with your professional idol.

'So I hear. Congratulations. It all sounds very exciting.' I'd registered Beatrix's name with Google Alerts years ago. I was in awe of how quickly she was climbing the publishing ladder. Whenever a new intern starts at Thoth, I always tell them to follow her blog. She's especially supportive of raising the profile of female authors, and frequently runs competitions for giving feedback on women writers' work. 'When exactly does it launch?'

'In September. I'm looking for some really stand out novels to make an impact,' she says without looking at me. She glances at Lenny instead and picks up her phone, punching at it with polished nails that look more like claws.

I stand waiting for Lenny to say something. Why is this encounter so stilted? I still don't understand why they've met up for lunch and how they know each other so well.

He shuffles in his seat. 'Beatrix loves Casey Wilde,' he blurts out as if to fill the silence.

What? Lenny's shown an editor the manuscript he's been most excited about in ages? Wilde is one of his agency's new authors whose book would be perfect for Beatrix's new imprint. But it's not out on submission yet and Lenny could get into trouble.

Her shoulders relax and she looks up. 'It's been a real honour to have a look at her work before it's quite ready for submission. *Alien Hearts* is a romantic masterpiece. And feminist. It's completely captured the emotions behind the Time's Up movement.'

I still can't believe Beatrix has enjoyed a pre-submission sneak peek. Lenny and I routinely let each other look at manuscripts not yet in the public arena, but that's just for the joy of reading and is kept strictly between us.

'I was almost in tears when I read that last chapter,' I say. 'It's incredibly sad when the alien is forced to kill the man she's fallen in love with.'

'I don't know anyone who's kept a dry eye during those final paragraphs,' says Lenny enthusiastically. 'Just imagine it as a film. Jennifer Lawrence would smash playing the lead.'

'I cried too,' says Beatrix. 'Tears of joy at the money Alpaca Books and Casey Wilde are going to make.' She looks at her watch and back at Lenny.

'Well, best of luck with *Out There Stories*,' I say brightly. 'And it would be great to see you at Thoth's twentieth birthday party in a few months. We've posted over one hundred invitations. I hope you received yours. It's all rather exciting.'

The invitations were written in scroll fashion and sent out in cardboard tubes thanks to Thoth Publishing's name having Ancient Egyptian origins. We'd booked a boutique hotel called Anubis opposite Hyde Park. Hoping that the party would raise the company's profile, Felicity had provided a more than decent budget.

However, Beatrix doesn't appear to have heard and taps on her phone again.

'I'll ring you later,' says Lenny with an apologetic look as I turn to leave.

Chapter 2

'You've hardly said a word since you got back from lunch. Shall I take you to A & E?' Irfan smiles and points to his watch. I give the thumbs up. In ten minutes, our meeting with author Gary Smith should begin. I put my jumper on the right way and focus again on my screen. Something about my encounter with Beatrix was definitely off. I'm still a little flummoxed as to why Lenny's never mentioned meeting her.

I decide to search on Twitter for clues, although I don't really know what I'm looking for. I log in and visit her feed. I scroll through the tweets about new authors' books, recently signed deals and publishing jokes. Then a couple from a few weeks ago catch my attention. Beatrix sent Lenny a humorous meme about acquiring new authors. He replied with a dancing alien gif.

I scroll further back to find more innocuous tweets that wouldn't merit a second glance to anyone else. What piques my interest is the occasional one that has nothing to do with work. I pick up my phone and open Instagram. I've only posted twenty-two photos in six months and haven't looked at friends' pictures since Christmas. I go to Lenny's page. He posts at least a couple a day. I skim the images of fancy food, book covers and launches.

I'm just about to log out when I spot a selfie of him and Beatrix. I screw up my eyes and stare at the surroundings. It's the cafe at Waterstones Piccadilly that looks more like a restaurant and is a favourite venue for book launches. Yet this snap strikes me as so personal. Lenny's arm is around her shoulders and they're cheek-to-cheek as if taking part in some intimate dance.

I take in her statement necklace, the perfect scarlet lipstick and matching nails. For the first time, I detail her appearance instead of her achievements. I take a deep breath and exit the app, observing how my nails looked stubby and cracked. Twenty minutes have passed and Gary hasn't arrived. Irfan and I head to the side room regardless. It's always been my dream to help writers realise theirs. When I was little, Uncle Kevin told me I could achieve whatever I wanted. I finger the silver book pendant around my neck that he gave me before he moved to New York.

I follow Irfan through the office and my eyes stray to the huge windows on the left. Fat snowflakes tumble through the air like polystyrene loose fill, as if I'm in a snow globe turned inside out. Kath won't be pleased. Her shoulder still isn't right since slipping on ice last month. I'll pop in after work to see if she's dared to venture out.

I push open the door and we enter the small room. I've already set out a selection of biscuits and the coffee is brewing. We sit down in the comfortable chairs and I slip a small circle of shortbread into my mouth. Whilst Irfan sorts through his paperwork, my thoughts are pulled back to Lenny and Beatrix.

It's like when I read an author's first draft and haven't yet pinpointed exactly what isn't right.

Irfan sighs and stares at the sweet treats. He pats the stomach that his doctor thinks needs to be smaller. 'I could do with cheering up since Farah's decided to tackle my diabetes risk and put me on a health kick.'

'Don't worry. I've just the thing for you.' I stand up and reach for a plate next to the coffee pot. 'Gary said that he's also under doctor's orders to change his diet, remember?' I put down a platter of neatly lined up vegetable sticks and dip. 'I got these just in case he doesn't want biscuits.'

'I might say something rude if I wasn't full of admiration – as usual – for your attention to detail.'

I like Irfan, as well as computer consultant Farah. Sometimes she meets him after work for a meal out or theatre trip. Now and again they invite me over for dinner. She makes the best onion bhajis. They melt in the mouth. I make them laugh with my lack of faith in dishwashers and insistence that I clean the plates by hand. Sometimes after work I'll take them for coffee. Farah and I drink ours unadulterated black while Irfan enjoys indulgent creations like hazelnut lattes. We pick her brain about computer problems. An avid reader, Farah asks us about Thoth's latest acquisitions.

The two of them look like a good match as much as Lenny and I don't. They both dress down for work in jeans, love musicals and spend holidays hiking in the wild.

Lenny and I once had one of those indulgent conversations that new couples enjoy. He'd wanted to know what I thought of him in bed. I said his oil massages were second to none and loved the fact that he didn't enjoy sex unless I had. Then I asked him what he liked about me. This was one year ago, just after we'd moved into the flat. Lenny said he liked the way I kissed. On a more practical note, he praised the way I made cheese and pickle rolls.

Eventually my probe burrowed through the surface.

'You're sort of like my… keepsafe,' he said. 'Moving to the capital was daunting. I missed the easy, cosseted student life. You made London feel like a home and helped me focus on my career.'

I had studied English in Durham, while Lenny went to Manchester Metropolitan. We met in The British Library almost two years ago, a few weeks after moving to the city and into tiny bedsits. We'd both been mature students, taking a gap year after the sixth form to do internships.

I guess I'm lucky. I've always enjoyed that feeling of being at home as long as there's a good book between my hands. Lenny's revelation made me realise I'm his go-to book in a way. I make him feel safe in a world of chaos. He said he loves that *about* me which must be the same as saying those three magic words straight. So I've written them in his Valentine's Day card. I feel like I should have reciprocated his declaration by now. We were in too much of a rush to exchange presents this morning. I can't wait until tonight when I cook him a special Valentine's dinner.

Irfan looks at his watch again.

'I'll go down to reception,' I say.

When I arrive, all is quiet. Snow is settling outside. 'Our author should be here by now.'

Hugo shrugs. 'Perhaps it's this weather. I can't say I'm looking forward to bracing it tonight. You must have had a large incentive to go out earlier – perhaps a romantic lunch?' He pulls a face. 'I'm helping Dad decorate his kitchen today. Not sure how I ended up without a date on the one day of the year a meal out is most likely to end with a shag.'

I shake my head and he laughs.

'You know I only say things like that to wind you up.'

It's true. Hugo's no misogynist. He's popular with the opposite sex because he shows respect. It's his commitment that's lacking and he rarely dates the same woman for longer than a few weeks.

His desk props me up. 'I wanted to surprise Lenny. Take him to lunch.'

'I hope he ended up paying as recompense for you braving the cold.'

'Not exactly. He was in the waffle house with someone else.'

'Business?' Hugo yawns.

What can I say? Casey Wilde's book isn't out on submission yet.

'Networking.' I gaze at Hugo. He knows everything about everyone, from professional achievements to random details. That includes me. A bookseller once emailed because Hugo told him I baked the best brownies this side of the Atlantic. He wanted the recipe for his Californian wife's birthday.

'Lenny was meeting Beatrix Bingham.'

It's not how Hugo reacts – it's how he doesn't, by concentrating on the signing-in book even harder, as if it were a newly discovered Dickens manuscript. He's remarkably quiet.

'Have you ever met her?' I ask and raise my eyebrows. Hugo and I get on well. Sometimes we eat lunch together. He'll give me the run-down on any agent I'm due to meet and of course, we'll talk books. Hugo loves Young Adult fiction. We're both huge fans of John Green. He'll try to show me photos of his latest date but I always refuse, citing no need. She'll have straightened hair, look athletic and well-groomed. We joke that his type is the antithesis of me.

'I've seen her a few times, most recently at Waterstones Piccadilly for a book launch last month.' He runs a finger down signatures and focuses on a name that didn't sign out.

'No doubt she's on your hit list even though she's way out of your league.' I keep the tone light.

'I'd probably be in with a chance. She likes younger men.'

We don't speak for a few moments and I realise I've folded my arms.

'What do you mean?' I ask eventually.

No response.

'Hugo?'

The phone rings. He picks it up. Expresses sympathy. Hangs up. 'That was Gary Smith. His bike skidded on ice. He's okay but the chain's broken. He'll have to reschedule.' Hugo shakes his head. 'What sort of idiot cycles in this weather?'

'An ambitious author who combines novel-writing with another job to pay the bills. Gary doesn't like spending money on public transport. Anyway, what were you saying about Beatrix?'

'Oh, nothing much. She's recently bought a Mazda MX-5.'

'Nice.'

'Don't pretend you have any idea what that looks like.'

Our eyes smile.

'What's more, next week she's moving into a penthouse flat overlooking the Thames. Her Instagram shots look amazing. It must have cost a packet.'

'She deserves it – but that doesn't explain what you meant about her and younger men.'

Hugo runs a hand through his slicked back blonde hair. 'Just another conspiracy theory. You know how publishing is full of them, like—'

'So what's the theory about Beatrix Bingham?'

He shrugs. 'It's just… take John Bennett—'

'Who wrote the *Earth Gazer* series?'

'Yes. He'd just left university. They dated for six months.' He stares at the signing-in book once more. 'Funny how she ditched him once the deal was signed.'

'Perhaps the relationship just came to its natural end. Or she felt their professional relationship was more important.'

'But then there was that young editor she dated who started out at Bloomsbury,' he continued, warming to his subject. 'All the books he worked on hit the Sunday Times List. He moved to Alpaca Books. Their romance ended shortly afterwards.'

'If you're implying that she was able to just use… I mean, really… these are intelligent men.'

'Who partly think with their pants.'

'Hugo. You can't say this about her. And would she really take such risks? It's a dangerous strategy that could so easily backfire.'

He shrugged.

'And it's slander apart from anything else. Beatrix's form as an influential member of the industry should tell you that her editing skills are attractive enough.'

'I'm not denying that. Nor implying she's falling back on womanly wiles. Really, I see her more as a ruthless player who's in charge and will use any extra tools in her arsenal to cut the deal when required. If anything, I admire her.'

'I still think—'

'Violet, this theory isn't something I've created. Speculation has been rife for a while. And you're right – it is dangerous, she should be more careful. Her reputation and professionalism could be at stake. There's a difference between ambition and recklessness. It's becoming increasingly obvious that if a younger man has got something she wants, Beatrix uses whatever assets she's got to acquire it. Not that she'd stand a chance with Lenny, obviously – what with him dating one of the most genuine people I know.' He gives me a good-humoured wink. 'And Lenny is only an assistant. It's not as if he's got his hands on anything for her to chase, right?'

He answers the phone and I head back to the lift, glad he can't see my face.

Chapter 3

I shuffle to get comfortable on the sofa, appreciating the soft velvet throw after an afternoon sitting on office chairs. I chose the yellow, terracotta and cream colour for furnishings to make our home look as cosy as possible, like it's a summer afternoon all year around. Flossie is lying next to me and lifts her head. We exchange looks before she curls into a cinnamon swirl.

The flat's layout is simple with two decent-sized bedrooms. The main one has a modest balcony, a favourite spot even though it overlooks a busy road. There is just enough room for my window boxes and a line of washing. I gaze at the wall above my fireplace. To the right of the rectangular mirror is my cuckoo clock. Uncle Kevin the financial whizz gave it to me years ago after a business trip to Munich. The wooden bird has just shot out to announce eight o'clock.

I stroke Flossie's back. She purrs and gives a shuddering stretch before her body pings back into a circle. I get up to check on Lenny's favourite lasagne. The kitchen is small but I prefer it enclosed so that cooking smells don't invade the living area. The tomato sauce is a bit dry now. It's a shame Lenny couldn't get home earlier, but he's doing everything possible to be considered for promotion. His agency normally closes its doors at six, but over the last month he has signed several new authors and Lenny likes to show goodwill by putting in extra hours. I consider taking the dish out of the oven when a key turns in the lock. I open the oven door and put in the garlic bread before going back into the lounge.

'That weather… I'm surprised the busses are still running.' He takes off his black mackintosh and shakes it in the corridor before coming in. Lenny hangs it up on the coat stand to his left. The cold air has made his skin glow. His eyes sparkle. I head over and we embrace. If I ever have a bad day and get a sinking feeling, Lenny's hugs are like buoys that keep me afloat. He wrinkles his nose. 'Mmm. Beef. Pasta.' He squeezes me tight for a second. 'You really are too good to me. I… I appreciate it.'

'Guess what's for dessert.' Nothing makes me feel better than making others happy. It started when I was old enough to look after Mum, in little ways, when she was working all hours. I did what I could to make her day easier, at first preparing straightforward meals like beans on toast. Eventually I progressed to omelettes. Mum was always so grateful and her worry lines became less deep if I also dusted or cleaned the bathroom.

'Not chocolate tart?'

'Opportunity knocked last night, seeing as you were out all evening at that book launch.'

'And thanks for ironing me a shirt for today. I'll just grab a really quick shower and then fetch your Valentine's present.' He disappears into our bedroom and comes back with a small gift bag. I don't need to open it. He always gets me the same book voucher and milk chocolates for birthdays, Christmas and Valentine's. It might not be the most imaginative gift, but it's perfect for me.

As promised, he's ready ten minutes later and we sit down to eat. Lenny uncorks wine and I serve the food. I've decided to broach the subject of Beatrix but I'm not sure how. It's still hardly sunk in that my idol could potentially be after my boyfriend. He needs to know about Hugo's claims and that she'll do anything to acquire *Alien Hearts*. He's on the cusp of becoming a fully-fledged agent and looking for that one big deal that will finally impress his agency. Lenny has been desperate for promotion. That makes him vulnerable to being exploited. He's already secretly shown Beatrix the manuscript. If she tells anyone, that could jeopardise his professional integrity. His agency won't want a partner who isn't transparent.

We eat the lasagne and playfully fight over the last chunk of garlic bread. After dessert we retire to the sofa. He pushes Flossie off and we snuggle up.

'Beatrix's imprint sounds interesting,' I say. 'Under her leadership it's bound to be a huge success.'

Lenny removes his arm from around my shoulder and picks up his glass of wine. 'She's a very persuasive woman – and a hard worker.' He clears his throat. 'Sorry about lunch time. I think the build up to *Out There Stories*' launch is taking its toll. I'm sure she didn't mean to be rude.'

I pour myself another glass of wine. Lenny touches my hand and his face splits into a grin.

'Two glasses? Violet? What's going on?'

As our skin touches, I feel the familiar jolt of attraction. In physics, neutrality is a rather wonderful thing. It produces stability. It's achieved through the attraction of opposites. Electrons and protons. Lenny and me.

I run my finger around the rim. 'Can I talk to you about something?'

'Everything okay?' He puts down his wine and gives me his full attention.

I tell him what Hugo said without revealing my source.

Lenny shakes his head. 'What absolute rubbish. Nothing but jealously spawns these rumours. You should know that.'

'I was surprised – but what other explanation is there?' Since talking to Hugo, I'd thought of more examples. Like the debut science fiction author she was known to have dated and snatched from HarperCollins. Word got around that they'd offered him a generous advance and the industry was flummoxed when he signed with Alpaca Books.

'Beatrix is at the top of her game,' says Lenny. 'She doesn't need to trade on her good looks. She'd heard about *Alien Hearts* and became so excited when I told her more about the plot. She didn't ask to see it, I offered. Beatrix is a complete professional. Showing her is no big deal. She'll keep schtum.'

'You know she's an absolute hero of mine. I just thought I ought to mention it. You've slogged hard to get this far and are on the verge of getting your own author list. I wouldn't want to see your reputation questioned in any way if the agency found out you'd shown the manuscript around.'

He pushes up his sleeves. 'If she's got a track record of ensnaring younger men, why doesn't she just go directly to Casey?'

'Because I realised at lunch time you haven't told her he's really a man.'

Like a starstruck fan, Lenny once showed me an author photo, saying he wrote so well about women that he must have been on hundreds of dates. Casey's tall, striking, with jet black hair and inky eyes. Lenny says Casey's ambitious and driven and is unsure whether to reveal his male identity, concerned that it might put off readers.

'Look, I'm not worried about Beatrix. Can't we leave it at that? Let's not spend our special evening talking about her – or Casey. How about I make coffee?'

He strokes my arm. Lenny's touch feels so good. From the first time we had sex, it was as if a switch had been flipped. It illuminated a universe of sensual pleasure.

I meet his boyish smile. Dean Martin's *Volare* plays in the background on one of the old CDs that Uncle Kevin couldn't take with him when he moved to America. I intertwine my fingers with Lenny's. We stand up. My hands slip around his neck. His go around my back. We sway side to side in perfect rhythm and I close my eyes. Our mouths meet. His hands trail my spine as we move as close as we can.

As the song comes to an end, I reluctantly pull away. We chat over coffee. I tell him about a new author we've signed who's well-known for her bestselling erotica. She's secretly always wanted to write children's stories and has been given a two-book deal under a pseudonym.

'And how was your day?' I ask.

'Busy. Sorry, again, that we couldn't have lunch.' He sighed. 'After meeting Trixie, things got a bit boring, to be honest. An afternoon spent sending out rejection letters is far from inspiring. It's hard, you know, still doing so much of the mundane stuff. If I don't get my own list this year…' His downturned mouth reflects the missing words.

'You will, Lenny. If not where you are, then at another agency. You've gained so much experience and got yourself out there, networking, in a way I never could. It'll happen, there's no doubt about it. Keep on keeping on.'

He takes my hand, lifts it and presses his lips against my palm.

'We've both come such a long way,' I say, gently. 'Remember when we first met and were still finding our way around the city?'

'It took me long enough to become familiar with the British Library. I don't know what I'd have done without you.'

I rub his arm. 'It won't be long before authors are queuing up to sign with you.' I kiss him on the cheek. Lenny clears his throat, gets up and disappears into the kitchen.

'I'll tidy up,' he calls.

I head into our bedroom to fetch his present, but first I pick his damp towel off the floor and drape it over the radiator. I drag the long, wrapped box out from under the bed. Lenny took up golf a while back so I splashed out and bought him a top-of-the-range putter. I'm just about to leave when Lenny's phone gives a low buzz on the bed. I pick it up to give it to him and the text notification on the front flashes at me.

It's from Beatrix.

Without thinking, I read the first line.

'I'm going to miss you, Violet,' Uncle Kevin says as we sit in the park near my new home. It's a place with blackbirds and robins, with twitchy-tailed squirrels and a rainbow of flowers planted to spell the word Welcome. Our legs are stretched out. We're both wearing odd socks. Uncle Kevin says life isn't about making things match up.

We've just eaten ice cream and I wipe my mouth with the back of my hand. Uncle Kevin rolls his eyes and points to my T-shirt. I look down and straightaway he catches my nose with one of his fingers. I giggle and pretend to look cross. There's no stain on my top. He catches me out every time with this trick.

One of the swings becomes free and Uncle Kevin jerks his head. I follow him over and sit down. He goes behind and reminds me to hold on tight. Then he pushes hard. I squeal as the swing rises high in the air. It's as if I'm flying and I pretend I'm sitting in Enid Blyton's Wishing-Chair.

Eventually we end up back on the bench. We talk about the latest book I'm reading and share a water bottle. Most of my friends won't because they worry about the spit. Uncle Kevin says I'm a practical person. He says that's a gift, but I'm not sure what he means. Sharing water bottles doesn't involve pretty paper or surprises.

The two of us fall silent for a moment.

'What are you thinking?' he says.

'That I'm going to miss you too,' I say and kick at the ground, almost taking the head off a beetle with a back so shiny that it looks like metal.

We're sitting underneath an oak tree in Applegrove Park, six houses down from ours. It's small with a slide and two swings. The fencing at the back is broken and behind it is the much bigger Applegrove Wood, which runs along the back of all the houses. It looks dark and exciting. I'm glad for the shade from the oak, my favourite tree. The curvy outline of its leaves looks as if someone has been doodling. My underarms are sticky and strands of hair stick to my face.

I've been dreading tomorrow for weeks. It's two days after my birthday. I turned seven yesterday. Mum says seven is very grown up. So I guess that means I mustn't make a fuss.

Chapter 4

I turn into a parking space outside the Sunflower retirement home. It looks more like a hotel, with the white pillars and regimented flower beds. It's a Sunday afternoon and three weeks since Valentine's Day. I drive forwards and then backwards a few times to get the angle of the car just right. My neighbour Kath is in the passenger seat and looks at her watch.

'Ten to two. You know the others. They won't be ready early. Let's just stay here for a moment.'

About nine months ago, I started to give Kath lifts here to see her friend, Nora. She introduced me and we got to talking about books. Another resident joined in. That's when I hit upon the idea of setting up a book club.

This is the first meeting I've felt up to attending since I found Beatrix's text.

'Perhaps we should wait in the reception area,' I say brightly and shiver. 'We'll catch our death staying in the car.' The door squeaks as I open it. A hand gently holds me back.

'How are things going? You've been a treasure these last few weeks, helping me with that shoulder cream as well as dropping off shopping as usual, but you've not mentioned Lenny. I've not pushed, but—'

'What is there to say?'

Spindly fingers poking out of a practical anorak squeeze my arm. 'I'm just worried, sweetheart. Are you eating properly? You just picked at the cake I offered you yesterday.'

'My appetite's just been off.'

'Has Lenny been in touch?'

I sigh and close the door. 'I told him to leave. He seemed to think we could still be friends.' A pain that's all too familiar grips my chest as if fists are wringing out my lungs. It's a pain I haven't felt for a long, long time. Not since what happened to Uncle Kevin.

At first I used to struggle with my strong emotional connection with Lenny. I've always been an independent woman – Mum drilled the importance of that into me. I pay my own bills. I speak my mind at work. I'm following my passion. I've gladly embraced the single life, having learnt that when you rely on someone, fate can snatch them away in the most decisive manner.

But then I met Lenny, and me became we.

'What did he say when you showed him the text? Talk to me, Violet. If my years of nursing taught me anything, it's that holding things in never did anyone any good.'

I study her soft white hair cut into a neat bob. She wears no make-up apart from a slash of pink across the mouth that rarely utters an unkind word. Concern deepens the map of lines on her face that betray years of working nights. She's wearing her usual fit-for-all-occasions slacks.

Normally Kath and I can't chat enough. We became friends after I found her in the ground floor hallway. She'd had a nasty fall on getting back from her weekly shift at a conservation charity shop. To thank me for taking her to the surgery, she'd baked a cake and invited me up to her flat, which is above mine. As soon as I saw her shelves full of books and framed photos of pets and safari holidays, I knew we'd be friends. She loves animals but her nephew, Norm, won't even let her have a goldfish in his flat. At the request of his mum, Kath's sister, he begrudgingly rents it to her at a low rate because her pension is so small.

We came to an agreement that she should bang her broom on her floor if she needs help. The flat feels so empty now, so quiet, and I wish feisty Kath would ask for help more often. When I knew last year that London would be my forever home, instead of renting I dipped into family savings put aside for me. It made sense for Lenny to move in.

'Violet?' Kath cocks her head and nods encouragement.

'In the end, Lenny didn't even try to lie. I read out Beatrix's text and he crumbled. I hadn't really believed it. I can't believe I told myself that her message must have been a joke.'

'Oh, darling…'

'I know. Talk about naive. Of course it makes complete sense now – all those late nights he spent supposedly at work. He spent half an hour saying that things had just been difficult, with him worrying about getting a promotion and having to put superhuman effort into his job. He mumbled some vague apology and gave a little speech about how we'd grown apart. How neither he nor Beatrix could fight the attraction.' My voice breaks. 'It makes me realise that he only really saw me as some sort of homely comfort in a strange city. After all this time, London doesn't feel unfamiliar to him anymore, and that makes me redundant.' I curl my fists. 'It's as if I've always, secretly, been second best. She's so glamorous, Kath. Really stylish. I could never—'

'Stop that this instant. No one lies on their deathbed wishing they'd had a wider thigh gap.' She lifts my chin. 'What counts is kindness. Honesty. Being true to yourself. You've got all of those things in buckets. The rest is just fluff. It truly is his loss.'

We get out of the car. She links arms with me. Her arthritis has been worse during the cold snap. As we approach the double doors, she gives me a sharp look.

'Don't you dare waste one more second worrying about Lenny. If he can deceive you like that, then you're well rid of him. Imagine the heartbreak if this had happened after you'd signed a marriage certificate and had kids.'

Mum said the same thing from Alicante last night. She told me to take a holiday and fly over to spend time with her and my stepdad Ryan. Oh, I was tempted, hearing the sound of cicadas and glasses that no doubt contained sangria in the background. My imagination ran free for a moment and I could practically smell sea salt and the sweet fragrance of vanilla orchids emanating from my phone. But I can't visit. She's finally living a carefree life full of sun and blue skies. Who am I to cast a shadow over that?

'You're right,' I say and do my best to put on an optimistic voice, having said too much. I don't want to worry Kath.

We are just about to go in when the others appear. Kath kisses her good friend and ex-colleague Nora. Both are in their eighties. She has short, dyed red hair and uses any excuse to wear her faux fur black jacket – much to animal-lover Kath's disapproval, who thinks it still sends out the wrong message.

Widowed Nora is a former hospital receptionist and loves a good old-fashioned romance. She's a fan of modern celebrity, loves gossip magazines and tries to keep up with the latest phrases. She's also probably the local cinema's most frequent visitor. Married Pauline, in her sixties, worked in admin within the police force and likes nothing better than a good detective novel. She wears a smart skirt and secretarial chignon and has a reputation for being handier with a screwdriver than Nick Knowles. A trip to a DIY store is one of her favourite outings. The book club is just made up of us four regulars, although other residents come and go, depending on the books.

They each give me a big hug. We head down to the pub – the women's choice of venue for the club. This week's read is a steamy romance.

'I've not slept much this week,' says Nora as we walk the short distance down the main road to the Frog and Duck. A cutting breeze blows, and I pull down my hat. '*A Fireman's Burning Desires…* goodness, this book has made me want to relive my youth.'

'Me too.' Kath tightens her scarf. 'Mind you, I'm not sure I could have kept up with his pace in the bedroom, and that's after years of working through the night making beds and giving baths.'

'That's what we like about you, Violet,' says Pauline as we enter the pub. Smart pine chairs with sage cushions give the place warmth. The carpet is dark green and the walls are painted magnolia. Glossy-leaved plants punctuate the room. The effect is fresh and cheerful like a sunny garden conservatory. 'You don't assume that because we're pensioners we're prudes. I mean, let's face it,' she continues and heads for a table by the window, 'with our decades of life experience, the last thing that's going to shock us is a bit of sex and rude words.'

'It's love-making, Pauline, love-making,' says romantic Nora and rolls her eyes as she sits down.

Kath and I smile at each other and I head to the bar to buy the customary four gin and tonics. All of us put in ten pounds a week, which supplies us with enough drinks and crisps. It takes me a while to attract the barman's attention. I carry the tray back to the table.

'Squad goals,' says Nora and raises her glass.

I'm the only one with any idea what that means.

'It's an interesting point,' I say. 'Is it love-making or just sex from the start?' We discuss the main characters' relationship. Without realising it, I zone out and stare through the window's glass.For Lenny, was it just sex with me and not true love? Self-doubt has filled the space he left.

'You okay, girl?' asks Kath. I meet her gaze and she offers me a Kettle chip before taking the last one. Three pairs of eyes stare my way.

'He's not worth it,' says Nora. 'You're a marvellous woman and deserve better.'

'It's true,' says Pauline. 'He'll wake up one day and realise what a gem he's lost. I was engaged to someone else, you know, before I married Bill.'

'What happened?' I ask. The others lean forward.

'He cheated on me. I found out from an anonymous phone call that turned out to be made by the other woman. She'd got sick of waiting for him to break off the engagement. He'd dragged it out for weeks – said he hadn't wanted to hurt me.'

'You've never told us that before,' says Kath.

'I don't often think of it – and that's proof that given time, hearts do heal.'

'Lenny said that – that he couldn't bring himself to tell me, although I have my suspicions that he was only waiting to move into Beatrix's new flat. I feel so stupid.'

'What an absolute rotter,' says Nora.

'I scratched my ex's car with my favourite screwdriver. Something I like to think I wouldn't do now. He had the audacity to call the police,' says Pauline. 'I got on very well with the officer. We got chatting… that's when I applied for a job in the force.'

'Something good will come out of this too, sweetheart,' says Kath. 'I dated a doctor once. It turned out he was married. To get over him, I decided I needed a change of direction. That's how I became interested in mental health and eventually specialised and became a senior nurse in that area.'

I smile at everyone. For the first time since Lenny and I broke up, I feel as if a dense fog of despair is thinning. That's one of the reasons I like friends from an older generation. They give you perspective. A number of years from now and hopefully I'd hardly remember Lenny.

I go to the bar and buy another round of drinks, determined to make the most of the rest of the meeting. Arms linked, the four of us eventually walk back to the retirement home, exhausting our memories of previous romances. My first love was an assistant manager at the local bookshop where I had a Saturday job. It was then that I realised the most attractive thing about a man was the width of his reading list.

As we arrive back, Hugo pulls into the drive. His gran lives there too, and now and again our paths cross. A week after Lenny left, I still hadn't mentioned the break-up at work. Then Hugo left for his annual two week skiing trip.

'How was the snow? Not as slushy as here I hope,' I say after greeting his gran. She goes over to the others and in minute detail describes the lamb shank Hugo bought her for lunch.

'Fantastic,' he says and looks me up and down. 'But it's you who looks like they've been on the slopes. I didn't know you were on a diet. Which one are you following? The 5:2? Or the South Beach? Whichever one it is, you look great.'

Diet? Hardly, but over the last week or so, both Kath and Farah have said I look drawn. I believed them. I can't sleep at night because I'm over-analysing where Lenny and I went wrong.

Hugo's the first person to indicate that the single life suits me after all. I look down. My trousers do seem a bit baggy and now I think about it, the waist slips from side to side in a way it never had before. If anything, surely I look a bit of a mess? Yet for some reason, along with my friends' camaraderie, Hugo's comment makes me feel just a bit more resilient.

We leave the park and get home before Mum, so Uncle Kevin and I play cards.

'Oh no. Not again!' Uncle Kevin shoots me a smile and holds his head in his hands.

I've won. I don't know how. His maths is much better than mine. Lately, I've got the feeling he's playing badly on purpose.

'Don't forget to take a pack of cards with you, Uncle Kevin. Your new friends might want to play.'

He gives my arm a squeeze.

'It's been a strange summer,' I say.

'Nothing wrong with strange.' He smiles. 'Sometimes that means exciting.'

Our tower block is being knocked down. I guess that might be exciting to watch. It was built in the olden days, when Mum was little. After another caught fire last year, it was decided that ours is too dangerous to live in. Mum says every cloud has a silver lining. It was a chance to move nearer to Uncle Kevin. She found another job waitressing. I said goodbye to my friends six weeks ago, at the beginning of the holidays – bad timing. Uncle Kevin picked us up in his shiny car and helped us move into our new ground floor flat. Really, it's the bottom half of a small house with a garden to play in.

But then a few days after we moved, our cloud ran out of silver. Uncle Kevin got headhunted. Sounds scary, doesn't it? Makes me think of my favourite Horrid Henry story about cannibals. It means he got offered a job in America, the place where people eat bacon with pancakes, do cheerleading and own guns. He was going to say no –

family was more important – but Mum told him not to be silly. It wouldn't be forever. She'd wanted a fresh start anyway.

So he took it and promised to come home as often as he could, starting with Christmas. Uncle Kevin said we should move into his house. With his new job, he could afford to keep paying for that *and* a new place abroad. But Mum got quite cross. She doesn't like to take things for nothing. So they *came to a compromise* – those are four of Mum's favourite words. He's selling his house but Mum accepted his car, huge telly and new freezer, like she's sometimes accepted holidays when he's taken us to Cornwall.

I tried to hide my upset but I think Uncle Kevin noticed because I came home from holiday club one day and he'd bought me a striped cat called Tinker. He got him from a place called the Cats Prevention Leak. Mum says I am old enough to look after something other than myself now. It is my job to give Tinker his biscuits and wipe his paws when he comes in from the garden if he's been covering up his wee. I promise Tinker will have the cleanest feet ever. I enjoy keeping things neat and tidy, like my room. Uncle Kevin says I must be the only child that does and teases me.

'Are you scared about starting something new?' I ask and stare at the scattered cards.

'I can't decide whether the feeling is fear or excitement. It's in the pit of my stomach. Sometimes it feels like water bubbles bursting and sometimes like heavy bowling balls dragging me down.'

'That's how I feel about tomorrow. I can't wait to see the school library, but then what if no one wants to get to know me?'

Not that I had loads of friends at my old school. And that didn't bother me. As long as I had my books, Mum and Uncle Kevin, I was happy. But it's nice to have someone to talk to at break. To sit next to in class. Someone to pull faces with when the lesson gets boring. Someone to have around to play and eat chips with in front of the telly, if Mum's in a good mood. And I had all of that in my old group of school friends. I was the quietest, but no one minded, apart from Lucy, the loudest. She said I should read less and concentrate on words that are spoken instead of printed.

Uncle Kevin leans across the table and takes both my hands. 'You will make friends, Violet. You're such a kind, caring person. Just give it time.' He says a few other things. I don't always understand what he means but there are three things he's drilled into me. To be myself, work hard and be kind.

Would a dad make me feel better like this? I'll never know because mine has never been around.

'I'm sorry to leave after you and your mum moved near,' he says and lets go of my fingers.

'I'm going to miss you,' I say. 'I've liked you, Mum and me always being a three. It's meant I don't miss having a dad. We feel like a family.'

He reaches across and gives me a big hug. I must be brave. It wouldn't be fair to Uncle Kevin to let him see me cry.

'But it's too good an opportunity for you to miss,' I say, because that's what Mum's been saying. Sometimes she sounds more like his mother than his sister, but then he is younger than her by ten years.

I'm glad Uncle Kevin hasn't noticed the wobble I feel in my lip. I can't do that to him or to Mum. She's been quiet all week. Those circles under her eyes look darker than ever. Despite the car and the telly and the freezer, I know she'll miss Uncle Kevin more than anyone. So when we get back home, I pretend that tomorrow isn't really happening. I'm not starting at a new school and Uncle Kevin isn't getting on a plane all the way to somewhere called New York City.

Chapter 5

Since I saw him at the retirement home last Sunday, Hugo has talked to me about things we don't usually discuss, like clothes and health trends. I feel like a ship that has sailed into unchartered waters. He complimented me again today; said he liked my outfit. I'd worn a skirt for a change – an old size fourteen I hadn't fit into for years.

I sit at my desk and straighten the keyboard. This evening, Lenny will be at a book launch for our author Gary Smith, who is represented by his agency. My stomach clenches. I haven't seen him for almost four weeks, except on social media. Not that I've looked at his profiles. Apart from a couple of times on Twitter. Yesterday he posted a selfie of him and Beatrix. Their relationship must be public now.

Tonight's launch is for Gary's Young Adult book called *Bubbles*. It's about a rich teenager whose family comes from nothing but ends up producing champagne. It's highly unusual – almost like a saga for young adults. The story spans several generations, from the penniless, hard-working ancestors to their modern indulged offspring. Early reviews expect it to be a huge hit. Translation rights sales are already dynamic. So Thoth Publishing is more than happy to celebrate in style. We've ordered in canapés and the interns are decorating our biggest conference room with gold streamers and balloons. Each guest will receive a goody bag containing a signed copy, luxury truffles and a mini bottle of posh lemonade.

Normally I'd make my usual excuses and curl up with a book on the settee. Old habits die hard. I did much the same during my university Freshers' week, despite everyone else partying. And there is never a shortage of editors happy to have a drink and talk publishing. However, the author, Gary Smith, is particularly nervous and he and I have worked closely these last few months. His agent can't make it tonight, which makes me think it is even more likely that Lenny will appear in his place. Plus Gary's wife has to work and his kids are away studying, so he's coming alone. I can't let him down.

Bubbles is his debut. Gary works on the bins, which was a surprise to me and everyone else at Thoth. He's a modest, middle-aged dad who plays snooker in the pub and goes to the football at the weekend. He left school at sixteen and took the first job he was offered. A swanky book launch is so far out of his comfort zone that we joke he'll need a geomap to get back. Gary wrote the story when his wife lost her job and had to take a position working nights. The local paper had run an article about a dyslexic teenager who'd just been published, which gave Gary the confidence to have a go as, on the sly, he'd always liked reading his wife's romance books. Inadvertently, his novel provides a moving insight into his impover-ished childhood. Without being preachy, the story sends a strong message that material gains and emotional well-being are not always linked.

So when six o'clock arrives, I head into the ladies' room to brush my hair. Perhaps I should make more effort, I think, as my colleagues change into high shoes and swap jumpers for blouses. Lipstick is applied. Squirts of perfume hijack the stale air. But I have no time anyway, having agreed to meet Gary outside the building at six fifteen. The party starts at seven thirty, but he needs to arrive early to sign books. I go to the lift and within minutes am downstairs in reception. I pass through the revolving door and stand outside for a few moments, blowing on my hands to keep warm.

I could have waited inside, but I need to quell my irrational fear that Gary will change his mind at the last minute and go for a few pints at the Red Lion next door. The sunny spring day is disappearing. Commuters rush by, swerving around Gabby, the homeless woman who sits leaning up against our building. She mouths hello at me. Most lunchtimes I stop for a quick chat and give her a sandwich bag. Lenny said she's probably one of those professional beggars and thought me naïve to make a spare packed lunch for her each day.

I look up and down the street. I don't want Lenny to come. Yet I do. Perhaps he's missed me. Maybe I won't feel anything and can let go of what he did. Will we talk to each other? How do I greet him?

It's a rickety bridge I need to cross, which makes me think of the ones on the jungle reality show Lenny liked to watch. If I reach the other side, the confidence boost I'll enjoy will make it worthwhile.

'Violet?'

I look up. Gary smiles nervously. We shake hands.

'You look great,' I say, making an effort to observe his outfit. I'm not that interested in clothes, but Gary needs a shot of self-esteem.

How similar our situations are this evening. I bared my soul to Lenny. Gary has bared his soul to readers. It's left us both vulnerable to rejection.

'You don't think the tie is too much?' He loosens his collar.

'Definitely not. You should see the fashion show being put together in the women's toilets.'

We head up to the first floor and into the conference room. Interns buzz around, tying balloons. A pop-up bar has been set up at the back. Caterers hurry to and fro, laying out glasses to fill and stacking small plates and napkins. I lead Gary over to a table where earlier I set up a pile of his books.

Gary sits down and runs a hand over his receding hair-line.

'Glass of champagne?' I say.

'Yes. No. I don't know. Perhaps I should keep a clear head.'

I sit down next to him. 'Try not to worry. I know this is your first event, but you'll be absolutely fine.'

I chat while he scribbles, but Gary is very quiet. I know him well enough to realise that means he's nervous.

I head over to Irfan. 'Our author could do with some moral support,' I say.

Irfan fills a glass with champagne for Gary and then carries that, and his own orange juice, over to the table. I help with the last minute decorations and dim the lights just as the first guests arrive. I chat with some bloggers whilst I sip my coke. I mustn't forget to give them goody bags when they leave. Their support for books is unpaid, and I tell my authors never to forget that. Music plays in the background and I gaze out of the windows at illuminated buildings, tired of trying to pretend to myself that I'm not looking out for Lenny. I'm glad to escape the gloss of the party. My job gives me a sense of belonging that only falters at such glittering get-togethers.

'Do you think he's jumped?' says a familiar voice in my ear.

I turn around. Irfan pulls a face. 'Gary's disappeared. People are waiting to talk to him – especially some of the youngsters.'

'Toilets?'

'Irfan's looked there,' says Farah, with a sparkle on her face that complements the book's fizzy drink theme. She's like a teenager at her first disco every time she attends one of these events. Gold tassel earrings shake as she speaks and she's wearing a blue embroidered silk top with sequins around the neck.

A blogger collars me for an early copy of a picture book she's eager to see and it's the perfect excuse for me to leave and look for Gary. I head up to my office. A light is on in the side room. I head over and open the door. Gary and I stare at each other. We've held many a meeting in there while discussing changes to his manuscript. I go in and sit down opposite him.

'Lovely. Peace and quiet,' I say.

'Not much of a party girl?'

'No. I'm more of a hot chocolate on the sofa, book in my hand, cat on my lap kind of person.' He smiles. Good. 'I often bypass these events, but seeing as it's you…'

'Thanks, Violet. I appreciate that.'

'I also accept that it's part of my job.'

'Now I feel like a school kid who's in trouble and has been sent to the headmistress.'

'Not at all. I didn't mean it like that. Quite the opposite, in fact. Your main job is the writing – albeit alongside a bit of promotion. But book launches, well, some authors don't have them at all – and the effect they have on sales is negligible. It's just that we want you to enjoy tonight. You deserve it, Gary, and I've already spoken to two enthusiastic young readers who are really keen to meet you.'

He stares at his drink. 'But what if they find out I'm a fraud?'

'What do you mean?'

'People aren't interested in what I've got to say, Violet. I'm not well-read. You know what I do for a living. I'm not a proper author. I just liked my kids' books and wanted to write one.'

'And it's one of the best Young Adult books I've ever read.'

'You really mean that, don't you? I can tell that you're not the sort of person to bullshit.'

'Take a few deep breaths and just be yourself. No one can beat you at that. It's going to go great. A night to remember. I promise. You wouldn't be a real writer if you weren't wracked with self-doubt.'

'Really?'

'Even our biggest authors get the collywobbles every time a new book goes out for review. And trust me. I've never known a writer not to feel on top of the world after doing a reading. Come on. I believe the champagne is top notch.'

He gives a tentative smile. We head downstairs. I take him back into the conference room and guide him towards the youngsters who wanted to chat. Fifteen minutes later, I see a group of them hanging on his every word. Gary has undone his top button. I give him the thumbs up.

My evening's been worthwhile just to see him lap up the attention and relax. I'm tempted to leave early, but stay in case Gary has another wobble. I am just about to check on the goody bags when I feel a tap on my shoulder and smile. The last time I saw Irfan he'd gone into telling jokes mode. Parties always do that to him.

He taps again and I turn around.

The teacher, Mrs Warham, puts her arm around my shoulder and guides me inside. She's got short grey hair and lines. She must be at least a hundred years old. My stomach untwists a little as I take in the friendly room. The walls are covered with colourful paintings and letters. On the left, in the corner, is a carpeted area with cushions. As the rest of the class file in, they sit down there. Mrs Warham calls over a girl with pigtails that are straighter and shinier than mine.

'Alice, this is Violet. She's joining our class. Could you keep her company today? Her coat peg is already named.'

'Yes, Mrs Warham.' Alice smiles and holds out her hand. I take it and she grips hard, pulling me to the back of the classroom opposite the toilets. She points to an empty peg.

'That word begins with V. Does it say your name?'

I nod.

'What does it mean?'

'It's a flower. And a colour. Purple.'

'Like your glasses.' She giggles. 'Take off your coat and then we have to sit in a circle on the carpet whilst Mrs Warham takes the register. I'm the first to be read out,' she says proudly, 'because my second name starts with an A too.'

'My second name also starts with a V.'

'You'll be read out last, then,' she says in superior tones.

Quickly I take off my coat and hang it up with my bag. Alice takes my hand again and drags me over to the navy blue carpet. We sit down. Everyone stares at me and heat floods into my face. A boy with jam around his mouth sticks out his tongue. Alice looks at two friends and the three of them grin. Alice seems to find a lot of things about me funny. Like my odd socks. The way I blush. And the pencil case she saw sticking out of the top of my bag. It's in the shape of an elephant. Alice whispers something to her friends about that but I don't hear and they all laugh. At break, she and her friends giggle in front of the boys. At lunch they do handstands on the field to show them their knickers. They shoot me pitying looks when I say I don't understand why anyone would want to do that. It's the longest sentence I've said all day.

'You don't speak much,' says Alice, after the end-of-school bell goes and we collect our coats.

'You're a shrinking Violet,' says her friend Georgie, and beams as if she'd just solved a maths problem. 'That's what my aunt calls her dog. His real name is Patch but he's very shy and hides behind the sofa when I visit.'

'Shrinking Violet, Shrinking Violet,' call the others and clap their hands.

Georgie looks at me guiltily. I bite the insides of my cheeks so that I don't cry.

That night I have a quick chat with Uncle Kevin on the phone. His voice sounds tired but he can't wait to start his new job on Friday. He asks how school went. I say it was okay. I don't mention the laughing or handstands. At least tomorrow I won't have to stay by Alice's side. And after-school club wasn't awful. We did craft work and then I was allowed to read my book. I'm reading *Charlotte's Web* because it was one of Uncle Kevin's favourite books when he was a little boy. I still don't like spiders but they don't seem as scary as before.

I don't mention my new nickname to him or to Mum. Perhaps those girls will have forgotten about it by tomorrow.

–

Mondays never used to bother me. It was just another day of the week. But I think, from now on, they are going to make me feel sick. I squeeze Mum's hand tighter as we hurry onto the playground. I couldn't sleep last night. My first three days at Applegrove Primary have been horrid. Last Thursday and Friday, Alice just wouldn't leave me alone.

'Where's your dad?'

'Why is your skirt so long?'

'Does your mum let you use her phone?'

'Have you ever worn lipstick?'

'Why do you like books so much?'

The questions go on and on and Alice never waits for an answer because she thinks she knows it all. When she said that my mum and dad must be divorced, I couldn't be bothered to say no.

I don't make a fuss, though, because Mum's new job isn't going well. I heard her tell a friend on the phone that her boss tells really bad jokes and wears too much aftershave. At least my teacher is nice. She smells of pretty flowers like the perfume Mum sometimes wears if we're dressing up smart.

So I chat about Alice with Tinker instead of Mum. He's a great listener and says I should be cat-like, in other words dignified and silent. I decide to take his advice. After all, I learnt at my old school that the Egyptians thought cats were gods, so they must be very wise. I keep my head up and ignore Alice. Problem is, she can't bear that and pretending she isn't there just makes her shout "Shrinking Violet" louder. At the end of school last Friday, she even pinched my arm. I did my best not to show how much it hurt.

'Goodbye, darling,' says Mum and kisses my cheek. 'Have a lovely day. Remember we're talking to Uncle Kevin again tonight. He's got an office party at lunch so we'll chat to him after, at seven o'clock our time – it will be two o'clock there and the celebrations will have just finished.'

The thought of that will get me through the day.

'Who's your Uncle Kevin?' says Alice, on the way in. 'Your mum's boyfriend?'

Alice has the strangest ideas. 'No. Her brother. He's in America.'

'I've been to America,' says Alice and she puffs out her chest as if she's flown to the moon and back.

She waits as if expecting me to ask lots of questions but I go straight in and hang my coat and bag on my peg. She sits down next to me on the carpet. I look at the date on the calendar up on the wall. Mrs Warham crosses off each day as it passes. It's a long time until December when term ends.

'Dad took me and my brother to Florida. I saw Mickey Mouse. It was amazing. And Cinderella. Beauty and the Beast too. I got all their autographs.'

Georgie gives me a smile as if to say sorry for Alice. Georgie isn't so bad. Or at least I didn't think so, until she and Alice and their other friends cornered me on the field at lunchtime. All I wanted to do was to read. They thought I should do handstands with them instead. I said no so Georgie ran off with my book. I chased her and she threw it into a puddle. It was the last thing Uncle Kevin had given me, apart from the silver book necklace that I wasn't allowed to wear to school. Other children from our class saw her do it but pretended they hadn't. I didn't cry. I just managed not to. I didn't want them to see me do that.

When I get home, I use my towel to dry my book. The pages smell funny and some stick together.

I sit by the phone and at seven o'clock exactly it rings. Mum puts the phone between us and we both listen. I ask what the party was like and his words go all bubbly as if they are orange squash that has been turned into orangeade. He talks about the colourful table glitter and cocktails. Apparently waiters walked around carrying trays of miniature food like burgers, hot dogs and salmon and cream cheese bagels. I don't know what bagels are, but Uncle Kevin had three of them.

He says the company has just signed a big customer and that the party for this was also a good way for him to get to know everyone. He works on the hundredth floor. We used to live on the eighth floor of our tower block and could see across the whole city. Perhaps from his office Uncle Kevin can see England. Mum and I tease him when he talks about a woman called Cindy who showed him how to work the coffee machine. I say she makes his voice sound gooey. He tells us about a team-building trip they are all going on next weekend. There's a pizza school in New York and they will spend the day spinning dough and choosing their own toppings before eating them.

Uncle Kevin hasn't got long but quickly asks about us. I go quiet whilst Mum talks about her new boss and all his rules. She calls him a rude name. That doesn't happen often. The doorbell goes and Mum hands me the phone before leaving the room.

'And how are things going with my best niece?'

'I'm your only niece,' I say and manage a smile at our usual joke. I wish he was close enough to hug. 'Things are okay.'

'Is your teacher nice?'

'Yes.'

'And the other children?'

I don't say a word.

'Violet? It's me. Come on. No secrets, right?'

I nod even though he can't see.

'Have you finished *Charlotte's Web* yet?'

'No. I've got to wait for it to dry.'

'What happened?'

I still keep quiet but Uncle Kevin always could read silence.

'Give it time, Violet. It's not been long,' he says, softly. 'You'll make friends. Remember the books you haven't liked to start with – but eventually they've become favourites?'

I think for a moment. 'Yes. Like *Where the Wild Things Are*. I was too scared to look at the pictures to start with.'

'And friends often appear from the most unexpected places. Perhaps you'll get close to someone in after school club who isn't in your class. Or someone in your street. Remember, my best friend in England is one of my neighbours, not a colleague.'

Uncle Kevin and his friend got to know each other when a water pipe burst.

Mum comes back to the phone and we say goodbye. Uncle Kevin tells me he loves me. I say it back. He always makes me feel better. He's right. Alice may not think I'm on the same level as her and her friends but it doesn't matter. I might find the best friend ever away from Applegrove Primary.

Chapter 6

Lenny. And Beatrix. Tight silver and blue dress. Bright pink lipstick. Beatrix Bingham reminds me of one of my favourite childhood books, *The Rainbow Fish*. I never wear anything tight. Comfort has always been my top priority. In the past, without wanting to emulate, I've marvelled at women like her, willing to put in such effort – although her glamour looks effortless.

'Violet. Congratulations on a wonderful launch,' says Beatrix in a well-managed tone. 'I've heard great things about the book. In fact I really must congratulate the author.' She sashays off.

'Hi Violet,' says Lenny. 'How are things?'

I don't know what to say.

'Great party. Sounds like one hell of a story.'

Finally I find my voice. 'Gary's a very talented author.'

'How's Flossie? Liking the quiet no doubt. Not the liveliest of cats, is she?'

I go to leave. Lenny takes my arm.

'Look… have you found a new flatmate yet?' He takes a large mouthful of champagne. 'I came across a junior editor yesterday who's looking for new digs. If you like—'

'No thanks,' I say abruptly. I study the face that used to be able to liquefy my insides. The gut-wrenching ache I've suffered this last month rips through my body, accompanied by a home-movie of all our best moments playing in my head. Like the day we moved in together when Lenny took my hands and spun me around and around and said he never thought he'd get out of his bedsit. Like walks in the park talking about work and the amazing careers we were going to have.

Lenny's face flushes. 'There's no need for all this awkwardness. Things change. It doesn't mean we can't be friends. We move in the same circles so it makes sense to at least be civilised.'

I shake my arm loose.

'Okay. I get it. I've been a shit.'

'At last some clarity,' I say in a tight voice.

'But we had grown apart. Perhaps I did us a favour, right? Our relationship could have stagnated for years before one of us was brave enough to make the break.'

'So now you're the hero? Oh, please.' I shake my head.

'Don't be like that. I didn't mean—'

'How do you expect me to be?' I snap. I could pretend not to care and make small talk but I miss him. I do. Before this evening, I'd googled how to cope with meeting your ex. I'm not always that good at dealing with the emotional side of things, like when Uncle Kevin… when he… sometimes it's best just to carry on as if nothing has happened. I think back again to my online research. One website said to remain poised. Polite. Keep it short. I could just about manage that. But as for demonstrating that I've moved on, how was that possible? He was the one with a new address and relationship.

'You'll meet someone else. Someone who's a better match than me.'

'You mean someone loyal, with principles? Damn right, she will,' says Farah, who's appeared at my elbow. 'You've got a nerve, turning up like this – with Bingham. Haven't you got one ounce of decency?'

'It's okay, Farah,' I say. 'Just leave it. Please. I'm okay.'

Farah looks at me and I nod. She glares at Lenny and leaves.

'Beatrix has a history. She might be using you. Just watch yourself,' I say to Lenny quietly, annoyed that despite everything, I don't want to see him hurt.

Lenny drains his glass and places it onto a passing tray. 'You don't need to worry about me. If you ever change your mind about being friends, I'm always—'

Beatrix reappears and takes his arm. She shoots me a pitying look. 'Jealousy is such an unattractive quality.' The two of them move away. I hurry out of the conference room and into the toilets. I lock the cubicle door and sit on the loo seat. A sob rises in my chest and I manage to suppress it. I take off my glasses. I don't really understand how this has happened. Lenny and I were so happy.

Night after night I've sat on my sofa with Flossie and a book, but four weeks on and I still find myself staring into space. I miss the things that used to irritate me, like him leaving drawers open or never checking the date on food he purchased. Lenny would leave his socks on the floor and not tidy away dirty mugs. I never thought unwashed crockery could leave such a gap. If I'm honest, at the back of my mind, I'd seen a future with a wedding and children.

Now I just saw me in my flat with a cat and shelves of books. That used to be enough – more than that, great – until I met Lenny. They say you don't miss what you haven't had. The hardest part is you can't go back.

I take several deep breaths, smooth down my jumper and put on my glasses again. As soon as I reappear at the party, Farah heads over and raises her thick brown eyebrows.

'Irfan's fuming,' she says. 'We can't believe Lenny's being so insensitive.'

'I'm okay.'

'Come around to dinner next week. Help me convince Irfan that quinoa doesn't actually taste like soil.'

I wish my eyes weren't drawn to Beatrix. Lenny can't take his eyes off her. Nor can anyone else, including Gary, who's never looked at me like that.

Across the room Lenny basks in Beatrix's popularity. She catches my eye and kisses him full on the lips. Irfan goes to the front and shushes the crowd. He says a few words. I look for Gary, to give him some last minute encouragement, but it isn't needed any more. He's standing next to Beatrix and her hand rests on his shoulder. Gary's face looks shiny as if she's somehow polished it.

I about-turn and head up to the office to fetch my coat and bag. I fasten the multi-coloured buttons and pull my bobble hat out of my drawer. Even though the weather is warmer now, it feels like a comfort blanket.

Lenny has moved on. That's very clear. Now I need to do the same.

Chapter 7

'Gary's here?' I ask Irfan. Authors never just drop into the office. We always make appointments if a meeting is required and usually, if they have one like Gary does, they are accompanied by their agent.

Whilst Irfan goes downstairs to collect him, I put the coffee on to brew in the side room. Gary appears at the door, holding a soggy umbrella. April is proving its reputation for showers. He takes off his jacket to reveal a smart shirt. On the front pocket is a designer logo.

Irfan follows him in and shrugs at me before sitting in the chair to my right. Gary sits opposite. I pass him his usual coffee, milky with one sugar. Gary smiles and hands me a plant. He glances through the glass wall and waves at one of the young interns. I haven't seen Gary since his signing and he seems to have acquired a degree of aplomb in those three weeks.

'I couldn't resist it,' he says.

'An African Violet?' I smile at the purple flowers. 'Thanks, that's lovely. But what have I done to deserve this?'

Gary takes a sip of coffee and puts the mug on the table. He stretches out and puts his hands behind his head.

'I don't believe in getting anyone to do my dirty business, so I've come here alone to tell you both myself...'

Irfan leans forward. 'Everything okay?'

'First up, I just want to say how grateful I am to you two. It's been quite a journey, this publishing lark, and you've both made me feel so at ease.'

This sounds like a goodbye. I don't understand. We've just drawn up a second contract after talks with his agent.

'It's thrilling to work with you,' I say.

'Yes, the support we're getting from retailers and the independents is fantastic,' says Irfan.

We've invested a lot of our time in this author who needed instructing, from scratch, about keeping his writing tight and adding emotion, about marketing and social media platforms. Nothing pleases us more than seeing all that hard work pay off.

'Thank you, but I won't be re-signing.' He takes another mouthful of coffee.

I take off my glasses. 'Gary, we have big plans for you. Have you discussed this with your agent?'

'It's my decision,' he says abruptly.

Irfan rubs a hand across his forehead. 'I don't understand. Your debut is doing so well. We saw this as just the beginning of a very successful career. Like Violet says, we've got the next two years mapped out with strategies to take your career forwards.'

'And I really appreciate the opportunity you gave me when no one else would take a chance. However, I've decided to sign with Alpaca Books.'

I flinch. 'Let's talk about this. What can they offer that we can't?'

'I've met with Beatrix Bingham a couple of times – if you remember, she was at my launch.'

Irfan and I exchange glances.

'She introduced me to Alpaca's children's fiction editor. Beatrix reckons within the year I could give up my day job.'

I'm speechless. So is Irfan for a second before he does his best sales pitch for Thoth. Poaching other publisher's authors happens, but more discreetly than this – and not by making unsubstantiated promises. Children's fiction isn't even Beatrix's area of expertise. As for Gary, Irfan and I have seen this before. A debut author has some success and develops a sense of entitlement that feeds their ego. They don't understand that to grow and maintain a long-term career takes time and that one hit guarantees nothing.

When Gary leaves, Irfan heads for his desk, angry. For him, this means sharpening his pencils with vigour. I pick up the bin and brush the shavings into it as he calls Gary's agent, who is equally unimpressed. Apart from anything else, he knows that his client's naïve announcement could deter me and Irfan from giving his debut the continued attention it needs.

I try to lose myself in another author's edits for the afternoon and finally pack up my things at five. I turn off the screen and stare at the blank rectangle, immediately missing the distraction of the words and cursor. I've worked so closely with Gary. Bolstered his confidence where I could. Felt so proud as I've watched his writing and promotional skills grow. But just like that, he's cut ties. Just like Lenny.

I put on a lilac anorak and try not to think about this anymore, that it might be because of something I do, or something about the way I am. The weather is warmer now despite the rain and I've finally discarded my bobble hat. I step out of the lift. I blush as Hugo wolf-whistles and mouth at him to be quiet. Hugo complimented my new trousers yesterday. I had to buy them because I've gone down a dress size. At lunch all I could manage was a couple of the low-fat samosas Irfan brought in. The trousers are more fitted than my usual style. It's the first time I've ever worn anything that isn't completely comfy. That's why I've never been a fan of stockings, high shoes or underwire bras, but I had to do something as much of my old wardrobe is now too baggy.

I head outside and go over to Irfan and Farah who are still hanging around, despite leaving fifteen minutes earlier. I take a deep breath and wish I could walk straight past.

'I was just thinking about my lunch,' I say to Farah. 'You're such a good cook. The spices in those samosas are so subtle.'

She gives me a hug. 'That must be Irfan's excuse for eating the lot – they were supposed to last a couple of days.' She stares. 'How are you doing? It seems like ages since I saw you at the *Bubbles* launch. Have you been in contact with Lenny?'

Lenny. That word didn't hurt quite so much as it did seven weeks ago. At first, similar words jumped out from everywhere I looked. Like the John Lennon album in the supermarket. The historical thriller a fellow editor was reading, featuring Lenin. Then there was the Lenny Kravitz concert poster stuck on the wall outside the train station.

'No. I've unfriended him on Facebook, but photos mutual friends have taken come up on my newsfeed. It's just as well I don't go there very often.'

Farah raised her eyebrows.

'They feature him and Beatrix out for meals or drinking or at publishing events.'

'Glad I unfriended him too,' she says.

'And me,' mumbles Irfan. He's hardly said a word all afternoon.

'We've been waiting – hoping you'll come for coffee with us,' says Farah and threads her arm though mine.

'Please do,' says Irfan. 'I need help persuading Farah that there is no health scare big enough to warrant switching to soya milk.'

I manage a smile. 'Sorry but I've got plans tonight.'

Farah holds me by the shoulders. It took me a while to get used to her way of touching people when she talks.

'Does this mean… have you met someone else?'

'Farah, please, mind your own business. Come on. Let's leave Violet to get on with her evening.' Irfan looks at me apologetically. 'Now you know why our children chose universities as far away from London as possible.'

Farah gives me the thumbs up before punching her husband's arm. Guilt pinches my chest as I walk towards the tube station. I didn't exactly lie. I do have plans. They just don't involve going out or romance. I'm starting a new book tonight. Then I will watch *Charlotte's Web*. Children's movies never fail to cheer me up. Tea will probably be a sandwich if I can face it. Last night Flossie and I shared a can of tuna, hers served in a bowl, mine on a slice of toast. I can only face the company of a cat at the moment.

Friday used to be pizza night if Lenny was in – his was a Meat Feast, mine a Margherita. We'd order potato wedges and garlic bread on the side. Afterwards Lenny would drink beer whilst I ate chocolate. Had he become bored with our routine? As I sit down on the train, I add this to the list of unanswered questions, although they are all asking the same thing: why wasn't I good enough for him?

One hour later I'm at the front door of the block of flats I call home. Spits of rain hint at an oncoming downpour. Stormy clouds have assembled across the sky. It's as if I've breathed them in and they've darkened my mood. I rummage in my handbag and can't find my key. I've become good at losing things. First Lenny. Now Gary. Is this how it's going to be? A doomed love life? A failed career? Just when I thought things were going so well.

I look up at the sky. The atmosphere feels weighted and close. It makes me want to scream, to run, so that somehow I can cut through it. Perhaps that's the answer. Leaving my job. Leaving London. Starting again abroad. I could stay with Mum and Ryan. No one need know that I'm the woman who lost her boyfriend and most promising author to boot.

I sigh and shake myself. Kath wouldn't approve of a pity party. I finally find the key right down at the bottom and slide it into the lock. I wipe my cheeks with the back of my hand. It must be months, years since I last cried. I'm just about to push open the door when running footsteps approach from behind, accompanied by deep breaths. I turn to see a woman around my age bent over, hands on her knees, gasping. It's almost like someone is chasing her. I glance over her shoulder but no one's there. She straightens up, cheeks red, forehead perspiring, and looks at her watch. Her catwalk cheekbones contrast her casual jogging gear.

'Everything okay?' I ask as she goes onto the lawn and stares at the building before sitting on a bench. It's positioned in front of a cherry blossom tree, next to a high wooden bird table that residents keep supplied with crumbs and seed.

'What? Oh. Sorry. Did I startle you?' Her face breaks into a smile.

'Can I help you?' I ask.

'Not really. I should have rung whoever placed the ad first, but thanks anyway. I've come about a room in one of these flats. I thought I'd suss out the building first before ringing. I shouldn't have worried. It's a quiet, lovely area and this front garden is so pretty.' The jogger gets up and walks over across the lawn edged with peonies and roses in blossom.

'Actually, it's me who placed the ad. I'm looking for a flatmate. Would you like to come up to take a look?'

'Pleased to meet you.' She gives a white smile. 'I'm Bella.'

'Violet.'

'Well, if you're sure it's not inconvenient. I have a habit of calling on people at the worst moment. Like when Gran's in the middle of putting on her tights or my brother has just plastered his face with shaving foam.'

I laugh. 'No. My diary's completely empty of late.'

She raises an eyebrow.

'I recently broke up with my boyfriend.' Why did I say that? Bella's just got one of those faces that makes you want to tell the truth.

'I'm so sorry.' She pulls a sympathetic face. 'That's why the room is available?'

I nod and she follows me in and up the stairs.

'Would you like me to take my shoes off?' she asks as I open my flat's door.

I think Bella and I will get on very well.

'Would you mind? Thanks.' I take her anorak and hang it on the coat stand. 'I'll just put the kettle on. Do you take sugar and milk?'

'Could I just have a glass of water? I'm gasping after that run.'

When I come back, she is on the sofa tickling Flossie's ears.

'I see you've made friends with the most important member of the household.'

Chapter 8

I smile at Bella as she sips an unappealing juice that is brighter than the well maintained lawn outside. While I might aspire to improve my health, I prefer smaller steps, such as eating plants instead of drinking them.

'Don't worry. I haven't made cocktails for two,' Bella says and smiles as if she can read my mind.

I can't believe she's only been living here for three weeks. We already seem to know each other so well.

'Thanks goodness. It was traumatic enough binge-watching that old *Love Island* series with you over the weekend – it's enough, at the moment, to have my taste in television challenged, thanks very much.'

She gives me a grin that exudes inclusiveness and understanding.

'You enjoyed every minute. Don't tell me you didn't.'

She flashes her white teeth again and turns away to wash up before leaving for the spa where she works. That's one of the many things I like about her – she constantly does the dishes, tidies and vacuums.

'Want me to make chicken stir fry tonight?' she asks.

'That would be great. Thanks. And I'll make the dairy-free rice pudding you showed me on that website for afterwards.' Bella has introduced me to healthier cuisine. And no one's more surprised than me to say I now do three runs a week. They are only short and I'm dripping with perspiration afterwards, but she promised the adrenaline high would make me feel so much better. Despite today's aching limbs, she was right.

Hugo is baffled later on as I pass him on the way out of work.

'Violet Vaughan,' he calls, 'what is your secret?'

Blushing, I head over.

'Is there a special pill I can take to get your bright eyes and skin?'

'I wish,' I say and grimace. 'It's the result of several tortuous jogs.'

'You? Running?' Gym fan Hugo laughs. 'Well, all I can say is that as time passes, it looks as if your life without Lenny is the best thing that could have happened.'

I'm still getting used to compliments about my appearance.

'You know, Hugo, you could have been right about Beatrix. I should have listened.'

He puts down his pen. 'You mean it's not simply lust that's brought Lenny and her together?'

'Have you heard of *Alien Hearts*?'

'Get with the programme, mate – that's old news. I just wish Wilde's agent would hurry up and submit it.'

'Lenny let Beatrix have a sneak peek for her new *Out There Stories* imprint. She's desperate to sign Casey Wilde. I can't say for sure, but that could be why she's interested in him.'

Hugo doesn't respond. Doesn't say *I told you so*. Instead he stands up and his long arms stretch over the desk. As best as he can, Hugo gives me a hug. 'Then it looks as if

Lenny is going to get what he deserves. In my experience, cheaters usually do.'

I head home whistling one of my flatmate's favourite Beyoncé tunes. Between them, Hugo and Bella are making me believe that I'm an okay person.

In fact, she's the ideal person to live with – easy-going, a real team player and passionate about looking after yourself. Bella is qualified to do facials, pedicures, manicures, aromatherapy massages, all sorts. She's fond of her regular clients and works with some of them, over months, to do a complete make-over, covering diet, hair and make-up. She says there is nothing more rewarding than unveiling the end result – not so much because of what she's done to their appearance, but because of the difference it makes to their self-esteem. Also, we both love coffee shops and she never stops talking to Flossie.

When I get home, she's chilling on the sofa, which is a rare sight. Bella's so full of energy. Although she has got her pink jogging suit on, which means she'll soon go out for her evening run. I tell her what Hugo said.

'Beatrix needs her come-uppance as well, in my opinion,' she says and pulls a face.

'That's never going to happen. Her career's on fire. She's just been nominated for another award.'

'You're more than a match for her, Violet. Why don't you beat Beatrix at her own game?'

We went to the cinema last night on a rare night she was free, and I told her more about Lenny and Beatrix. The film was a romance. Not my usual genre, but since Lenny left, I've found myself fascinated by other people's relationships, even if they are fiction. I'm looking for signs of where I've gone wrong and, if I'm honest, a sense that

I'm not the only one ever to get hurt. Bella and I both cried at the same moments – and we both found the ending disappointing. She reminds me of my childhood best friend, Flint. I've never really had one since. On the day she moved in we sat talking until gone midnight. She told me her ethos was to be the best possible version of herself. We discuss that again, now, as Beatrix's name comes up.

'It means keeping fit. Respecting your body,' she says. 'And being well-groomed – keeping your image current. It's all about making a statement that says I mean business and I don't need anyone else to make a success of my life. My friends are great. Colleagues too. But I'm not depending on either to give me a helping hand. You know, one day, I'm going to open my own spa.'

I don't doubt it.

'Something of a perfectionist, aren't you?' I say, teasingly.

'Takes one to know one. Look how orderly your food cupboards are; how your books are shelved in alphabetical order. And it's obvious you put everything into your job to push your career forwards.'

It's true. Nothing less than A grades would satisfy me at school, even though Mum said I worked too hard. I'd been in awe of Uncle Kevin as a child. How his world was so much bigger than Mum's. I set my heart on widening my horizons. Going to a top university. Getting a great job. A tidy room means a tidy mind, Mum used to say, and she was right. Often, when she worked late, I'd spring-clean the whole house. Then I could rest my mind and finish homework, do extra reading and plan out strict timetables for revision.

Irfan always praises my attention to detail and I've never really thought about it before, but in my own way I'm not unlike Bella – I want to be and do my best.

Truth be told, I want to be *the* best.

'I'm no stranger to heartache, you know,' says Bella.

I sit down next to her.

'My ex cheated too.'

That makes me feel better. I wonder if anyone has ever cheated on Beatrix. Somehow I can't imagine it.

'I felt like such a fool. I thought we'd be growing old together – had constructed the whole story in my head. We'd get married, barefoot, on a beach in The Maldives. Our kids would have ginger hair like him – a boy and a girl, twins so that I'd only need to give birth once. When I found out he'd slept with our neighbour, I felt humiliated to think I'd planned our future in such detail.'

'I was the same. Lenny and I were going to be legends in publishing. I imagined us married for fifty years and the industry lauding the union of such a successful agent and editor…' I sigh. 'So how did you cope?'

'I made even more effort at the gym, got my hair re-styled and revamped my make-up. I cut out processed foods. Plus I worked all hours at the spa and got a pay rise and permission to build my own client list so that those customers had continuity. It was my idea and the boss loved it. Believe me, I made sure my ex would regret what he'd thrown away. I bumped into him a couple months later, at a pub where we used to hang out. I was with the girls, celebrating my success at work.'

I take off my new belted trench coat and drape it over the back of the sofa. 'What happened?'

'He sat at the bar staring. Eventually he came over, just as everyone toasted me. You should have seen his face. He looked like a little boy who'd lost his favourite toy.'

'What did he say?' My stomach flutters.

'That I looked even better than usual – the actual word he used was stunning. He was so fickle, he kept shaking his head and then tried to win me back. Said he'd made the biggest mistake of his life – that our neighbour wasn't half as driven as me and not the sort of woman he wanted to spend his life with.'

'That must have felt so satisfying, to knock him back.'

Bella stands up and stretches. 'Yes, but to my surprise I let him down gently. By that stage I no longer felt the desire to hurt him. My confidence was back. I just felt sorry for him; said I'd moved on and wished him well. But I felt calm inside – as if I'd achieved a degree of closure.'

That makes sense. Sometimes I lie awake at night, thinking about what Lenny has done, and it feels like the rushed bad ending to a novel – as if more chapters need to be written to properly tie up all the loose ends; to present me not as the victim but as a strong, self-reliant woman.

'Just think about that article in yesterday's newspaper about people to watch in the publishing industry…' Bella reaches down to touch her toes.

'It listed Beatrix as a perfect role model for young women.' And she is for me – or was. My jaw clenches. But not anymore.

'If only people knew what she was really like. I don't care how much she's achieved, she's no role model if she ploughs through other women's lives to reach for her own means. At the very least, she slept with your boyfriend whilst he was still living with you.'

Bella stretches her arms into the air. I've never exactly heard her badmouth friends or colleagues or family and we've talked a lot, but she has a sharp edge if there's the hint of injustice in the air. Her ponytail swished vigorously from side to side when I told her about Kath's condescending nephew. And the more I talk about what happened with Lenny and Beatrix, the higher her pitch becomes. With it, my sense of anger towards them increases, as if she's turning up its volume.

'Go and look in the mirror,' says Bella.

'That's not my preferred activity.'

Bella gives a mischievous smile. The more I get to know my new friend, the harder she is to resist.

Take last weekend. My clothes had become even baggier. Turns out I'm now a large size twelve. Bella insisted we go clothes shopping, which is an activity I've never enjoyed. I usually just head straight into M&S and stay there. But she insisted I should be more adventurous, so, heart pounding, I ventured into several boutiques. It wasn't as bad as I thought. With the music blaring, I felt less conspicuous and picked up several items for work and new jeans, all tighter than my usual style. Bella tried on clothes as well. I enjoyed giving her my opinion and listening to her advice. For fun we tried out platform boots and posed in wedding hats. I also looked in the window of a hair salon. Bella reckons my brown hair would look great with blonde highlights.

Reluctantly I get to my feet. It'd been a busy day at work. Bella yawns. She's always more tired when her day includes doing lots of massages. I head over to the mirror above the fireplace. Bella stands next to me. I look from her face to mine. Perhaps if I paid more attention to fitness, my face would have more shape – more character, like hers. Her cheekbones and defined jaw line are two striking features that made her look like a determined, assertive person.

I've never been bothered about my looks before. Not in such detail, anyway. I believe in being smart and making the best of myself but I have no interest in contouring my face or having my eyebrows threaded. I don't really see how that can make me a better or happier person. Or at least I didn't before. Bella is raising doubts.

'You've got amazing eyes,' she says. 'One's slightly bluer than the other.'

The only people to ever have noticed that are Flint, Mum and Uncle Kevin.

'Wouldn't it give you satisfaction to make Lenny realise you can look even better than Beatrix – with your amazing personality intact?' She nods at my reflection. 'Wouldn't he feel a fool for letting all that go? For losing someone who is the whole package?'

It would be like giving a book a new cover. A refresh, while keeping the contents the same.

'But I wouldn't want him back. Not now.' Or rather I *won't* take him back. Want is a different matter – despite my feelings of injustice.

'This isn't about going back. It's about moving forwards: holding your head high and coming out winning. Imagine the first time he sees you with a glossy new image. Can't you almost taste the sense of control? His realisation that you don't need him anymore?'

'I'm not sure. Maybe it is best to let things lie.' Something inside me solidifies, though, at the prospect of being in charge, of triumphantly steering my own destiny again despite the hurt and the knock to my confidence.

'Best for whom? I don't like to judge people, Violet, and this isn't judging – it's *fact*. You need to realise, for the sake of your self-respect, that Beatrix has been a bitch. He's acted like a bastard. There's no respect. You shouldn't let them treat you like that.'

'But we're not at school. Tit for tat, that's not my way…' I say, but with uncertainty now.

'This isn't about getting back at him – you're not sabotaging his relationship or career. It's simply showing him what he couldn't see before. That you're the best catch. It's about making him and Beatrix eat their words about how you look.'

Bella clears her throat and stops her stretches.

'I think I know a way to help you move forwards. Thoth Publishing – the twenty year celebration you told me about that's in the middle of June. Five weeks from now. Just picture Lenny's face. You walk in looking amazing. We'll find you an A list dress.' She takes my hands. 'Oh Violet, you'll feel on top of the world. I hate to see you lost in your thoughts and looking depressed. How you stare out of the window or at an upside-down newspaper. I'm so grateful for having my room and a flatmate who's such fun and cares for her neighbours. And you work harder than anyone I know.' She squeezes my fingers. 'You've done nothing wrong. You didn't deserve what happened. What you do deserve is to feel fabulous and untouchable.'

Someone like Bella sees me as fun? A lump forms in my throat.

I sit on the carpet and try to ignore Alice, who is behind and flicking my hair. Tonight I am going to start my plan to find a proper friend. I'll start in after school club. It might mean I have to put my book away.

If Alice wasn't so mean, I'd be perfectly happy. I don't need a best friend. I can share my problems with Tinker and my teddies. I've got my books. My drawing. My favourite telly programmes. It's just that it bothers Mum. She thinks I don't know, but every day, when we walk home, she asks the same questions.

Who did you sit next to in the lunch hall?

Did you play any nice games at break?

Would you like anyone to tea?

She hasn't made lots of friends in her new job yet, so I don't understand why she's worried about me. It hasn't even been one week, although it feels much longer, with Alice and her stupid jokes. At break she comes up and presses a bit of chewing gum into my hair. Mrs Warham has to cut it out.

At lunch time, one of the boys accidentally kicks a football into my face and it cuts my lip. I don't understand how, since it hasn't got any sharp edges. It's a bit like Alice. She hasn't punched me in the face or jammed my head down the loo. It's just all the little things and comments add up and damage my time in school.

I don't mind about the football even though the boys laugh. It means I get to go to first aid. One of the dinner ladies dabs my cut with something that stings. She asks if I want to rest inside for a few minutes. I say yes and ask if I can go to the library. What a treat. I enjoy tidying up all the books and then I read. It's exciting to listen to the grown-ups talking in the office opposite. As the end of play nears, at two o'clock, the teachers keep gasping. One woman even rushes to the toilets after listening to the radio. Her voice is full of tears. I hear the words aeroplane crash. Something about a tower. And New York. Teachers must get to watch movies when we are all outside. That's so cool. Today's must be what Uncle Kevin calls an action movie – a scary one, because I peek, and the head mistress keeps covering her eyes.

Uncle Kevin loves those films. I watched one with him, once, about a big wave. Mum got cross and said that it wasn't suitable.

Mum worries too much.

At five to two, the dinner lady comes to find me. Her face looks funny, as if she's holding in words that she's afraid to say. She tells me to run along to class. I get into the room early. The bell hasn't been rung yet. The other children file in and we settle down to maths. It's not my favourite subject but I don't find it difficult. I take after Uncle Kevin that way. The girl next to me copies my answers.The afternoon drags, unlike when we do story-making and it flies. Finally the last bell sounds. I get my coat and am ready for after school club, but in a weird jelly voice, Mrs Warham says my mum is in the playground and that I'm going straight home.

I hurry out. Her eyes are red. She must be poorly. I give her a big hug. Some of the other parents stare. One of them pats Mum's arm.

'Are you okay?' I say as we leave the playground.

A strange noise comes out of her throat. Like a cross between a sob and a snort.

So I don't ask her again. Instead I tell her all about my lip. I explain it was my best lunchtime yet. She doesn't talk as much as usual. Doesn't even ask me those questions about whether I've made friends. When we get home she won't let me watch telly. She says something about it being broken, so I sit with Tinker on my bed. He listens whilst I tell him about my day. Then I write a story. I like doing that. Today's is about a hedgehog called Pinhead. Mum stays downstairs on her computer. But finally I get hungry. I go to see her. She's got her head in her hands.

I clamber onto her lap and put my arms around her. We hug each other tight.

'What's the matter, Mum?'

Tears stream down her cheeks.

'Nothing. I… I'm just not feeling very well.'

It's as I thought. 'Do you want me to make a marmite sandwich? Or peanut butter? And a glass of squash?'

She shakes her head. 'How about I get you a takeaway pizza? And tomorrow, I don't think I'll be up to going into work. You can have the day off school if you like.'

My eyes widen. Today really is the best day ever.

I hug my knees the next morning as I sit in bed. No school. No Alice. Just me and Mum. The sun's shining. And my book is all dried and less smelly now, so I can finish *Charlotte's Web*. Mum spends the day making phone calls and fiddling on her computer. Somehow the telly is working for videos now but not the telly channels, so I watch two of my favourites. I eat biscuits. At lunch I help make sandwiches.

I ask if we can go to the park but Mum doesn't feel up to it. So I go into the garden and play with Tinker. When

I come back in, I huddle on my bed with my drawing. The sun is setting when Mum finally comes up.

She sits on the bed and takes my hands.

'Mum?'

Her eyes fill.

'What's wrong?' I say. 'Have you got to go to hospital?'

She shakes her head. 'It's Uncle Kevin. I'm sorry, Violet. So sorry, but… there's been an accident. Uncle Kevin… he's died.'

What? That doesn't make sense. Just yesterday he was at a party. Mum's got muddled.

'What happened?'

'The big tower where he worked. It fell down.'

'How?' Lego towers fall down. Not huge ones made from bricks.

'An aeroplane flew into it. Lots of brave people like police officers and firemen did everything they could to help, but the damage was too much.'

I try to digest this news but it's hard to swallow. Just like carrots, my least favourite food.

My mind flicks back to yesterday at school. The woman crying. The words I heard about an aeroplane and New York.

'But he's only just started his new job. And he was going to bring me American candy home at Christmas. He said maybe next year we could visit and…' My brow knots. 'Who will I talk to about books?' I pick up the copy of *Charlotte's Web* and hold it to my chest. I think about the tower that caught fire and why that meant we had to leave ours. 'Towers are dangerous things.'

Mum squeezes my hand. 'What's happened to Uncle Kevin's tower is very, very rare.'

'Like that limited dishun book he bought?'

Mum nods.

'But why couldn't the police help? They are supposed to keep everyone safe.'

'It was too smoky. Too many steps to climb.' Mum gets up. 'Come downstairs. Let's have dinner. It's pasta with garlic bread. Your favourite.'

'Uncle Kevin loves garlic bread. We should have it when he gets back.'

Mum skims her thumb across my cheek. 'He loved you very, very much, Violet. And he'll always be with us through the fun memories and good advice he gave.'

But I'm not listening. Uncle Kevin can't be dead. Mum's just being silly. She's not well. He will be home for Christmas.

I'll be able to tell him all about horrid Alice and hopefully by then I'll have a new friend to introduce.

'It'll be all right. You'll see, Mum.'

To make her feel better I take out my felt tips and draw her a picture of her, me and Uncle Kevin. We are in the park. Tinker's there too. The sun is shining.

–

Before school the next morning, I draw another picture of Uncle Kevin standing next to a tall pile of books. He's wearing his silly Christmas jumper and laughing. I'm going to school today. Mum is going back to work.

People look at us when we reach the playground. Mrs Warham takes me inside early. She asks if I'm okay. She must have heard that Mum's been behaving oddly.

The day carries on as usual. Assembly. More maths. Painting. Except Mia with red hair gives me a chocolate bar. Her mum thought I might like it. And the head-mistress comes in. She admires my picture. Then Mrs Warham gives me a gold star for tidying up the pencil pots.

At break, Alice comes over with her friends to where I'm standing in the playground, near the boys playing football. I'm hoping to get hit again so that I can go indoors and read. Alice's face looks pinched as if she's eaten something disgusting.

'Bet you think you're special with all this attention just because your stupid uncle died.'

Where did she hear about that? 'He's hasn't. My mum's got it wrong.'

Alice laughs. 'Of course he has. My older brother told me all about it. Mum wouldn't let me watch the telly so he showed me on his computer.' She shakes her head. 'His tower got hit by a plane. Bad people were flying it. There was a fire. It fell down. Another tower did too.'

'It's not true,' I say and jam my hands in my coat pockets.

Her bottom lip juts out. ''Tis so. I watched it happen. Mum thought it would scare me but it didn't. Not even the people jumping out of windows or the scared faces with flames behind them. What a horrible way to die. I'm never going to America again.'

Her friends pull her away and I run – run as fast as I can down to the bottom of the field. I hide my head in my lap until I hear footsteps approaching.

Mrs Warham sits down. 'Everything okay?' she says, gently.

'Alice says it's true,' I whisper. 'Uncle Kevin's tower fell down. She saw people jumping out of windows.'

Her face colours for a moment.

'Is she making it up?'

'What did your Mum say?'

'She said the same as Alice – without the jumping bit. She said the police couldn't save him.'

Mrs Warham bites her lip. 'It's true, Violet. Lots of people from the tower went to heaven yesterday. Your uncle wasn't alone.'

I stare at her. She looks well and doesn't seem like the sort of person to lie.

'Do you think he was with his new friend Cindy?'

'I'm sure he was with people he knew.'

'I want to hug him.'

Mrs Warham hugs me instead. We sit in silence for a moment.

'What if Mum dies? What will happen to me?'

Mrs Warham thinks for a moment. 'I don't expect your mum will die for a long, long time – but if she did, there would be lots of kind adults to make sure you were okay.'

I crush the blade of grass in my hand. 'Secretly I didn't want Uncle Kevin to go to America. Do you think this is a punishment for me being selfish? Am I a bad person?'

'No, Violet. No, and you mustn't ever think that. These things happen.'

'Well, I'm never going to die.'

Mrs Warham doesn't argue with that and I feel a bit better.

I thought last Wednesday when I started school was the worst day of my life, but it's not. It's the second.

Chapter 9

'The shit's really hit the fan this time.'

Irfan doesn't often swear. We've just come out of a meeting with Felicity.

'How can this have happened?' she said. 'We've lost Gary. Irfan? Violet? I want an explanation.'

We didn't know how to reply.

'Did you share our vision with him? Our comprehensive ideas for his branding? Is there anything that he's not been happy about that you haven't mentioned to me?'

Felicity queried the communication between us and our authors. Do we respond to their emails in a timely manner? Do we understand that the small things matter so much to writers like a card or a bunch of flowers on publication day?

'I built up this business from nothing,' she said. 'Coming from a family of self-made entrepreneurs, I know more than anyone that the journey down is far quicker than the journey up. We can't ever afford to lose great acquisitions for no good reason. I thought Gary had a long future ahead of him with Thoth.'

'So did we,' said Irfan, 'but—'

'And of all the publishers, we had to lose him to Alpaca Books,' she interjected. Her short silver-streaked hair normally suited her sallow skin, but today it made her look older than her fifty years and accentuated the lines.

Felicity had gone into publishing because of her love of science fiction. She gained experience at the big houses and then set up on her own. Her family invested the necessary money. She's always been proud of having paid that back within five years. She's now one of the most respected independent publishers in the industry. Yet her appetite for success is still sharp enough to smart from disappointment, like when she lost the *Earth Gazer* series to Beatrix. From that point forwards, she's seen her as a personal rival.

'She spoke to us as if we were interns fresh out of university,' says Irfan and sharpens a pencil ferociously. 'And as for Felicity scheduling that meeting next week, for us to go through all our authors and reassure her that we're doing everything we can for them and their books… you'd think she'd give us some credit for those who sign again and again. Maybe it's time I thought about moving on.'

'She's just disappointed, like us.' I get up, walk around to his side of the desk and take away the sharpener. I squeeze his shoulder. 'You're a fantastic editor, Irfan. It's been such an honour to work with you. I've learnt so much. This is a knee-jerk reaction from Felicity. Don't respond in the same way.' I'm glad I'll have Bella to talk about it with when I get home. That prospect makes me feel better already. Before, when things went wrong at work, it was so hard to return home to an empty flat.

'But—'

'Think of me, if nothing else. If you left, I'm not sure I could manage without Farah's low-fat vegan beetroot brownies.'

He puts down the pencil. 'Well, if you put it like that…'

We smile at each other.

'Seriously. Don't worry. She's on the phone right this minute to Gary's agent. He's as angry as her. She'll soon realise there's no logic to his decision and that there is nothing we could have done.'

Irfan sighs and nods as I return to my desk.

'It doesn't help that Thoth's profits have taken a downturn this last quarter,' he says. 'Those hardback publications were a bad call. Thoth needs something big. Did Lenny… I'm sorry to mention him, but—'

I hold up my hand. 'I'm okay. It's been nearly two months.' My gold nail varnish shines. Bella encouraged me to buy it. We are going shopping again today as it's Friday and the office closes early.

He studies me. 'You do seem a bit brighter, of late – does that mean I can tell Farah to stop worrying?'

'Please do! So, you were saying…?'

'Did Lenny ever mention an author called Casey Wilde?'

'I've read his manuscript. There's no doubt about it, *Alien Hearts* is pure brilliance.'

'*His*?'

'Yes – although keep that to yourself.' I didn't care about getting Lenny into trouble but coming out about his gender was the author's right, not mine. Lots of male writers write as women. It isn't unusual. But it's Wilde's decision when to reveal the truth.

Irfan lets out a low whistle. 'It's created such a buzz. I'd heard on the grapevine that Alpaca Books is a strong contender. But we're another smaller publishing house and haven't even received it for submission. Why Alpaca? They haven't got the financial clout of one of the Big Five. If only we could sign that book. What a coup that would be. A dream come true. It would mean so much for Felicity and would make up for losing Gary.'

All day I mull over Irfan's words. He talks about Wilde again when Farah comes into the office. She finishes early on a Friday as well. She doesn't express much interest, however, because she's staring in my direction. A not unpleasant sensation buzzes in my stomach lately when someone notices the change in my appearance. At first, when Hugo started to praise me, it felt uncomfortable – like the high strappy sandals I bought last week. I practised wearing them at home and almost fell over. But now these comments feel like an affirmation that I am moving on from being the person Lenny felt he could treat so badly.

When Irfan disappears to check on one last pricing issue with sales, she helps me put my coat on. Farah is thoughtful like that.

'And how are you?' she says.

'Good, thanks. Well, you know, apart from Gary not re-signing. You?'

'Excited that one of the kids is actually letting me visit their university digs. We go tomorrow. In fact, tonight I'm making a batch of Amira's favourite sweet pistachio barfi. I'll get Irfan to bring you some next week. It must be an effort to bake for one.'

Farah makes the most amazing desserts. A couple of times I've been invited to family bashes and my senses of taste and smell have been overindulged.

'I'm glad you are feeling better,' says Farah cautiously.

'I am. Since Lenny left, it's been an opportunity to start afresh. I've started a fitness regime. I don't have much time to think about him these days.'

Farah raises her eyebrows.

'I know. Me, running. This must be a parallel universe. Care to join in?' I ask and suppress a smile.

She doesn't need to reply. Her face says it all and she pretends to punch me.

'I'm glad you're looking after yourself, but I hope that includes good home cooking because—'

Irfan appears at her side. 'Farah. For goodness sake. If she wanted to eat chocolate for breakfast, lunch and dinner that would be her business, not ours…'

Farah looks sheepish. 'Sorry. With the looming weekend, maternal mode is firmly switched on. It's only because I care.'

'Honestly. I'm fine. In fact I've got a new flatmate.' That should reassure her.

'Really? Since when?'

'A few weeks.'

'You've kept that under your hat.' Farah's shoulders relax. Her eyes shine. 'Is that because there is more to it than you're letting on?'

Irfan groans.

'No. It's a she. Bella works in a spa. She's been helping me clean up my lifestyle and has taught me some really healthy recipes. We go shopping together and watch movies…' I consult my watch. 'In fact, sorry, I've got to get going. I'm meeting her now.'

I grab my coat and bag, turn off the computer. Farah gives me a hug that lasts longer than the usual few seconds. I hurry out of the building and take the underground to Oxford Street. On the train, a man accidentally steps on my foot. We start chatting. Even share a joke. He waves goodbye from the platform after he's got off.

When I tell Bella, she winks. 'You're going to be an absolute knock-out at the Thoth party – like a real Egyptian goddess. Look in that shop window. Go on.' She nudges my elbow with hers.

The woman staring back doesn't look familiar, even though I see her in the mirror every day. I can't get used to the subtle changes. The smaller bottom. The glossier hair. She feels like an imposter, as if the outside isn't real and I'm not showing my true self, like *The Emperor's New Clothes* in reverse.

We head into the nearest boutique. Bella inspires me to try on outfits that I've always allocated in my head for other people. Like the clingy jeans. The short tailored jacket. The brightly coloured blouse. Bella has given me the confidence to realise there's a whole lot more I can do to attain my potential, aside from improving what was going on in my head. It never occurred to me that a person's wrapping was as important as their content. I should have known that from my job in publishing. A great cover can make a good book a bestseller. I pose in the changing room and swivel from side to side as chart music plays. I stand on tip-toe to imagine what the outfits will look like with high heels. Bella catches my eye, gives an impish grin and laughs.

'Look at you. We'll make a catwalk queen of you yet.'

She helps me laugh at myself. We hug.

Next stop is Boots the chemist. I browse the shelves. Bella and I try on a couple of lipsticks, both of us having wiped the tester with a tissue first. The make-up assistant chooses the right foundation for my skin. She insists on applying it and selects an appropriate blusher, eye shadow and lip gloss to match. Then she sends me over to another counter where I have my eyebrows threaded.

I can't believe the difference a few products can make to the shape of my face. I look so... executive. Bella is in her element, surveying the beauty products. She hands me a couple of face packs to add to my basket and says she'll give me a pedicure when we get back. As we walk out of the shop, a man wolf whistles at *me*.

'How did that make you feel?' asks Bella and links her arm through mine. I look down at our wrists. She'd suggested we bought matching friendship bracelets from an accessory store. They didn't cost much but couldn't be worth more to me.

'Of course, it's highly inappropriate, I mean...'

Bella catches my eye.

'Is it wrong that I liked it?' I say in a half-whisper.

She rolls her eyes. 'No. Context is everything. He was simply expressing his appreciation.'

A wolf whistle isn't anything I've ever aspired to receive. In fact I used to wonder why any woman would want that unsolicited attention. Yet now I feel as if it's some sort of tick. A tick in a box that was never completed for the old Violet. A tick that brings expectations.

With aching feet, we end up in a coffee shop off the main road. Bags hang from my hands. I never realised

84

shopping could be such a workout. Bella will have to give my shoulders one of her massages. The cafe has simple wooden tables and chairs and sells hot drinks in old-fashioned sized cups with saucers. The cakes are traditional English fare – scones, Victoria Sandwich and toasted teacakes. It's not the sort of place Lenny would like to be seen in, but it's quiet and straightforward after a couple of hours navigating the stores. I'm drinking black coffee and am surprised after purchasing small size twelve jeans. I'm not sure if it's that or the caffeine that makes me feel taller than Big Ben. Sixteen, fourteen and now twelve – these numbers are important. They represent how I'm counting down to success; how I'm moving on from heartbreak.

I never understood that word before. How could a heart break in two? The physical pain of Lenny leaving took me unawares. A sharp pain in my chest. Not a stab but a sheet of agony that pushed down, as if I was undergoing a medieval execution and being crushed to death. People say a good cry helps. I found it only made things worse, whereas meeting Bella has given me a goal again. Shedding old clothes and lazy habits – it feels like shedding a weaker version of me.

Farah is great but hasn't encouraged my change. I know from the way she speaks of her fashion-conscious daughter, Farah probably thinks I need some "meat on my bones". And Kath says my hair colour is lovely as it is and did I know peroxide will ruin its condition?

'There's one explanation for Farah,' says Bella and puts down her cup. 'It's quite simple. She's jealous. You're looking, quite simply, fantastic.'

'I'm not sure about that…'

'You have to watch out for people sabotaging your hard work because the new you makes them take a long look at their own flaws.'

Could she be right? Now that I think about it, Farah is a little overweight.

The barista approaches and we stop talking. I like the way his fringe flops over his brows. He hands me a paper bag containing three cherry scones. 'They go out of date tonight. Please take them. They'll only go in the bin.'

'Thank you so much.'

'My pleasure. And by the way – you have the loveliest smile I've seen today.'

Bella gives my arm a squeeze as he grins and leaves. 'See. What did I say?' she whispers. 'I'm far too proud to be jealous!'

An hour later we're back home and I hang up my new clothes. As I go back into the lounge, there's a knock at the door. Kath has just got back from her Friday bingo with Nora. It's almost nine o'clock.

'Fancy a scone?' I say and tell her about the cafe owner. I make us a nice pot of tea and sit down next to Kath on the sofa. She admires a red dress stretched out on an armchair.

'Goodness, that's tiny,' she says.

'It's Bella's.'

'Is she in? I'd love to meet her.'

'She hurried out for her evening run. The roads are emptier at this time.' I pick up the dress. 'I'll just put this in her room.'

I walk in and lay the dress on the silver polka dot duvet cover. Bella's slippers sit on the floor, neatly by the side of her bed. This space used to be Lenny's. It's comforting to see it's no longer empty.

Chapter 10

I wake up Monday morning feeling guilty after eating pizza. This is new for me. What triggered it was the sight of the takeaway box with its lid still flipped open. All the clues were there – the skid marks of tomato topping and crust crumbs.

I'd celebrated after spending yesterday afternoon with the book club. We'd gone to the garden centre for lunch. It was the fourteenth of April – exactly two months since Lenny and I split.

I still miss the shape of him in bed. Each morning, I reach out for his warmth and am met by cold sheets that dwarf me. I need to continue filling the gap he's left: make my life as full as Bella's with her work, her friends, her health regime.

I suggested setting up a book review blog for Kath, Nora and Pauline. Now and again they talked about how they missed using the computer skills they acquired in their jobs. This was the perfect solution. They keep up-to-date. I keep busy. We finally settled on a name: Vintage Views.Excitement bubbled as we decided the blog, as well as reviews, could include posts on subjects they were interested in that were connected to books. And friends of theirs could write guest posts.

Nora would contribute reviews of movies that had been adapted from novels. She's always secretly fancied being a cinema critic. Former nurse Kath was interested in stories that dealt with mental health.

'And I'm keen to review any book, film or television programme that's even remotely linked to Benedict Cumberbatch,' said Pauline, which led to us all confessing our celebrity crushes. I've agreed to meet them in the pub after work tomorrow to get started on the website, since they are too keen to wait until the weekend. Over recent months, without even realising it, the book club has made me feel as if I'm more on the inside of something than out. It's a place away from work where I also feel like I fit in. Yesterday afternoon I didn't think once about my failed romance or my makeover. It was just me being me like before. Hence the pizza.

And now, instead of seeing the new sleeker me, I suddenly feel big. Before starting my new health programme, I never felt like that about my body or thought much about anyone's physicality. Whilst I found Lenny attractive, it wasn't his figure that registered first. It was always the eyes. How they made me laugh. How they made me feel like an attractive woman in a way I didn't feel embarrassed about. It's hard to look back now and realise it must have been different for him. Eventually he'd stopped seeing me, the person inside. Instead he saw someone who didn't suit the glittering life to which he aspired; a home bird who'd offered him a refuge from the scariness of striking out as an adult, on his own, and wasn't needed anymore.

To make up for my *slip* – that's what I'm calling the pizza – I get off the bus early and walk an extra mile to the office. Plus I take a brave step and call into a hairdresser's near work during my lunch. They've had a cancellation at four thirty and if I can leave that early will be able to fit me in for highlights. Blonde streaks will mark another benchmark along the way to a new me who doesn't need anyone else to make her life complete.

Except the hairdresser straightens my hair as well. I can't help gasping when she's finished. She gives a low whistle. 'Just look at who's been hiding under all that brown frizz. You look like a cover girl.'

I can't take my eyes away from the mirror. I feel big-headed thinking it, but it's true. I wouldn't look out of place in one of Bella's fashion magazines.

The hairdresser gives me a glass of prosecco and sells me a pair of straighteners. Out of politeness, I sip for five minutes and then hurry out, arriving at the retirement home just in time. My friends are meeting in the reception area before we all walk down to the pub. I stand outside nervously.

After a deep breath, I push open the door and step in. Kath stares. She walks over. The others join us.

'Your hair looks terrific and so much longer without the curls,' says Nora. 'You look like a young Lauren Bacall.'

Pauline shakes her head. 'You'd make a great under-cover agent. I mean, that's some transformation.'

Kath says nothing. She understands that I don't want a fuss. To my relief, as we walk the short distance to the Frog and Duck, talk moves from me to Vintage Views and the best look for the front page banner. Nora fancies a pink background with flowers. Kath favours a pragmatic look. Pauline insists photos of our faces across the top would look best and we say we're not taking mug shots.

We find a table in the corner and Kath pats the head of a golden retriever sitting nearby. A jazz CD plays in the background. It's seven o'clock and a handful of business people nurse drinks. I head to the bar for our usual crisps and gin and tonics. This time I get served straightaway and the barman keeps me talking and then offers to carry my tray.

'We need to order the food,' says Kath. 'If I eat too late I'll be up all night.'

The others murmur their agreement and we scan the menus. I'm getting used to looking for the healthiest option instead of what I really want. Normally, I'd enjoy fish and chips with buttered white bread and mushy peas. Instead I order the superfood salad that contains spinach, quinoa and lean chicken breast. I mumble something about having a high cholesterol level.

Lately I'm finding life's easier with the occasional small lie.

When I get up to fetch napkins and cutlery, plus table sauces for the waning taste buds of my friends, the barman appears at my side and strikes up another conversation about the weather. The movies. Food. A whole gamut of things. He even laughs at one of my jokes.

When I make my excuses as the book club members stare our way, the barman delves into his pocket and pulls out a paper napkin with writing on it. He passes it to me.

'Here's my number. We could catch a movie or eat out. Whatever you want.'

Before I can reply, he disappears. As I hand out the cutlery, the others want to know exactly what he gave me.

'His phone number,' I say, in disbelief.

Dinner arrives and when we're finished, I take a few headshots. Even if we don't use them in the banner, as Pauline suggested, they will prove useful for the individual profile pages. Then I take a few candid photos of the group as they sit chatting, just as practise. I scroll through them and really like one of the casual group shots.

'Look at this. It's perfect for the banner.' I pass around my phone.

The photo captures all their different personalities but in a natural, uncontrived way. With Nora, she has her fur coat draped around her shoulders and is sporting immaculate make-up. Animal lover Kath is talking to the golden retriever. Pauline's glasses perch on the end of her nose and she studies the menu as if reading a police report. They look happy. Relaxed.

'What do you think?' I ask. 'Wait. Let me put it through a sepia filter. That will give the shot a real vintage feel.'

I fiddle with my phone for a few moments and then pass it around once more.

'We look like movie stars snapped by the paparazzi,' says Nora and beams.

I ask the dog's owner if she minds us using the shot. She gives me her business card and says she'd be delighted, and asks could I send her the link for the blog when it's ready so that she can take a look? Then we talk through the rest of the website's design features. I promise to get it all up and running by the weekend, and on Sunday will set up a Twitter account and show them how to use it.

At the end of the night, everyone gives me a hug. The book club members' enthusiasm feels better than a sugar rush. And I didn't think once about Lenny. In fact, that rather nice barman asked me out. I won't ring him, of course. I don't feel as if my inside matches the new outside yet. He might be disappointed.

'You should believe more in yourself,' says Bella, who's exhausted after an afternoon pampering a hen party. We're both in our pyjamas, on the sofa with Flossie. 'The blonde hair brightens your whole demeanour. It's a tip I give to clients who want to refresh their look. The final piece of the jigsaw is to make an appointment for contact lenses. And, I've been thinking—'

'How about we concentrate on you for a moment,' I say. 'You've been so supportive and encouraging. I wish I could give something back.'

'But you do, Violet.' Bella sits more upright. Her tone softens and her eyes crinkle around the corners, eyes as green as her healthy diet. 'You and all the clients I help. That's the thing about empowerment – it's contagious. Empowering you empowers me. There's nothing better than opening someone's eyes to the fact that they came into this world alone and at some level that's how they should remain – without relying on another human being.' She ruffles the top of Flossie's head. 'We leave this world on our own, too, so shouldn't we be able to face the middle bit without the interference of others? Isn't that the goal? To get stronger as a… as a spirit, between the start and finish points? I'm not saying don't form a strong bond with people or fall in love, but don't look to anyone else to validate who you are. We are here to maximise our own journey. That's what I think, anyway.' Her eyes shine with the passion of someone who's got complete confidence in their beliefs.

She does make sense. Lenny, Beatrix, Kath, Farah… if I don't agree with them in my heart, none of their opinions should matter. Bella does like a project. I've worked that out. I'm her latest one. It's flattering that she thinks I'm worth it after the way Lenny made me feel. And she's renewed my faith in the concept of women supporting each other.

'The flirty barman should prove to you there's more than one way you can hit Lenny and Beatrix where it hurts.'

I sip my drink. Is hurting them what I really want to do? Revenge? Payback? In the past, I didn't think those words were for me, but lately I'm not so sure.

'The icing on the cake for Thoth's party night,' continues Bella, 'is that not only do you turn up looking fabulous, but on your arm is the perfect date.' She leans forward and whispers, 'Casey Wilde.'

'Me? And Wilde? That's a joke, right?'

Bella's expression doesn't flinch.

'As if that would be possible. Apart from anything else, Beatrix has probably already got him hooked.'

'She may still not know his true gender. Lenny has to be careful. From what you say he's already taken a big enough risk by giving her a sneak peek. You can find out Casey's email address. Arrange to meet. You have lots in common that you can talk about.' Bella sits straighter and rubs her hands together. 'For starters, you've read his book – from what you've said about that Gary, authors love to have their egos massaged.'

Would a man like him really be interested in me? Lenny made it clear he thought Wilde was something of a womaniser.

'You're any man's type, believe me, the way you look,' says Bella as if she can read my mind.

'It would certainly be a coup if I could persuade him to sign with Thoth. Felicity would be over the moon and Beatrix…'

'…would be furious.' A smile crosses Bella's lips.

Nervous questions pinch my stomach. What if Casey and I did meet up? What if we did get along?

Bella squeezes my arm. 'You've got four weeks to look even more amazing and land the most exciting science fiction author this year. It will be Violet Vaughan people are talking about, not Beatrix Bingham. Sassy. Invincible. Powerful. No one will be able to touch you then.'

Yesterday Mrs Warham's calendar said Friday the fourth of October, so today must be Saturday the fifth. One good thing about Mum's job is that she doesn't have to work on the weekend. Her boss isn't quite as yukky as she first thought. Apparently Ryan lost a sister a few years ago, so he knows how Mum feels. It's funny how adults say people get lost when they die because we know that they've gone to heaven.

Mum's eyes are still red most mornings and she sleeps a lot. It's nearly lunch time and Mum hasn't got up. I made myself cornflakes and orange juice for breakfast. I took some up to Mum. She didn't open her eyes and told me to watch telly. She was just feeling tired. She'd be down later.

Yesterday Alice cornered me in the playground and wanted to know about Uncle Kevin's funeral. Her brother said it won't be for ages because all the bodies are in pieces and no one knows who is who. She wants to know if he'll be burnt or buried. Her brother said Uncle Kevin would just be dust now, mixed up with everybody else.

Thank you, Mrs Warham, for walking past and sending Alice to the headmistress.

I stand in the garden and breathe in grassy smells. Mr Jones next door is very neat and has mowed his lawn, even though the summer is over. That's what I'm going to be like when I'm older. The sun is doing its best to cheer things up, but angry-looking clouds keep covering its smile. I wear my fleece. Zips are fiddly and I'm glad it pulls over my head. It's purple like my glasses. Like my name. Like Ribena, my favourite drink.

Our fence is broken, which feels like an invitation to sneak into Applegrove Wood. I haven't done that yet because Mum says I mustn't enter alone. But dog walkers pass through it, so it can't be dangerous. I look back at the house. Mum's curtains are still drawn. It won't hurt to have just a little run around. I wish I had a friend to play with at weekends. I've tried hard to find one at after school club but it's so noisy and everyone already knows everyone else. Mia, whose mum gave me chocolate, is nice. We've done jigsaws together and she stuck her tongue out at a boy who made fun of my glasses. But Mia is very popular and there aren't many children on my street apart from a two-year-old who is always crying and a teenager who scowled at me for no reason.

I hope to miss out the teenage years. Teenagers always listen to music. Maybe they think it sounds better than real life. Lately, I can understand that.

I walk up to the fence and squash myself between the two broken slats. Seconds later I'm on the other side, under the shade of a tree. I love conker trees. Their leaves are boring, but their prickly green cases contain the shiniest, smoothest jewels. I pick one up and squeeze the hard green shell, being careful not to scratch my hands.

'Do you want me to show you how to easily open that?' says a voice.

I look up. A boy stands next to me. His hair is the same brown colour as Uncle Kevin's, but it's tied back in a ponytail. He's wearing a jumper that looks as if it's been knitted by a gran. His trainers are really dirty. I like his smile. And, unlike Alice, he sounds kind.

'Put it on the floor and stand on it really gently,' he says. 'Squish your foot from side to side and it should burst open without breaking the conker inside.'

I do as he says and then bend down and prise open the cracked case. There are two small conkers inside, like twins in a mummy's tummy, but not identical. One is bigger than the other.

'One each. My name's Violet,' I say, feeling my face heat up.

'I'm Flint. Want to play catch?' He tags me on the shoulder and starts running. I put the conkers in my fleece pocket and follow as fast as I can, darting around tree trunks and jumping over piles of twigs. He trips over and I catch up.

'You okay?' I say, in between breaths.

With grazed knees, he stands up and laughs. 'You got lucky. I fell over some roots.' Flint's still wearing summer shorts.

'Are you allowed to play out here often?'

'Mum lets me and my brothers and sisters do what we want. We don't even go to school. She teaches us at home.'

I gasp. 'Now you're the lucky one.'

'We also get to wear what we want. And choose our own food. I had biscuits for breakfast.'

Sounds like he is lying, doesn't it? But I believe him. Mum lets me stay up later than usual right now. She switches the telly on. We eat in front of it. I get to watch programmes I'm not usually allowed to. One was called… what was it? *No Rules Kids* – about parents who let their children do whatever they want. Like Flint. They can make their own meals. Decide when they want to go to bed. It sounds great. I'd never have to see Alice again. Or eat carrots. I could stay up until midnight.

'My turn to catch you,' says Flint.

I start running. Piles of leaves squelch under my feet and mud flicks up against my legs. I couldn't find a pair of trousers to wear. Mum hasn't done the washing all week. So I'm in a summer skirt with ankle socks but it doesn't matter. I'm nice and warm in my fleece. We come to a really big trunk with a treehouse in the branches. Its roof has a hole in it and a grey squirrel stands next to it. Its tail twitches. The house's wooden sides are a bit lopsided and covered in moss and bird poo. There's a ladder going up to it. Me and Flint look at each other. He starts to climb. I follow.

We sit inside on the floor. Perhaps this place can be our secret. Mine and Flint's.

'Awesome,' he says. 'My brothers and sisters will never find me here.'

'Are you trying to hide from them? I'd love to be part of a big family.'

'Be careful what you wish for, my granny always says. My brothers are cool. My two sisters can be annoying. I guess they are all okay but sometimes it gets too noisy. I haven't got my own room so there is nowhere to go and just read. I love books.'

'Me too. Maybe… maybe we could both read here. I'm reading *Fantastic Mr Fox* at the moment.'

'That's an awesome story. The farmers are so mean.'

We talk about clever Mr Fox and I tell Flint about *Charlotte's Web*. He says he likes spiders and will ask his mum to get the book from the library.

I shiver. The sun has disappeared and the woods are chocolate cake dark. I tell Flint that perhaps I should head home. Mum might be up.

We run to the bottom of my garden. My chest relaxes as I see that Mum's curtains are still closed.

Flint waves and I push my way through the fence. Humming, I reach into my fleece pocket and hold onto the two conkers as I go inside.

Chapter 11

It's Friday and with only just over three weeks to the party, I feel shattered. I've gone all out to reach my target of creating a more professional image and found some great websites that give all sorts of tips. I've actually juiced for breakfast, done squats and sit-ups, I went for a facial and Bella helped me transform my feet with a loofah and nail polish. Farah and Irfan asked me to go for a coffee after work but I didn't feel up to it. She's beginning to irritate me with her comments about how *peaky* I look. And she brought in some home-baked muffins and made a big fuss about me taking one.

Yet in the toilets, yesterday, two editors complimented my new style and asked where I'd bought my outfit. I can only conclude – and I don't like to – that Bella's right: Farah's jealous. Goodness knows why, because it takes a lot of work to achieve the changes I'm making. Irfan's not worried. He asked for my secret formula to getting fit as all his best efforts weren't having much effect on the size of his belly.

I yawn and gently nudge Flossie to one side before putting my laptop on my knees. It's only two o'clock. I'm back early from work because of hours owed to me. I sink back into the sofa and click onto Facebook. I know Casey Wilde is friends with Lenny on there. I could look at his full profile through my ex's page, seeing as I know the password. Perhaps I could work out places he likes to frequent or make arrangements for a rendezvous and accidentally bump into him. As an editor of children's fiction, I have little professional excuse to contact him.

It all sounds rather childish, but Felicity deserves Thoth to do well and over the last couple of months I've realised that, sadly, there's more to success than hard work and integrity.

I log out and type in Lenny's password. It's not something I'd ever done before. I've heard women in the office talk about how they secretly read their partners' texts or track them on social media. However, I'd always trusted Lenny and been brought up not to snoop in people's private business.

Lenny once told me he uses the same password for everything: Aston Martin. I used to find it endearing that he saw himself as some kind of James Bond. But looking back, I realise his glitzy dreams were a symptom of his immaturity. As Bella's pointed out, it was me who paid the bills. Did the washing. Got in the groceries.

I scroll down his page and try not to stare at the photos of him and Beatrix; how his default position is to drape his arm around her protectively. I put Casey Wilde's name into the search bar. His profile photo is of a quill. He has more than one thousand friends and posts about writing, books or the gym – and parties. There is no mention of *Alien Hearts*, just his *work in progress*. Clearly, he is being careful until he decides on his official author identity. Perhaps if I look at the messages sent between him and Lenny, I'll find something.

I hesitate, then remember Bella saying that sometimes you have to step out of your comfort zone. Flint was the same, encouraging me to be brave enough to take risks. I've thought about him a lot lately. It took me a long time to forgive Mum for what happened to him. It was her fault and so cruel. So brutal.

I feel sick for a moment, and then shake the memories away, taking a deep breath.

I click into messaging. Top of the screen are the latest conversations between Lenny and Beatrix. My finger hovers for a moment. It's no good. I can't resist. I scroll down mundane talk about work and shopping. My cheeks feel hot as the conversations become more intimate. They talk about the new underwear she's bought from Victoria's Secret. I can't seem to turn away.

> *Hey gorgeous. I'm in the Gents at work, feeling decidedly heated. I'm thinking about you between the sheets. Me showing Beatrix Bingham who's boss* ☺

Lenny's never spoken to me like that. I read her reply.

> *We both know who calls the shots and you love every minute. So little Lenny needs to learn to do as he's told. Perhaps tonight he'll be more obedient.*

I feel empty inside. The memories of our gentle love-making evaporate. Looking back, we did have a kind of routine. Lenny would reach his height of pleasure and please me afterwards. Usually I was in the missionary position but I thought that suited us. For me it was just about getting close. The smell of his skin. His breath on my face. The full, satisfying feeling of him moving inside. The sweet sound of his moan. Whereas these messages make me think his and Beatrix's love life is so much more varied. Once again, I ask myself if Lenny had become bored. If… if I'd never been good enough, not even at the start.

My finger pauses as I decide whether to scroll down further to when Lenny and I broke up. It's like squeezing a spot. You know you'll regret it but can't stop. The conversations move backwards in time and my eyes feel impossibly full. In February, she teases Lenny about having feelings for me after he bought the Valentine's present. Beatrix says perhaps she should withhold sex. He replies by saying not that, as it's the best he's ever had.

Maybe I'm bad in bed.

I think back to the hours we spent under the duvet. I never felt shy but always thought it was the emotions that mattered, not the mechanics or positions. Should I have tried to spice things up? Has he had an affair before? Was he only with me because I had a nice flat?

My insides crumble like a dry leaf screwed up in the middle of his hand. Flossie moves nearer as if she knows I'm upset. She pushes against my side and purrs. I take a moment before clicking into his conversations with Casey Wilde. There is just one message: Lenny welcoming him to Facebook and Wilde giving him a new email address he'd just created.

An email address. What if I wrote and told him how much I'd enjoyed *Alien Hearts*? I wasn't meant to have seen the manuscript, but why should I protect Lenny anymore? Heat flushes through my limbs and for just one second, I consider throwing the laptop across the floor as I think of the photos of Lenny's arm draped protectively around *her*. My heart thuds and I take a deep breath. He would have to finally grow up and take responsibility for giving me an unofficial sneak peek. I copy the email address. Just in case.

Now I can't stop myself scrolling through all of Lenny's messages. One from his mum was written just after I first met his family. She says I'm a lovely girl. I sit a little straighter and click into another from his brother, dated the same day. He says I'm not Lenny's usual type.

Lenny replies.

Looks aren't everything.

Is this proof Lenny *never* found me attractive? An indignant spark burst into flames in my chest. How *could* he talk about his girlfriend like that? I log out of his account and go into Outlook. Without hesitation, I open a new email and paste in Casey Wilde's address.

I'm just about to type when there's a tap at my front door. I put the laptop to one side, get up and open it.

'Kath. How are you?'

'Okay, love. There's nothing much on the telly and I wondered if you fancied a game of Scrabble. Violet?'

'Sorry. My mind was elsewhere. Come on in.'

'Are you sure?'

'To be honest, I could do with the company.' My throat catches as I shut the door.

'Everything all right?'

I screw up my eyes. I don't do crying. Not since we lost Uncle Kevin. Nothing seemed as bad in comparison. Not until now. I loved Uncle Kevin. I loved Lenny. In different ways, they've both left. But I'm a grown-up now. I should be able to cope. Mum going to bed all the time after the

Twin Towers didn't do her any good. Just because Lenny and I broke up doesn't mean I can't carry on as normal.

We sit down on the sofa and I snap the laptop shut.

'Just ignore me,' I say to Kath. 'I've had a tough week at work. How about I put the kettle on and—'

She squeezes my hand. 'It's okay. You don't have to explain. I just worry about you, that's all. For the last month or so… I don't know… something seems different.'

'Things are. I am.'

'How?'

'I don't know, more confident, better than I was before. Bella's been really good for me.'

I head into the kitchen and put the kettle on. When I come back out, Kath has stood up and is peeking into Bella's room. She will see the make-up laid out smartly on the dressing table and a stack of celebrity magazines. The Jack Vettriano print on the wall of a stylish couple walking along the beach. And a couple of pairs of really high heels in the corner of the room. Bella and I are the same shoe size. I tried them on once and was amazed at how much slimmer my legs looked.

I head back into the kitchen and clear my throat to distract Kath. I wouldn't want her to know I'd caught her looking. I don't blame her. She must be curious.

When I come back out with coffee, Kath is back on the sofa.

'So, this Bella… She's making things better?'

'I'm so glad I've got to know her. She's tidy. Disciplined. A real inspiration. And tough – she doesn't let anyone mess with her. And what she doesn't know about style…'

'That's important?' Kath cocks her head to one side.

'Yes. I realise that now. In the past I've always gone for comfort first.'

'Like me.'

'And there's nothing wrong with that – but I work in the publishing world. Bella has helped me see that I need to be savvier. You know how passionate I am about my job. I work as hard as possible and can't do anything else on that score. A new image could really push my career forwards that extra mile.' I doubt Beatrix lost many authors. Would Gary have left if I had her slick business reputation? No.

Kath nods.

'You're always telling me you wished many of your patients had thought to look after their health when they were young. Just think of it as a reboot – the old Violet needed an update, that's all. And I'm sure she can still beat you at Scrabble.'

We play the game accompanied by a plate of biscuits, although I can't face eating after reading those messages. A ball of heat still glowers in my chest. How dare Lenny.

Even Kath's appetite is off and she looks more tired than normal. On Monday, she has an appointment to see the doctor. Her painkillers aren't doing much for her arthritic pain and she has trouble picking up the Scrabble letters. She needs an extra lift. So I do what I'd never done before: let her win on purpose.

After walking Kath up to her room, I return to my flat. I put on a new top which is low cut, I brush my highlighted hair and apply make-up like the assistant in Boots showed me. I stand under the standard lamp to take a photo. It's a trick I found online. I switch my phone's camera to selfie mode and take about twenty different photos.

Finally I find one I like. It includes cleavage but has an air of professionalism and emphasises my cheekbones. I like to think I look serious but approachable. My stomach flutters as I notice the shadow of my collar bone that has never been visible before. The lamp's light gives my highlights a Fifties movie starlet feel and the lipstick accentuates my mouth. Yesterday I had my contact lenses appointment. I'm allowed to wear them for a few hours every day, to start. They'll be ideal for a night out with Casey Wilde.

I go into Instagram and put the photo through different filters. I hardly recognise myself by the time I've finished. I share it with my followers and immediately start getting likes. I'm surprised what a boost that gives me, as if I've had a sip of the headiest champagne. I block Lenny and Beatrix's accounts before coming off. I want my new appearance to be a total surprise.

I return to the sofa, flip open my laptop and go into Outlook. The ball of heat in my chest ignites again. *Looks aren't everything*? I load the new photo as my email signature, and write Violet Vaughan, Editor, Thoth Publishing. Punching at the keys, I start to type.

Chapter 12

Dear Violet Vaughan,

Thanks so much for your email. I'm delighted that you enjoyed Alien Hearts. More than that, I'm extremely grateful that you sent me my very first piece of fan mail. Let me assure you it will be duly printed out and framed. ☺ Really, I'm thrilled that my work made you cry and realise I have possibly the only job in the world where saying that is acceptable. After years of rejections, I still can't get used to people in the industry saying I've done a good job.

However, I am surprised your friend Lenny gave you a copy to read and revealed my gender identity which is currently Top Secret – I'm aware that makes me sound like the biggest idiot. I'm just worried readers may not take the book seriously if they know I'm a man – although my agent tries to reassure me that I don't need to worry about that.

As you wish, I won't mention that you've emailed to Lenny – or to the agency. I agree, from what I know of him, that he was probably just being overenthusiastic and I wouldn't want him to get into trouble either.

Oh, by the way — your photo looks kind of familiar. Have we met before?

Thanks again.

Yours truly,
Casey Wilde

Heart pounding, I lean back in the sofa. He responded quickly. On first reading it, I feel an inexplicable anxiety and can't face my morning plateful of fruit. But then I take a step back and tell myself I can deal with flirting. I stop overthinking and light-heartedly email back. It doesn't come naturally and I try to give my words a tone that matches the filtered photo in my email signature. As for him thinking he recognised me, this is good. It means I must look more like other young women and don't stand out anymore.

Dear Casey,

I'm moved to tears at the prospect of my words framed and hanging in your house. Thank you. It's truly an honour. ☺ But seriously, Alien Hearts is unique. Bold. Romantic. Gripping. Emotional.

I wonder if I may tempt you with an invitation to meet up. I'm so excited about your writing and would love to discuss your methodology and how you researched. And I know a lovely coffee house next door to a vintage bookshop. Perhaps I could meet you there one day after work.

Yours equally truly,
Violet Vaughan

I hug the laptop to my chest, as if it's a best friend. This is fun. I get up to take a shower. Will he bother to reply? I'm almost in my bedroom when an email landing in my inbox pings. I hurry back to the sofa.

> *Dear Violet,*
>
> *That would be great. Meeting a fan will be good practise for when I undoubtedly become a household name. (I hope you realise I jest!) Jokes aside, I appreciate your kind words. But I drink more than enough coffee during the day – how about cocktails?*
>
> *Yours,*
> *Casey*

Of course. The suggestion of a cafe next to a bookshop is too like the old me. I don't want to appear ignorant and think hard of a cocktail bar I can suggest. They aren't the kind of place I visit often, but one comes to mind. Months ago I went with Farah. We'd been chatting about the fact that she didn't drink and I didn't much either, so we found a place called The Olive Bar where the mocktail menu was wide-ranging, including a lavender spritzer and virgin ginger mimosa.

> *Dear Casey,*
>
> *Do you know The Olive Bar in Covent Garden? I'll remember to bring my autograph book!*
>
> *Violet*

I smile.

Dear Vi,

May I call you that? I feel we are friends now, since I made you cry and you're aware of my gender dilemma!

That sounds perfect. I know it's the weekend, but dare I hope that you are free tonight? Eight o'clock? I'll even wear my new leopard print shirt.

Yours as ever.
Casey

My hands feel clammy. Can I really do this? Faceless exchanges online are one thing, but what about meeting him in the flesh?

But then I think of Bella. She'd tell me to go for it. And she's right. I'm an editor. Casey's a writer. We'll have lots of talk about. It'll be all right. And besides, more than anything, I'm doing this for Felicity and Thoth.

I press send on my reply to confirm. What should I wear? I wish I was as small as Bella. She has such exquisite clothes that literally hang on her. Luckily she gets home early and we go shopping. Eventually I find a bright green dress. Normally that colour would complement my purple glasses, but after a week of getting used to contacts, I hardly wear them now. It's cinched in at the waist – not a body part that's been in my vocabulary much before. I stare at the full-length mirror. The dress is low cut at the front but not too revealing. I buy a bright red lipstick. Bella has a pair of high nude shoes I can borrow.

I'm so grateful for her help. She does my nails, make-up and hair. I promise her a trip to the cinema next week, my treat.

At seven thirty, I look down at myself. I take a few selfies for Instagram and carefully choose the best filter. As soon as it's shared, the likes start to come in. It's helped that I've researched the best hashtags and add on #weekendvibes.

I scroll back through the few photos already uploaded on my account. Before heading out to the underground, I delete all the shots of the old me.

I was glad to leave school yesterday. Fridays are my favourite because they mean the weekend is here and this week Alice has been more horrible than usual. She keeps talking about America. About burning bodies. About people jumping to their death. Her older brother keeps showing her videos on his phone. I don't think he should. They sound like horror movies. Mum tries to keep her newspaper away from me, but I've seen some of the photos.

It's scary. My knees feel funny when I think about Uncle Kevin helpless. Adults in uniforms are supposed to keep everyone safe, but in America they didn't. What if it happens near us? What if the bad people fly aeroplanes into school or where Mum works or our street? I don't want us to die in a fire. I don't want to have to jump out a window. And with all the noise, Tinker would run away.

I thought I couldn't hate Alice any more than I did until yesterday because she started to be nice and for a while stopped calling me Shrinking Violet. I couldn't work out why, at first, but then it hit me. It's because she's sick of me getting attention from Mrs Warham, the dinner ladies and even the boys who asked me to play football yesterday. I got a goal and some of them clapped just as Alice was walking past.

Later, Alice walked with her arm around my shoulder and looked important. I pull a face at Flint as I tell him about it. We're sitting in the treehouse. It's late Saturday morning. October is colder but such a pretty month with red, orange and yellow leaves. Mum is still in bed. I run home every hour to say hello to her and pretend me and

Flint have been in the garden with my toys. She'd be cross if she knew I'd gone over the fence.

'Alice sounds like a real dragon fart,' he says and lets a beetle crawl over his hand. Half of his hair hangs loose from his ponytail and his anorak is covered in grass stains. His mum lets him play outside most of the time.

'She even helped me tidy up the pencil pots, one of my favourite jobs. But she just kept yawning and didn't bother sharpening the ones that had gone blunt. I couldn't take it anymore, after lunch, and shook her off; told her to keep away.'

Flint hugs his knees. 'What did she do?'

'Pinched me really hard on my leg and then ran off to her friends saying that I smelled bad and must have pooped my pants like a baby.'

Flint shakes his head. 'Who does she think she is? You need to let me help you think of a revenge plan.' He sits up straight. 'If my brothers and sisters get me into trouble – blame me for something they did – I always get them back. It's not like I'm being mean. It's only fair.'

I put down my book. 'What have you done?'

'Once Skye ate all the bottoms of the carrot muffins Mum made. She thought no one would find out as you couldn't really tell when they sat the right way up. Skye said she saw me do it. Put a bit of muffin in my coat pocket as evidence. I got my own back. Our rabbits like carrots and that gave me the idea of mixing their poo pellets in with her muesli. They look just like raisins.'

My eyes widen. 'She didn't eat them?'

He laughs. 'Yes. One. She was sick. She hasn't got me into trouble since.' He shrugs. 'Sometimes you have to stand up for yourself. I can help you think of a way to get back at that idiot Alice.'

I hug my knees too. It feels good to have someone on my side. We meet up outside most days, either in the woods or out front. Flint's allowed to walk to my house and I was really happy on Monday because Mum let him come inside to play. She poured us drinks and cut two slices of cake, although she gave Flint a funny look. I'm not that surprised. He was wearing one of the jumpers his mum knitted. It had gone wrong and the neck almost came off his shoulders. But Mum's polite and she didn't say anything. Then we went up to my room. Flint said it was cool because it wasn't all pink and he thought the cuckoo clock from Uncle Kevin was amazing.

Flint gives me a cheeky grin and points in the corner of the treehouse. There is a big hairy spider. After reading *Charlotte's Web*, I don't mind picking it up.

'They are probably more frightened of us than the other way around,' says Flint.

'That's what Uncle Kevin used to say. Alice hates them. She screamed louder than a fire engine the other day when she saw one run out of the school games cupboard.'

'Really?' Flint leaned forwards as I release the spider and it scurries away. 'Then you know what to do. It's Halloween soon.'

'You mean catch one from the woods and—'

His head nods up and down really quickly. 'You could put it in her school bag or,' His eyes gleam, 'down her back.'

'I can't.'

'You can. It's only fair after all the things she's said about your Uncle Kevin.'

I think about Flint's idea when I'm tucked up in bed that night. He's the best ever friend. He's looking out for me. And he's right. It's time I stood up to Alice.

Chapter 13

I sit inside The Olive Bar. It's eight o'clock and the place
is already half-full. Despite my new clothes, on the inside
I feel like a can of cheap supermarket lager set amongst
glossy liquor bottles. I perch on a stool by the bar and pull
down the hem of my dress. Coloured lights swirl across
the room's walls. If Flossie was here, she'd go for the kill,
convinced they were some kind of rainbow mice climbing
the walls. A disco beat thumps loudly in the background
and a circle of friends by the window sing along whilst
taking selfies. I tap my foot in time to the music and
study the drinks menu. Do people even use the word *disco*
anymore? Uncle Kevin taught me my first dance steps. I'd
stand on his feet and we'd hold hands and move at the
same time until I found the confidence to jump off and
try some of my own moves.

The barman ignores a group of women waiting at the
other end of the bar, beams at me and asks what I'd like
– or rather shouts. The latest tune must be playing above
the legal number of allowed decibels. Yet I don't mind.
Somehow it makes me feel less conspicuous and as if I
belong here.

'What do you recommend?' I ask in a raised voice.

'What's your name?'

'Violet, I mean… Vi.'

He thinks for a moment. 'I've got it. I'll make you a Vi-tai. How about that?'

I've had a Mai Tai before and like rum. He blends ingredients in a silver shaker and ice clatters as he moves it up and down, as if he's the lead performer in a percussion band. He seems oblivious to the frowns of the other women waiting.

I sway side to side along to the song until my drink arrives in a tumbler with a small spring of mint. Kath's so excited to blog about conservation and wouldn't approve of the plastic straw.

'Thank you. What a lovely colour.'

The barman winks.

'I'll have one of those too,' says a voice next to me.

The barman gives the thumbs up and calls a colleague over to deal with the other customers. I turn around to face the most penetrating eyes and a chest full of leopard print.

'That shirt is actually for real?' I ask before I can stop myself. 'I mean…'

Casey bursts out laughing. It's a delicious sound. Full, warm, with notes of mischief like a spiced gingerbread latte. Not like Lenny's, which is always a bit too loud, as if he's trying to convince other people that he's having the best time. Casey's head jerks towards a table near the window, with two seats and his jet black fringe flops down. His long fingers smooth it back. I take my drink over. The music is a little quieter here. He waits for his, having insisted on paying. I try to concentrate on the Saturday crowds outside surrounding a street juggler, but my eyes are drawn back to Casey. He's just as striking as in the photo I saw. Nora would say he belonged on one of her

Mills & Boon covers. A loud voice from behind catches my attention. A man is on his phone and telling someone to hurry up and get here.

Casey strides over, sits down and his legs fall apart as if that's his default position. Our glasses clink together. The man talking into his mobile walks past, squeezing in between tables, and accidentally knocks Casey's shoulder. As an apology, he offers a tattooed high-five. Casey presses palms with him and the man moves on.

'Lovely to meet you, Vi. I'm thrilled that you liked *Alien Hearts*.'

'I couldn't put it down,' I say. We talk about the plot. Casey tells me how long it took to write. And how it's really the fifth book he's written. The others are firmly under his bed.

His legs move further apart. 'So, I'm assuming you want to meet because Thoth is interested in acquiring me.'

My eyes widen and his rich laugh attracts the attention of a group of women behind.

'I don't see any point in playing games – although I'm not sure my agent would approve of this clandestine meeting.'

'I'm just a fan. That's all,' I say and suck up refreshing fruit juice and rum.

Casey pulls out his straw and tosses it on the table before taking a mouthful. 'So you're not here in an official capacity? Who cares anyway? I'm sure my agent won't mind me meeting editors on my own. And if he does…' He shrugs. 'I don't see how he really can object. I wrote the thing, after all.'

My eyebrows rise of their own accord.

'What?' he says.

'How long have you been signed to your agent?'

'A couple of months.'

The alcohol is already loosening my tongue. It probably doesn't help that I was too nervous to eat before coming out. 'You've not earned your agent a penny yet. The work he's putting in before publication is based on his belief in you and your work. So…'

Casey leans forward. Thinks for a moment. 'You're right. I need to show him some respect. I'll call him straight away.'

'No, I didn't mean—'

'Gotcha there, didn't I?' His generous mouth upturns. 'You've got a point, though,' he says more softly. 'I didn't mean to sound like a twat. It's just… all of this is new. I don't want to upset anybody.'

What a difference from Gary Smith. Casey stares. 'Sorry if I sounded conceited. Is it always like this – books causing so much interest before they've even gone on submission?'

'Only exceptional ones. Frankly, I think it's a work of genius, so don't consider me the person to keep rein on your ego. And I don't think it's conceit – you should be rightly proud of yourself. And it takes any author a while to understand how the publishing process and its players work.'

Casey smiles so I decide to go for it and give him my best pitch, tell him why I think Thoth Publishing would be a perfect match. How Felicity lives and breathes science fiction, starting with a childhood defined by *Battlestar Galactica*, *Star Trek*, *E.T.* and *Star Wars*. How it inspired her to set up her own publishing house – how she worked night and day for twenty years to make it the solid business it is. How making *Alien Hearts* a success would mean everything to Thoth and not just because of the clinical aspects like sales and Amazon rankings.

Casey hears me out. Puts down his drink.

I keep my voice light. 'Has anyone else approached you yet?'

'Just one editor. She has an excellent reputation.'

'Beatrix Bingham,' I say, guessing he'll equally appreciate my openness.

Casey tilts his head. 'How did you know that?'

'I've done my research. She wants to sign you to her new imprint *Out There Stories*, an imprint with no solid record. It's an unknown entity.'

'But *she* isn't. I've done my homework too. Thoth isn't doing as well as it could…' His inky eyes dance. 'But you're bold.'

Am I?

'And I admire that. But I have my career to think about. Beatrix is already talking foreign rights and screen adaptations.'

'That's all pie in the sky before you've even signed and investigated all your options.'

Casey calls the waiter over. 'Same again for me. Vi?'

I like that. He's not assuming. If Lenny was drinking beer, he'd get us one each before I could object.

'Yes please.' I give the waiter my credit card. I need to take charge. 'Could you open a tab with that?'

'You're not at all what I expected,' he says as the waiter heads to the bar.

'You're a penniless debut author, Mr Wilde. I couldn't possibly expect you to buy more than one cocktail.'

'Penniless? Hardly. I own a hairdresser's.'

The waiter arrives with our drinks and hands me my credit card.

'That doesn't surprise me,' I say when we're alone. 'It makes sense, now, why you understand women so well. I'm presuming they're the bulk of your customers – that we're not talking a barber shop? What made you go into hairdressing? How do you fit your writing in alongside work?'

He's so easy to talk to – is that because of him or the drink?

'Yes, I style women's hair. I was also brought up by a single mother and two older sisters. As for your other questions…' He grinned. 'You know, Beatrix only wanted to know one thing when I told her.'

'Enlighten me.' Even I'm impressed by how together I sound.

'She asked what I thought of her hair and angled for a reduced price cut at the salon.'

'Do you want to give up the hairdressing and eventually become a full-time writer?'

'No. For a start, I could never do that to my staff. Over the years, they've become friends and depend on their employment with me.'

'I bet your mum wouldn't want you to, either. Imagine getting free haircuts for life.'

'Hardly. Despite my objections, she's always insisted on paying. Mum's no freeloader. My dad developed cancer soon after I was born. He died within a month of being diagnosed and had no life insurance. Mum had three children to provide for and held down two jobs for as long as I can remember.'

I pause for a moment and give this news the time it deserves to sink in. I sip my drink, before I reply, feeling able to share with Casey what I rarely share with anyone.

'I'm sorry to hear about your dad. Our backgrounds aren't dissimilar. My mum worked several jobs too. My dad was never on the scene. Even when my Uncle Kevin died and left us a load of money, she didn't touch it for years. She saw it as blood money. He was in finance and died doing his job.'

'What happened?'

Normally I avoid the subject. People either don't know what to say or try to find out if he'd been a jumper.

'He died in The World Trade Centre attacks.'

Casey squeezes my hand. For someone who crafts words day in, day out, he knows when not to use them.

We talk more about our childhoods. How we both developed a love of reading. He wants to know why, like most editors, I don't write. I ask what turns him on about science fiction. The evening passes so quickly it's as if it's a book I can't put down. We order bar snacks. I pick at olives and crisps. The style of music changes.

Casey grabs my hand. 'I love soul music.'

'But—'

Before I know it, we are facing each other on the square dance floor, if you can call it that. Really it's just a space at the back, between the toilets and bar. It means that everyone moves very close together. Normally I'd feel self-conscious, but for some reason I don't. The women around me twist their bodies, drop to the floor and spring up, they curve their arms in the air and sing along as the chorus plays. Moving my feet side to side has always been a winning formula. Casey grabs my hand and swirls me. I grin and nearly lose my balance. He slips one arm around my back. It's almost as if he can sense I've not had much practise.

Then suddenly the alcohol hits me. I feel more unsteady and my mouth feels as if I've eaten a handful of crackers. I make my excuses, telling him about the Sunday book club and how, tomorrow, I'll be setting up the website and Twitter account.

'Good luck with it,' he says as we step outside. It's quieter now, more like my usual Saturday nights. 'How about we do this again? I don't feel you've worked hard enough to sell me Felicity as an editor,' he says in that mischievous gingerbread latte voice.

'Felicity sells herself.'

'Have you shown her my manuscript?'

I shake my head. 'I wouldn't want to get her hopes up if your agent decides not to formally let her read it.'

'Maybe I'll mention Thoth to him. See what he says.'

'Don't mention me though, will you? It's best that he contacts Felicity,' I say quickly.

He looks down at me. 'I can't make you out, Vi. Something just doesn't add up.'

I feel different again. Purple. Frumpy. 'What do you mean?' Perhaps he's discovered that the person he's looking at isn't really me. That underneath I'm the woman Lenny thought was boring in bed; the woman he felt he could cheat on and take for granted.

'I don't know, but I'll get to the bottom of it. There's nothing I like more than a puzzle – and a beautiful one at that.'

I look away.

'And that's what I'm talking about,' he says and with his hand gently guides my chin back to face him. 'A woman like you can't be unaware of her good looks – and yet you genuinely seem to doubt yours.' My pulse speeds up. 'It's a mystery I'd love to unravel. So, I propose we get together again – how about it? You and me? Let's make it a date.'

'Is that what it is?'

He grins. 'If you prefer, we don't have to label it. Have you ever heard of Chapter Battle? It's happening in Camden Town next Saturday afternoon. Writers stand up and read out their first chapter. The winner is the one who gets to the end without being booed down. It starts just after lunch. I think you'll find it fun.'

'It sounds brutal.' But what an unusual idea. 'I know a cafe there that does a great brunch.' It used to be one of Lenny and my favourites. I'd have maple syrup pancakes whereas Lenny would pretend to love trendy mashed avocado and poached eggs on toast. He wasn't so keen on the Camden vibe. It was too bohemian for him and not enough designer labels. But he'd heard that celebrities ate there, so it was often our weekend trip of choice. The chances of Lenny being in the area were small. On the grapevine, I'd heard that Alpaca Books would be holding an all day meet and greet event, on that date, starring its top erotic romance authors with champagne and luxury goody bags and male pole dancers. There would be too many Instagram opportunities for him and Beatrix to miss.

'Perfect. We'll meet for lunch first. Let's email this week.' He kisses me on the cheek and checks I'm okay getting home. I watch him stride into the distance and, feeling like royalty, treat myself to a black cab. Smiling, I have to move my phone away from my ear as Bella squeals when I tell her the evening was a great success.

Chapter 14

I love my job, but Monday mornings are a challenge even for me. Many authors work at the weekend. They have no concept of time if inspiration strikes and for those that hold down other full-time jobs, they set aside Saturday and Sunday for writing. This means they also carry out their administrative tasks on those days and my inbox is usually full when I get in. Today is no different and I scroll down, glad it isn't yesterday morning. I woke up feeling jaded after the alcoholic cocktails I'm not used to drinking. I re-read *Alien Hearts* after a long bath before heading to the Sunflower retirement home.

I've given my friends an old laptop I'd held onto after shelving it for a more compact model. Everything's getting smaller these days. Like girlfriends. Or so it seems. It didn't take me too long to set up the Vintage Views website, since I've often helped authors and interns. Then we set up a Twitter account. Pauline will be able to show the others how to use that. Plus she and ex-receptionist Nora can touch-type and have offered to write up the blog posts. Due to her arthritis, Kath is grateful, along with other residents who are keen to write guest posts.

'So what's the subject of the first post?' asks Irfan and yawns as he sits down opposite and passes me a mug of tea. He turns on his screen.

'Nora's is on how Mills & Boon has modernised and moved with the times. Kath's will be next. She's reviewing a non-fiction self-help book about coping with anxiety. Pauline has taken control of the Twitter account and I told her what I could about hashtags. There's so much to explain like how to use gifs and add tags to blog posts, but for complete beginners, they're doing brilliantly.'

Irfan stares at his computer.

'Everything okay?'

'What? Sorry, Violet… have you looked at your inbox yet? Something's just dropped in.'

I click onto the relevant page. There's a new, unopened email at the top. From Felicity.

> *Dear Irfan and Violet,*
>
> *I'd like a brief meeting with you both this morning, if possible, to further discuss the loss of Gary Smith. 11 o'clock if that suits. Please RSVP to let me know.*
>
> *Best,*
> *Felicity*

I look up at Irfan. 'We haven't had time to prepare our notes about the other authors and everything else Felicity wanted to know, like how we support them on social media and what we do to strengthen the editor/author bond.'

'It's too late now. I've got a meeting with marketing first thing and then must brainstorm with design about the cover for the latest Little Starfish story.'

For me, though, the next two hours pass slowly – surely Felicity didn't truly doubt the children department's efficacy? We had seven books shortlisted for prizes last year and have continually innovated, including putting together a starter pack to help debut authors get the most out of signings and school events. With the help of the publicity department, we're proving increasingly successful at getting interviews into the national media. Many of those have brilliantly raised authors' profiles.

It makes me realise just how much I want, no, need my job and how important this makeover of mine would be if I ever found myself back on the job market fighting against other editors to get a position.

By the time eleven o'clock arrives, I have a mental list, at least, of why what happened with Gary was just a blip.

'After you,' says Irfan and gives a brief look to the ceiling as we head towards Felicity's office. Like the side room, the walls are made of glass so that she can see through to the open plan area. The pinched look on her face doesn't alter as we go in.

'Sit down, both of you,' she says and nods towards the two chairs on the other side of her desk.

I've always liked Felicity. She is honest and down-to-earth. When she hired me, she said I still had a lot to learn about publishing, but my passion for children's books won her over. During the interview, we'd had an animated discussion about whether it had been the right decision for Enid Blyton stories to be edited for a modern audience. She is also a huge fan of Paddington Bear and we chatted about whether the recent films had done the character justice.

If she were an item of stationery, she'd be a stapler. Uncomplicated and unassuming but holding everything together.

Felicity pushes away her keyboard and rummages underneath her desk. My stomach rumbles. I haven't had time for breakfast and now wish I'd accepted one of Irfan's low-sugar biscuits. Felicity sits back up, gets to her feet and hands us a bag each.

'This isn't the redundancy equivalent of a retirement clock, is it?' mutters Irfan and cautiously peers in.

His face adopts a quizzical look. I inspect the contents of my bag. There's a box of chocolates in the shape of a bookshelf, a beautiful gilt peacock notebook and mug that says Best Editor in the World on the side with an arrow pointing upwards.

'I do hope you'll both accept my apologies for what I said about Gary,' she says and rubs her forehead. 'I was completely out of order. Truth be told, I was having a bad week with one of the kids. And discovering that Beatrix Bingham was instrumental in poaching him… well, let's just say the whole *Earth Gazer* debacle still feels raw. I shouldn't have taken it out on two of my best editors. I apologise. I let my professionalism slip.'

'I don't know what to say. I thought I was in here to collect my P45,' says Irfan.

'I'm so sorry I gave you that expectation. Business is steady, although we can't afford to get complacent. We're only as good as our authors. As for Gary, well – perhaps this would have happened sooner rather than later, anyway.'

'Remember Callum Phinn?' says Irfan.

Felicity and I nod. The three of us had been knocked sideways by his sensitive story of the gay son of a macho weapon systems operator in the RAF. He almost signed with us but, in the end, went for another publishing house, despite our clear marketing passion and long-term vision. Callum was a debut author and signed for a one book deal offering more money instead of our two book deal that showed more commitment. His novel didn't do as well as expected and the publisher lost confidence and didn't re-sign him.

'One of a successful debut author's most important skills is to realise they are only as good as their next book,' says Irfan. 'The five-star reviews and the raving publicists mean nothing if you don't keep on top of the writing. Like Grace Webster.'

We all smiled. A former television newscaster, she wrote laugh out loud young children's books and despite her global success, was the most conscientious of all our authors.

'I like Gary,' continues Irfan. 'I wish him all the best. I would have liked to publish his next books, but for lots of reasons authors move on – we all understand that. I just hope he stays on track.'

Irfan and I stand up and thank Felicity once again for the gifts. She asks me to stay behind. I sit down again. She waits for the door to close.

'This is awkward for me to say, Violet, and I do hope you won't take it the wrong way.' She picks up a biro and fiddles with it. 'I can't help but notice… lately… you…' Her fingers grip the biro more tightly. 'Okay. I'm just going to say it. Please don't take offence for me making such a personal remark. Your appearance, it's very different. And good for you,' she adds quickly. 'I mean, you looked great before and do now, just in a different way. I'm just concerned that, well, it's a very glamorous look and—'

I squirm. This is worse than Farah's clumsy remarks. 'I just wanted to get healthy and—'

Felicity holds up her hand. 'Violet. I'm pleased for you, but I need to know… is this all part of a plan to leave Thoth and push your career forwards with one of the Big Five? Because I truly value you as an employee and if you are thinking of leaving, I'd like us to discuss what I can do to make you stay. Perhaps—'

I digest her words. The changes I've made seem to have already pushed my career prospects forwards. 'Please don't worry on that score. I love my job here and hope to build on what I've already achieved. Honestly. My new look… I just, I don't know – thought that it was time for a change.'

Felicity's shoulders relax. 'Really? What a relief. Thoth wouldn't be Thoth without Violet Vaughan.'

For some reason, hearing those words makes me want to tear up.

'And you are quite right. Change can be a good thing. I've had all sorts of different hairstyles over the years. Perms. Highlights. I even had dreadlocks as a student.'

I smile.

'I'm so glad you aren't leaving us. You'd be sorely missed.'

Suddenly Mondays don't seem so bad after all. I head back to my desk. Irfan looks like a guilty puppy as he sits behind a half-eaten box of chocolates. I shall leave mine in the office overnight. I don't want the temptation. Although I might just have one with a coffee, seeing as I didn't have breakfast. I settle back in front of my screen and take a double-take at my screen. A message from Lenny has dropped into my inbox. This morning is full of surprises.

Hi Violet,

How are you? I hope everything is okay.

I'm sure I don't need to mention this, but me letting you read Alien Hearts was done as a favour and I'd appreciate it if you didn't talk to anyone about this manuscript. Casey Wilde has found out that it's been read before submission. I'd only let a few people take a look, like Hilary in accounts who's a huge fan of dystopian novels and Dan in marketing. However, annoyingly, I lost a printed-out version I was taking home last month. I took it out of my briefcase at a book signing when I was looking for my phone charger and must have left it there. Casey says he had drinks with some woman at the weekend who's seen it. He messaged me on Facebook but seemed reluctant to give more details, although it's obvious he really liked her. Anyway, I know you wouldn't do this to me, but I do need you to delete the file.

Cheers.

All the best,
Lenny

My appetite disappears and is replaced by a dull ache at the way he emails me in a friendly tone as if nothing has happened. And what about the comment making it clear that I didn't figure as a contender for being the sort of woman Casey would like?

I haven't looked at Lenny's Facebook page again, but now can't resist. I wonder how Casey and Lenny have talked about me.

Is it possible he could fancy me?

I log in to Facebook with his password and click into the message Casey sent.

> *Hey Lenny*
>
> *I'm messaging you privately on here so that – for your sake – our conversation doesn't get picked up in your office. I met someone at the weekend who's read Alien Hearts. It's not even on submission at the moment. She said you were the source. I don't want to say anymore. She's a lovely person.*
>
> *Casey*

A lovely person. Liquid heat fills my chest and for a moment expunges the cold Lenny left.

> *Hey Casey,*
>
> *I'm sorry. You're right – I was just so excited about the manuscript and appreciate you keeping this to yourself. I promise it won't happen again. I can't think who you're talking about. But get used to it, Casey. You'll have to get used to female fans fawning over you once this book is released.*
>
> *Cheers.*
> *Lenny*

I grin when I see that Casey doesn't feel Lenny's comment dignifies a response.

'I'd almost forgotten what that beaming smile looked like,' says Irfan opposite me.

'Just something stupid on Facebook.'

Perfect. I can relax. Casey's a good sort. This makes me all the more intent on acquiring him. And that'll teach Lenny for assuming it couldn't possibly be me that he met. I deliberate over whether to now share his manuscript with Felicity and decide not. I'll ask Casey on Saturday. Clearly he likes things doing by the book. I lean over the desk and pluck a single chocolate out of Irfan's box and then put it back, recalling the low wolf whistle Hugo gave me this morning before he moaned that it was weird suddenly seeing someone in the friend zone as hot.

I click into Instagram. My last photo got more than sixty likes. That extinguishes the anger building over Lenny's insensitive email. I lift up my phone and take a selfie in my work clothes. Irfan shoots me a strange look. I smile and go about the important task of choosing the right filter.

Chapter 15

'That cafe is wonderful. A place built to make memories. I can't believe I've never been in there before,' says Casey as we walk towards Camden market. I try to keep up. Bemusement crosses his strong features and he slows. His long legs are wrapped up in tight black jeans to match his hair and leather jacket. There's a hint of Danny Zuko. Does that make me Sandy? I watched *Grease* as a child with the acceptance that I'd never be the kind of girl that boys raced cars for.

I'm wearing a new pair of blue jeans. The style is skinny. At first I thought there was some mistake. The thrill I enjoyed when fitting them on in the changing room last night matched the high of acquiring a new author. Bella encouraged me to buy a matching denim jacket. She bought one too. Underneath is a white blouse that's practically see-through and reveals my bra straps. A subtle floral pattern masks my cleavage.

'You know this area well?' I ask, fighting an unexpected urge to link my arm with his. It's almost out of my control in the same way that I haven't been able to stop remembering those penetrating eyes or the intelligent, confident tone of his voice.

'I lived near here as a teenager. My family moved down from Manchester. It reminded me of the indoor market there, Afflecks Palace, and the Northern Quarter. Best of all, I could buy cannabis-flavoured lollipops without a Proof of Age ID card. It's one of my favourite parts of London for a day out.'

'You haven't got a strong Mancunian accent.'

'No. Mum grew up in London. I guess that rubbed off.'

Camden is my favourite part too, with its diverse shops and market stalls. It's probably one of the places I used to feel I most blended in. Over the years, I've bought a purse made from leaves and a hand-knitted dress. I've browsed through second-hand bookshops and watched customers have feathers sewn into their hair. I've eaten a wide selection of authentic street food and drunk from coconut shells, while accompanied by the smell of joss sticks in the air.

Another reason I like it is that in an ever-changing world, its free spirit has never changed. Except that now as we walk along, and I stop to thumb through a rail or taste a free sample of fresh juice, the male stallholders treat me a different way. One compliments my pink cat-eye style sunglasses. Another glares at a male pedestrian who accidentally bumps into me and asks if I'm okay. Stallholders were always polite in the past, but some of the young, good-looking ones had even started to call me madam. Not anymore.

'So where is the Chapter Battle being held?' I ask and wish I hadn't bought boots with such high heels. I smile to myself. Every now and again the old me makes a comment like that.

We turn down a side street. 'Just here. I'm glad you could come. It's no fun on your own.'

We stop outside a Tudor pub. Suitably, it's called Canterbury Tales. I follow Casey in. The bar is crowded and all the scratched mahogany tables are full, apart from one in the corner with a sign marked reserved. At the back is a small laminate dance floor with a mike in the middle. Customers face it expectantly, drinks in their hands. To the side stand a group of people – the authors, presumably – holding sheets of paper and notebooks. They shuffle nervously on their feet. The walls could do with a lick of paint and the layout is ramshackle, but the atmosphere is warmer than an English beer.

'Seeing as you insisted on paying for lunch, drinks are on me,' says Casey.

'Diet coke, please.'

'I'll need a whiskey to steady my nerves.'

It turns out that the reserved table is for us. Casey is good friends with the landlord who takes us to our table and pulls out the chair for me. He wishes me luck sitting next to an ego as big as Casey's. He says I'm more than welcome to sit with him at the bar instead. Playfully, Casey throws a slow-motion fist and his landlord friend ducks. I glow from tip to toe. I was lucky if Lenny even introduced me to his friends.

'You're taking part?' I remove my sunglasses, feeling like a VIP after the barman's attention. 'No wonder you wanted moral support although you're remarkably calm.'

'I thought I'd read out the first chapter of *Alien Hearts*. Or the prologue, to be exact – that's allowed as well.' He sipped his drink. 'It went out on submission this week. To a few indies and two of the Big Five. My agent wants to test the water.'

I pick up my glass, drain it and stare into the bottom. Casey's agent hasn't submitted to Thoth. Felicity would have mentioned it.

I'm failing. Failing with the plan to sign Casey. That must mean I'm failing in the glamour stakes as well. For a moment, it's as if I'm back in the playground of Apple-grove Primary with no friend group. I glance down at myself and all of a sudden miss my odd socks. Who am I kidding? As if I could carry off a transparent top and tight jeans. I must look a right joke.

'Vi?'

'What? Sorry. It's all very exciting for you. Great news,' I say brightly, without giving him eye contact.

He takes off his jacket and fully displays his Jackson Pollock style T-shirt to the room like a peacock fanning its tail. I'm embarrassed to think back to my flirting now over cocktails. Talk about out of my league.

'Look, Vi, I'm working on my agent about Thoth,' he says. 'It's clear from what you say that they'd have a real vision and passion and honestly, I—'

'Don't worry. Really. I don't have any expectations.'

Casey says something else but I hardly hear. As if I could compete with Beatrix Bingham. It's not as if he's asked me out on a date. It's a Chapter Battle. I need to get a grip.

I breathe a sigh of relief as the landlord announces the start of the proceedings and amongst the clapping it's too noisy for anyone to talk. The first author takes to the dance floor. His hand shakes as he holds the mike as if it could predict the boos that were going to arrive after just two paragraphs.

'Too many adverbs,' whispers Casey.

'And not a gripping enough start,' I say without looking away from the mike, inwardly waging a battle against my negative thoughts.

My pulse rate slows as I feel the welcome embrace of my comfort zone now that we are talking about words. The next author takes position and starts to read. She lasts longer and even garners a few laughs.

'Not bad. That was funny,' says Casey and waves to her. She blows him a kiss.

'She just needs to make the dialogue sound more realistic,' I say. 'Of course, there's no doubt you'll win.'

'Don't jinx it. Look, about the submissions,' he says but is interrupted as the landlord calls his name. A chink of sunlight breaks through the side window and I put on my sunglasses as Casey begins.

The barman takes a break from pulling pints. A man next to me stops scrunching his crisp packet. Silence falls as Casey begins to read. The prologue is a sensuous scene of two characters dancing. It's not obvious until the last paragraph that one of them isn't from this planet and that revelation draws gasps.

A woman whistles and claps just before he finishes, as if she knew the end was imminent. I turn left to look and my mouth goes dry.

Beatrix? And Lenny?

It can't be.

It is.

My heart pounds.

I'm amazed they've spurned the glamorous meet and greet at Alpaca Books. This isn't happening. He must be carrying on our weekend tradition of Camden lunches. Wearing funky shorts and a stylish halter neck top, she heads over to Casey and kisses him on both cheeks. Perfume wafts across the room and smells like the most expensive thing in the pub.

It chokes me as if it's poisonous gas. I inhale and exhale, trying to take back control of my emotions as she moves her arm up and down his shoulder and pulls his collar gently. He bends down and whispers something in her ear. Casey's laugh drifts over to me.

My chair scrapes as I stand up and feel dizzy for a second. I navigate the chairs and head for the door. Just as I pass, Lenny steps backwards and into me.

'Watch where you're going,' he mutters without turning around.

I lower my head and escape into the spring air. Please don't let him recognise me. I head up the side street and then left towards the station. Footsteps sound behind me. Instinctively I quicken my pace. Lenny must have turned to look. This isn't part of the plan. I need to look my very best when he sees the new Violet Vaughan – not this half-baked version who, at the moment, hasn't convinced Casey to give Thoth Publishing a chance. I still have a few weeks left to turn things around. However, fingers curl around my elbow. I try to shake it off but the grip becomes tighter.

'Vi?'

Casey. Thank God. Oh no. He darts in front of me. I can't meet his eye.

'What's the matter? Why did you leave? Is everything all right?'

'Yes. Sorry. I should have said goodbye. I just don't feel well. I didn't want to cause a fuss.' I force a smile. 'Well done on the reading, Casey. You were fantastic. Best of luck with *Alien Hearts*. I'm sure it's going to be a smash hit.'

'Vi, about submissions. Look at me for a minute.'

No. Because that means he'll be looking at me. I couldn't bear that – not after he's been looking at the vision that is Beatrix Bingham.

'Sorry. I think I'm going to be sick.' I shake his hand briefly – keep it professional – and then run as best as I can in my heels.

I don't mind school today because Flint is coming around tonight for Halloween. Mum said we could go trick or treating together. She has to come with us – even Flint's mum insisted on that – but she's promised to stay at the end of each house's drive so that we don't look like babies. He came to tea at the weekend. Mum made us chicken and vegetables. I prefer fish fingers and chips but Flint said it was really yum. His dad has a vegetable garden and they have chickens, mostly for eggs but sometimes for meat. We talked about what outfits we'd wear.

Flint is going as a skeleton. Mum bought me a glittery witch's hat and a cape from the supermarket. She's not sleeping so much now, so it's more difficult for me and Flint to sneak into Applegrove Wood. We have to go at the weekend. I crawl through the gap in the fence when Mum is watching telly. Her eyes aren't so red. It's strange but she somehow seems better since last weekend when she got a phone call saying Uncle Kevin had been found. He was on the second floor of his tower. Masonry (I wonder what that is) had fallen on his head. Mum didn't tell me, but I heard her repeating what the person on the phone said: that Uncle Kevin must have got to work seconds before the plane hit and not been high up and at his desk. So he started to walk back down the tower again. Being found on the second floor meant that he almost got out.

I cried a lot, in secret, when I heard that. Thinking that he nearly lived makes his death much worse.

But not for Mum. I heard her talking to another friend. Listening in is the only way I find things out these days. Mum said she could cope now that she was no longer in a place called limbo. I don't know where that is – perhaps it's near work and she goes there when I'm at school. It can't be very nice because all these weeks it's made her so miserable.

'Let's go, Violet,' calls Mum.

I pull open my bedroom drawer and take out a sandwich bag. Inside is Muffet. He's not the spindly sort of spider but has lovely thick, furry legs. I'm so happy that he is still alive. I took one of Mum's sewing needles and made holes in the plastic so that he could breathe. I found him down the bottom of the garden last night near the woods. Last weekend Flint and I talked through my plan. I almost chickened out but Flint kept on encouraging me to be brave.

Halloween is the perfect day to do it. Alice is such a scaredy-cat. And it serves her right for not asking me to her party. I'm the only girl in the class who didn't get an invitation.

'It's not personal,' said Alice, who likes to use grown-up phrases. 'But you're such a Shrinking Violet I know you'd rather stay at home. You'd only cry at the biscuits Mum has bought with monsters on the front. And me and everyone else will be doing pretty Halloween make-up. It wouldn't show behind your big purple glasses.'

As I wave goodbye to Mum, my stomach hurts as if I want to eat. But I had a big breakfast. Mum bought half-moon shaped pastries with chocolate in the middle. She hasn't done that for a long time. The pain must be because I feel a bit nervous. What if Alice finds out it was me? And I don't want Muffet hurt. I hope he manages to run away. Flint said Alice deserves it. I know he's right. She's been so unkind.

145

I make sure I am one of the last to go in the classroom. When I get to my peg, Alice and her friends are already sitting on the carpet. I wait until everyone else has hung up their coats and then quickly I pull out the sandwich bag. I tug off my bobble hat and jiggle it over my peg. I turn around to check no one is looking. Everyone is listening to Alice showing off about the games her mum has organised for the party tonight. Apple dunking sounds like fun.

Alice's peg is at the other end of the wall near the toilets. I put the sandwich bag on the ground and hang up my coat. I head for Alice's bag. It doesn't take me long to let Muffet escape. I do her bag up again and go into the toilets where I pretend to wee.

Heart thumping, I return to my peg, stuff the empty sandwich bag in my coat pocket and sit on the carpet. That's the good thing about having a second name beginning with V. It gives you a bit of extra time when Mrs Warham is calling the register.

After what seems like a whole year, we come back from assembly, fetch our bags and sit at our desks. It's maths first today. I stare very hard at my notebook, not daring to look up in case I catch Alice's eye. My hands feel damp. Suddenly a loud scream echoes around the classroom.

Alice stands up quickly and falls back onto the floor. She flashes her knickers. They are red with white spots today. Alice likes to do that if it's her choice, but not when it's an accident and everyone giggles.

'A huge spider! It jumped out of my bag. It ran onto my book,' she says in between sobs.

'Calm down, Alice, and sit back at your desk,' snaps Mrs Warham.

Alice shakes her head. It matches her whole body.

'Do as you're told this instant,' says Mrs Warham, who checks Alice's chair. 'There are no spiders here. You must have imagined it.'

'There was.' Tears run down her face.

I've never seen Alice cry before. Lots of her so-called friends grin. It's a relief to see that her face gets blotchy and swollen too. But I can't help feeling sorry for her. Her tears make me realise that underneath she's just like me.

At break she is still crying. But then, Muffet was quite big. And especially hairy. As we all hurry into the October sunshine, I go up to Alice and give her a tissue.

She sneers. 'You think that is going to make me invite you to my party?'

'No, I—' I'm stuttering. I only wanted to make her feel better.

Flint is right. There's no point in feeling sorry for Alice.

'I'd rather invite that spider,' she says and seems to feel better when the others laugh at her joke. She stuffs the tissue down the front of my jumper and, holding hands with Georgie, skips away.

But I'm not bothered. Her tears have shown me that Alice isn't as brave as she likes to think.

Chapter 16

After getting back from Camden, I changed straight into my pyjamas and take refuge under the magnolia and pale lilac duvet despite the afternoon sunlight. Bella is sitting on my bed. My room isn't as stylish or vibrant as hers, with the overflow of dog-eared books from the lounge stacked on the floor. On the wall is a yellowing framed photo of Mum and Uncle Kevin, taken when they were little. He's sticking his tongue out. Before these recent weeks, the only visible cosmetics were a powder compact and clear nail varnish – now I've converted a small writing desk into a dressing table and it's laden with colourful eye shadows and lipsticks, plus my new hair dryer and straighteners.

On the inside of my wardrobe door is a new full-length mirror. I came home from work one day to find that Bella had bought and installed it. I've never had one before. I was never the kind of person to rate their own appearance out of ten nor to ask their partner if their bum looked big. It didn't seem relevant. I peek out from under the sheets so that my voice sounds less muffled.

'I can't believe I saw Lenny. What if he recognised me?'

'From what you tell me, there's no way that happened,' says Bella and hugs her knees. 'He and Beatrix won't be able to believe their eyes at the party.'

'What must Casey think? I'm such a fool. And I've completely failed in persuading him to offer his manuscript to Thoth.'

'You assume too much. Did he actually say that?'

'He said he was working on his agent, but that's no guarantee.' I pull the duvet up to my chin. 'My phone keeps bleeping. I know it's him texting. Casey will want to know that I got home okay.'

Bella gives me a stern look. 'Then you text him back, bright and breezy. Say you're feeling better. It must have been something you ate. He'll understand.'

'I can't do that.'

'Why not?'

'To start with, it's a lie — perhaps I should be honest. Tell him about Lenny and Beatrix and that it was just too much seeing them.'

'Tell him anything but the truth. And play down wanting him to send the manuscript. Make out it's his loss, not yours.'

I sit up and lean against the velvet headboard, fiddling with my watch. Bella lays her hand on mine and my fingers relax.

'There's something I didn't tell you about when I split up with my ex,' she says. 'Oh, I revamped my image and my career and yes, I knocked him back in the pub when he wanted to get back together. But even though I just felt sorry for him, I still hadn't quite moved on back at my flat. Photos of him were still up. I'd kept all the gifts from him, the jewellery, the perfume and scented candles he knew that I liked. One corner of my bedroom could have been mistaken for a shrine to him. However, if I'd let on in the pub that a small part of me pined… if he'd come back for a coffee or if we'd shagged… I wouldn't be where I am today building my own life, saving to buy my own house, writing my own story without waiting for a man to fill any potential plot gaps.' She squeezes my hand. Her slim fingers are remarkably strong. 'You tell Casey the truth. You admit seeing your ex upset you, then it's giving the power back to that loser and Beatrix. You don't need either of them in your life. All you need is your own agenda and self-respect. Get Casey on your side. Acquire his book. Take him to the party. This is all still possible.'

'You really think so?'

'We have two weeks. Let's pull out all the stops and really get you into tip top shape. By the time we've finished, Beatrix will look positively B List compared to you. I've seen miracles happen at the spa in fourteen days.'

'Is that what I need? A miracle?' I manage a smile.

Except that was the great thing about Bella. She didn't make it sound as if I looked awful right at this moment. Bella didn't focus on the here and now, she concentrated on the what ifs. She made me feel as if anything was possible and images fill my head of Casey and me having wild, passionate sex. My cheeks feel hot as I ask myself where those thoughts came from. *You fancy him, idiot*, says a smug voice in my head.

Bella continues to talk and my neck and forehead become less tight. She says the two of us are in this together and that she'll join me on a three day juicing detox. She'll give me two facials a week and insists I accompany her every night on her late jog. Plus, she's discovered some amazing rehydration cream to apply to my arms and legs every day, so that whatever I wear to the party, I'll look positively dewy – her words. I feel like a Hollywood star in the making as I listen to her grooming plan.

'First of all, though,' she says, 'text Casey. Suggest that you meet tomorrow. Subtly make him realise you're interested in seeing *him* and that you really aren't that bothered about the book. I mean, you like him anyway, right?'

As usual, Bella seems able to read my mind.

'In fact, let me do it.'

Before I know it, she's picked up my phone from the bedside table. I try to protest but she scrolls through my contacts, taps in the words and presses send.

'Come on. Time to get up. Feeling sorry for yourself won't achieve anything.'

I smart at her words but know that she's right. Whistling, Bella leaves the room, muttering something about googling new juicing recipes. I pick up my phone and read what she typed.

> *Hi Casey,*
>
> *Thanks for your texts. Sorry I haven't replied sooner. Please accept my apologies for leaving so abruptly. I suddenly felt very ill. How about we meet up tomorrow morning? Hopefully this is just a twenty-four hour bug. The weather is due to be decent. We could catch up in Phoenix Garden. It's very pretty – and then head to Foyles' Cafe afterwards. My treat. It's not too far.*
>
> *Vi*

He doesn't reply straight away and I do my best not to feel disappointed. Instead I open an unexpected text from

Farah. She's started inviting me out for coffee and cake or dinner more than usual. I swipe it away.

I take a shower and get changed into a pink jogging suit like Bella's. My stomach rumbles but instead of filling it with food, I fill my mind with images of Beatrix's jealous face when I walk into the party with Casey on my arm. That feels far more satisfying.

I sit on the sofa and my phone bleeps.

Vi,

I'm so glad you're feeling better. I felt like Prince Charming abandoned at the ball by Cinderella! Not that I see you as some sort of scullery maid. I'm sure you look just as fantastic after midnight. And you didn't leave a shoe behind – just your pink sunglasses. I was tempted to keep them for myself but my head's too big (please, don't make any observations about that). Sunshine and snacks sound great. How about ten thirty? I think that cafe opens at half past eleven on a Sunday. And we can discuss submitting Alien Hearts to Thoth.

Casey

Warmth courses through my veins. Bella may be a little overpowering at times, but thanks to her, everything is back on track. I message back my agreement without acknowledging the slightest interest in his manuscript.

Chapter 17

Getting ready to meet Casey takes a considerable while and half an hour alone to decide what to wear. In the past, I'd simply grab a pair of trousers and a top. When we first started dating, Lenny used to say it was a joy to be with someone who spent less time in the bathroom than him. Whereas now, I have hair to style and make-up to apply.

After much inner conflict, I choose shorts, a figure hugging T-shirt and a flowing white crocheted cardigan from a little boutique in Covent Garden. Shorts only formed part of my holiday wardrobe before. For the first time in my life, I shave above the knee and apply moisturiser with just a hint of tan. I could waste hours online studying beauty videos and reading reviews of products that promise to make you a ten out of ten. This is not something I ever thought I would say.

I glance at my watch. Nine o'clock. I've been up since seven. That's another thing that has changed. On a Sunday I'd often lie in, reading a book after cuddling up to Lenny, who'd feel snug and comforting. These days I am up with the birds doing my nails or cleaning the flat. By taking more care of myself, I somehow feel more efficient and time-table every hour.

There's a knock at the door. It's Kath. I haven't seen her much the last few days. Her smile looks a little forced and her movements are slow.

'Just checking you're going to book club this after-noon,' she says. 'We're all so keen and want to show you the blog posts we've managed to put up.'

'I've been following Vintage Views' progress online and have read them already. They look great. But of course I am, although is it okay if you get a taxi today? I'm out with a friend and won't have time to come back here before meeting at the home.' I hate letting her down by not giving her a lift, as her income is so tight. But increasingly I realise Bella is right and I need to put myself first. In fact, I'd managed to thwart a suggestion that the book club meet again one evening last week. I've been feeling shattered after work and it's always great to hang out with Bella.

'Okay, see you later then,' says Kath and she yawns. 'Goodness. I slept terribly last night – how about you?' Her eyes scour my face. 'Is work demanding at the moment? Perhaps you should ease off your fitness routine for a while. Relax more. You deserve it.'

In slightly clipped tones, I explain that I enjoy exercise, difficult as that might be to believe after her only ever seeing me wear trainers for travelling to work.

'How about coming around to mine after book club? I'm baking this morning, if my fingers allow it. Your favourite chocolate cake,' she added in a bright voice.

Trouble is, it's not my favourite any more. And my life's getting so busy. Slowly my priorities are changing – and certain people's inability to accept this is becoming increasingly irritating.

'That's really kind. Thank you, but I've got stuff to do here.'

Kath's shoulders drop, but I can't risk even a mouthful of cake. It might trigger all the old taste buds. I say goodbye more quickly than necessary.

As Bella says, my needs are just as important as anyone else's.

I head out into the warm May air. It doesn't take long to get to Tottenham Court Road and when I reach the garden, children are already running around, grateful for a spot of sprawling wilderness within the concrete capital. It's a community-run green space, a registered charity that strives to encourage urban wildlife. Sometimes Lenny and I would meet here for a sandwich and I'd throw the birds crumbs, whereas Lenny would wolf his bread down in seconds.

I sit on a wooden bench, engraved with the name of a regular visitor who died last year. It's a quarter to eleven. I take out my phone and am just about to message Casey but stop myself. Instead I admire the different shades of purple of clematis and heather. A vertical shot of yellow Forsythia separates the plants and contrasts the subtler blossom colour of the nearby magnolia. I study the different shades and shape of each plant. They look like a group of friends, each of which had maintained their identity, yet together they fit well. I've never fitted in. A girl from primary school, Alice, once compared me to a weed. She said I'd put down roots where I wasn't wanted. And that I ate too much food. Everyone else had laughed.

I direct the thought to a part of my mind reserved for the old Violet who had taken far too long to react to the bullies at school; who'd been naïve enough to let Lenny hurt her. Also snuck away there were the memories of me making him a packed lunch, ironing his socks and lovingly stroking his brow as he slept off yet another prosecco-induced hangover.

I squint in the sunshine and wish I'd brought a sunhat, just as Casey looms into view. I roll up my cardigan's sleeves. He's wedged my pink sunglasses onto his nose. They almost match his candyfloss coloured T-shirt. I grin and stand up as he hands them over. We hug. It seems over-familiar but for just a second I don't want to let go.

'You smell nice,' he says.

'Must be all the flowers.' I point to the magnolia.

Casey glances at me and smiles before linking his arm through mine. We stroll.

His hairs brush against my skin and the closeness of his chest makes me wonder how he'd smell if I pressed my lips against it. Carefully I avoid all talk of his manuscript and the publishing world. It's he who brings up the subject of the Chapter Battle.

'How did it go?' I ask with as much disinterest as I can muster, as we pass a squadron of sky-blue butterflies battling against the breeze.

'Need you ask?'

'No. Although I would ask where you got that confidence so that I can purchase some.'

'What can I say? All the interest from publishers, people like you… it must have gone to my head.'

'You were born confident. I can tell,' I say, steering the conversation away from *Alien Hearts*.

He laughs loudly and a nearby blackbird squawks and flies away. 'I'm afraid my mother and sisters would whole-heartedly agree. I recognised very early on that I was the man of the house and that didn't frighten me.' A shadow of emotion that disagrees with those words crosses his face. 'Not that I'd ever have called myself that in front of my mum and older sisters. And it took a while for me to grow into the role – a role that, I guess, sounds old-fashioned now. They have always been forces to be reckoned with, especially in my younger years. I wasn't allowed to play out until homework was done. As far back as I can remember, I had lists of chores but as I matured, the roles reversed a little and I began to feel a responsibility for family members. As soon as I could, I saved up for a car and I'd insist on picking my sisters up from nightclubs instead of them risking public transport home. They used to moan the way I used to when they supervised me doing my English or maths but, deep down, we all knew the concern sprang from love. We looked after each other.'

'My mum was the same,' I say as we approach a pond. 'Everything that seemed hard, I eventually realised was for my own good.' Apart from once. But I push those thoughts of Flint away.

We peer into the water and by a patch of bulrushes notice a cluster of frog spawn. A few tadpoles have already hatched and twist their bodies as they swim. I kneel down and scoop bubbles of clear jelly into my hand.

'When I was little, I used to imagine these threaded into a necklace – one I could wear as well as my daisy chains. The design label would have been called Mother Nature.'

'No surprise you've become a children's fiction editor,' says Casey and watches as I carefully tip the spawn back. He shakes his head. 'You're so perfectly groomed yet think nothing of sticking your hand in a muddy pond.'

Perfectly groomed? As I try to think of a witty response, a scream catches our attention and I jump up. Running towards us is a toddler, red in the face and holding his arm. His mum follows, pushing a buggy which jolts up and down as she veers from the path and its stones.

'Stop, Toby! Careful! You could fall into the water.' She shoots us a desperate look. I dart over to the little boy and crouch down in front of him. His whole body shakes. Casey stands by my side and runs a hand through his hair as if he might find the answer of how to help in there.

'Ow!' gulps the boy as his nose runs. His mum catches up. I reach into my pocket and pull out a tissue. I look at the mum as her baby starts to cry and gratefully she nods.

'Is it okay if I wipe your face?' I say gently.

Toby nods too. Job done, I look at the red lump on his arm.

'Did a bumblebee hurt you?'

Tears run down his face again. Gently I examine the lump. The stinger is still in. If left, the pain will increase. I'd been stung often enough as a child playing in Applegrove Woods.

'Is it okay if I give your arm just a little squeeze?' I say. 'It will help get rid of the pain.'

'No!' He pulls away.

'Toby! Darling. The kind lady is just trying to help,' says his mum as she lifts up the baby.

His bottom lip quivers. 'You won't squeeze hard?'

I shake my head. Reluctantly he holds out his arm. With another clean tissue at the ready, I gently pinch the inflamed skin. Toby winces, but thankfully the stinger pops out and I wipe it away.

'A really big bumblebee stung me once on my leg,' I say. 'But I realised that it was because I was flapping my arms. It got frightened and thought I would hurt it. The bumblebee told me it was very sorry but the little sting was its way of keeping safe.'

Toby wipes his face and looks at his arm. Then at me. 'It spoke?'

'Yes. It told me not to be scared next time. Just to keep still. It said bumblebees were much more frightened of humans because we were so big.' I reach into my handbag and pull out a handful of medication from a zipped pocket. Casey holds his hands out and I drop them in. Ibuprofen, paracetamol, hayfever tablets – I come to a small packet of antiseptic wipes. I look at the mum once more and she smiles. I pass Toby a wipe.

'Clean the sting gently with this. You are being so brave.'

Toby does as instructed and gives the wipe back to me.

'There. All done. If you look carefully around the gardens, you might find your bumblebee waiting to say sorry. Or sometimes they just make their friends buzz extra loud when you pass. That's an apology.'

Toby grins. 'Come on, Mummy.'

'Thanks so much,' she says as she pushes her buggy past.

I delve into my bag once more and pass her my business card. 'I work for a publisher. One of our new authors has just written a book designed to make insects like spiders and bees less scary. The illustrations are fantastic. Email me if you like, and I'll post you out a copy.'

'I don't know what to say. Thank you so much. Hey, Toby, listen to this,' she says and hurries after him.

Casey stares at me for a moment. I wonder if my make-up has smudged. He shakes his head. 'Talk about organised. You're a nurse to boot. Is there no end to your talents? So, talking to insects…?'

I put away the boxes of medication. 'I… I used to speak to animals a lot as a child.'

'I used to speak to my Action Men. They gave me advice about fighting. In return I'd set them up with my sisters' Barbie dolls.'

I grin and throw the dirty wipe into a bin. He catches my hand.

'We didn't finish our dance properly at The Olive Bar.' He pulls me close and I can't help smiling as a middle-aged couple walk past. The woman shoots me a wistful look as if recalling a scene from her past. Dancing in the park? How my life's changed. Before I know it, his lips are almost pressed against mine. My heartbeat accelerates as our mouths part. I shut my eyes. I forget Lenny and Beatrix. I even forget Bella. Right now, this is about me and a man whose qualities continue to open up in front of me like a beautiful lotus flower. His humour and kindness. His gentle ways. His ambition. His loyalty. His smile.

Just as our lips brush against each other, his phone rings. After an almost imperceptible sigh Casey pulls away.

'Great timing. Mum's not well, so I'd better answer it.'

Have I really nearly been kissed by a man who looks like him? I glance down at my outfit. The legs that Farah called slender last week and my blonde hair. My new and improved body parts feel like a toolkit that makes me invincible now. The sense of power feels more addictive than the creamiest chocolate bar.

'Sorry, Vi. I'd better head off. My sisters are both busy today and Mum sounds confused about her tablets. I won't be able to rest knowing that she's so worried.'

I meet his gaze and nod. 'Of course you must go. I hope she's okay.'

He takes my hand and kisses the palm gently before taking out his travel card. 'Text me?'

'I'll wait to hear from you,' I say with a fearlessness I'm beginning to feel.

'Okay. And, Vi? Spending time with you today… it's helped me come to a decision. Regardless of what he may think, I'll be instructing my agent to submit to Thoth tomorrow. If you in any way represent their values, then I want to be a part of it.'

Fireworks Night used to be a favourite date for me and Uncle Kevin. Whilst Mum made bangers and mash, we'd spell our names in the night air with sparklers out in the back garden. He'd buy me boxes of fun snaps and pretend to be really scared at the noise when I threw them on the ground. And he always found an amazing display to go to. Last year's had a waterfall with water drops made of white sparkles. Mum said it was the prettiest thing, like a wedding dress's train. A dress with a railway on it doesn't sound very pretty to me.

This year I want to spend it with Flint. It's next week. I asked Mum and she said he can come to tea. She wondered if he'd be doing anything with his family but they haven't got the money to visit a display and won't use sparklers in their back garden in case they frighten the rabbits and guinea pigs.

We're sitting in the tree house. It's a Saturday morning, which means hours and hours off school. Fireworks Night is next Friday – only six days to go.

'Mum's promised to make us bangers and mash, just like old times,' I say.

Flint puts down his book and his face splits into a grin. Today he's wearing one of his older brother's old jackets. It's a little bit big for him. 'That's awesome, especially as Sally has started trying to make us go vegetarian.'

Flint calls his mum by her name. It sounds very grown-up to me.

He pulls a face. 'Last night she served up burgers made of something called Quorn.'

I don't know what that is but it sounds disgusting.

'I couldn't eat more than a mouthful so just made myself a cheese sandwich instead.'

'I wish my mum would let me skip her meals. We had fried eggs last night. I don't like the white.'

'Me neither. But the yolk is yummy, especially with sticks of toast dipped in.'

We smile at each other. Me and Flint have so much in common. Unlike everyone in my class, he also doesn't much like The Spice Girls.

'Alice threw an egg sandwich at my jumper yesterday. It smeared across it. All afternoon she said I smelt like farts. Everyone laughed and made raspberry noises when they came near me.' I curl my fists. 'I really hate her. It's just getting worse. Everyone has forgotten about the spider.'

'You need to think of something else. She needs to be taught a lesson that will really hurt.'

'Like what?'

Flint pulls his ponytail tighter and thinks. 'If only we could get a firework. You could throw it at her feet. Watch her scream when it goes off.'

I gasp. 'Wouldn't that be dangerous? She could get burnt really badly and I'd get into so much trouble.'

'She was horrid about your Uncle Kevin, remember.' Flint shrugs. 'If it was me I'd get her back big time for that. The worst thing that could happen is that she might catch fire a little and have to strip off her dress.'

I can't help giggling at the thought of Alice standing in the playground in her stupid bra. We're only seven but her mum bought this fancy matching underwear and she struts around in the PE changing rooms acting like a pop star. She called me a baby for wearing Eeyore knickers.

'A firework would be really hard to find, though,' he says. 'We need to find another way you can scare her.'

Alice keeps going on about a party she is going to on Fireworks Night. It's at the house next to hers. She plays with the children even though they are older than her. Alice fits in at school and out. Nothing will ever break her popularity.

But I did hear Alice saying she isn't going to a display because she hates loud noises. Flint's given me an idea. I remember Uncle Kevin's fun snaps. I still have a box in my bedroom.

I say goodbye to Flint after we've played tag and think about next Friday. Flint reckons the idea of fun snaps is a bit tame but says to throw them at her during lunch. Hopefully the shock will make her choke. He's right. If they really frighten her, it will be a good payback. She'd know how Uncle Kevin felt when those planes crashed into his tower.

I wish the nightmares would stop. A few weeks ago I even wet the bed. But Mum didn't get cross. She asked me to tell her about the dream. It's always the same. Uncle Kevin is trapped inside the tower. At a window. He looks down at me. We wave. I feel sick with panic that I can't help him. He starts crying and takes off his jacket. The flames get nearer. He calls out in pain. With one last wave, he mouths *I love you* and then climbs outside the window and I wake up in a sweat.

It's Alice's fault that I have these nightmares and that makes me more determined to teach her a lesson.

Enough is enough.

Flint is right.

Next Friday I'll need to try something even scarier than the spider.

As he says, it's only fair that I make her jump as well.

Chapter 18

I walk into the Frog and Duck brushing my fingers against my lips, still shell-shocked that Casey Wilde's mouth has almost been there. I had to ring Kath and say I'd meet them at the pub instead of the retirement home as usual. After Casey left, I went into Foyles to browse and lost track of time buying a book about dating and then sitting in the cafe enjoying a black coffee. I did find it hard to resist the scrumptious looking sandwiches and cakes. It's difficult now, as time passes, to stick to my super healthy plan.

However, I know it's the right thing to do. Getting closer to Casey today has already proved that. A man like him wouldn't have looked twice at me before. I shouldn't feel validated by that attention, but it's impossible not to be swayed by something you always assumed was out of reach. Flint thought I was cool but we were only ever best friends and the boys at primary and high school never looked at me as anything more than different Violet who was clever and never spoke much. Now and then a boy would admire my maths knowledge and I'd help out with homework. Plus, a boy and I in year eleven used to talk passionately at lunchtime about an obsession with Manga that we'd both developed. And in the sixth form, I became quite close to Brett, who could relate to that sense of being on the outside of things looking in. I was the book nerd. He was gay. Somehow we were a good fit.

It's like the many books, over the years, that have attracted my attention due to an eye-catching cover. Their appearance has meant I've discovered new favourite genres and authors that I might have otherwise passed over.

Why couldn't I see before that looks do really matter?

I wave to the flirty barman who remembers me from last time. I go over to my friends and we hug. I half-listen to them speak as my mind replays my morning in the park. I ask if anyone needs a top-up before getting myself a gin and slimline tonic.

When I get back to the table, the conversation hushes. I know from the way I was treated at school that they've been talking about me.

'We can't wait to show you more blog posts we've drafted,' says Pauline in a cheery voice and opens the laptop. 'Kath's latest review is just brilliant. It's for a book called *Reasons to Stay Alive*.'

'It really resonated with me after working as a mental health nurse during the latter years of my career,' says Kath.

'We just need a bit of help working out how to edit them once they are published,' continued Pauline. 'Plus we could do with any useful suggestions for which Twitter accounts to follow.'

Kath takes out a present and card from her bag. 'It's okay, I know you are busy, so I forged your signature,' she whispers. Of course. It was Pauline's birthday last Wednesday. Kath told me about it a couple of weeks ago. How could I have forgotten? Over the last few months, I've always been the one to buy the present and card from me and Kath if anyone has had a celebration. And because of Kath's stiff fingers, I've done the wrapping.

'Sorry, I completely forgot,' I whisper back as Pauline eagerly opens the present – a box set of a new detective series she'd not stopped raving about.

Kath squeezes my arm under the table and her hand wraps easily around my wrist. A flicker of – I'm not sure what – crosses her features.

We chat about the blog and then move onto our own lives. I tell them about the little boy who got stung. They are more curious about Casey.

'So what did you have for lunch?' asks Nora. 'Asparagus, I hope. It's an aphrodisiac.'

'Just ignore us,' says Kath and shakes her head. 'You're entitled to your privacy.'

Pauline leans forward. 'But there'd be no harm in showing us a photo – have you got one of him on your phone?'

'No,' I replied, wishing I had.

'Isn't that refreshing?' says Kath. 'A young couple who don't record every single moment of their day via selfies.'

'Compare him to a film star then – just to give us an idea,' says Nora.

I feel happy talking about Casey, and that's a simple sentiment, but the way he makes me feel doesn't need highfalutin words.

'He's… a modern-day Gregory Peck.'

'So, tall, dark, macho,' Nora takes off her fur coat.

'Yes – although he does wear pink and leopard-print T-shirts.'

'You couldn't bring him along to one of our meetings, could you?' suggests Nora and I reply with a silence that makes the others laugh. We've focussed so much on Vintage Views recently that we decide it's time to get reading again. I ask for suggestions. Pauline wants us to try one called *Vox*, set in a dystopian future where women are only allowed to speak one hundred words a day.

'Imagine that.' Nora shakes her head at Pauline. 'We'd blow that in just five minutes sitting in the communal lounge.'

'It wouldn't be too difficult for me,' says Kath in a matter-of-fact way.

Never self-piteous. Always a brave face. In that moment, I decide I *will* go back to Kath's afterwards for that chocolate cake. An hour later, after I've finished troubleshooting a lot of the blog's problems, I call a taxi whilst Kath has a last minute conversation with the others. The group keep looking at me. Perhaps they want to ask for more advice and are worried about taking up my time. I've always told them running the club is a pleasure, but lately, my world has become bigger. Brighter. I'm moving in different circles. Bella has opened my eyes to endless possibilities. If I'm honest, having to spend part of my weekend with the book club is beginning to jar.

I pay for the taxi home and help Kath up to her room. I'd been thinking about the book *Vox* on our journey back.

Towards the end of our relationship, one hundred words a day would probably have sufficed in terms of chatting with Lenny. Mostly I listened to him talk about his work and the latest social event he'd attended. We communicated with grunts at weekends, whilst he watched the football or I read. Yet the spark still hadn't disappeared for me.

'It's not quite the same eating on my own,' says Kath and sits opposite me at her small kitchen table. Her teapot is covered in a hand-knitted cosy from the days before time caught up with her joints.

'In fact,' Kath pushes away her plate. 'I can't keep quiet any longer. I have to say something – because I care. We all do.'

'We?'

'The book club members. Violet. We're worried.'

'About what?'

'This new regime of yours. How you've coped after Lenny leaving and—'

'I think I've coped just fine. I don't understand, Kath – only last weekend Nora was admiring my hair. Everyone was complimentary. What's changed in seven days?'

'You have. It's frightening. It's as if you're disappearing before our very eyes. When I squeezed your wrist in the pub… Violet. There's nothing to you. What's going on?'

I fold my arms.

'Have some cake. For me,' she says. 'How can it harm? Surely your new lifestyle allows the occasional treat. What are you so afraid of?'

I'm not afraid of anything anymore. That's the point. Not Lenny. Not Beatrix. Not the feeling of being left out or not being good enough. Not anyone else's opinion. Perhaps I'm scared of intimacy with Casey, but that's only because I'm still getting used to my new skin.

'I wouldn't want you worrying,' I say. I cut myself a slice and eat the whole thing within minutes.

Kath blushes. 'Look, I didn't mean—'

'It's really delicious. May I have another slice?'

Kath sits in silence as I repeat the whole process. Then I ask for a slice for Bella. Just to make a point. I make my excuses to leave and carry it down to my flat on the cling-filmed plate Kath hastily provided. I go into my bedroom, close the door, get into bed and eat the lot.

A wave of nausea overwhelms me. I get to the bath-room just in time and throw up. For several moments I'm retching, glad that Bella is still at the spa.

'Nosy so-and-so,' I mutter and wipe my mouth with loo paper. Who the hell did Kath think she was? I drink a couple of glasses of water, put on my face pack and read an online article about a new beauty regime. Why couldn't Farah and Kath and the other book club members just mind their own fucking business?

I bite my lip. The F word never used to pop into my mind so easily. Maybe it should have.

I go back into my bedroom and sit on the bed. Two weeks isn't long to get Casey to accept that invitation to the party. I have no time to lose and need to be more proactive – whatever other people think. I take off a slipper and fling it across the room. My breathing becomes rapid and I exhale.

Bella has been dropping hints that I should work out some intricate plan to seduce him, but even the new me thinks that's going too far. Something like that, it can't… it shouldn't be forced.

I pick up my phone and find Casey's number. I'd had trouble finding a hair appointment this week. Perhaps he could help. I couldn't think of any other excuse to meet.

Hi. How is your mum? I hope all is okay. I'm hoping you can help me out – but no problem if you can't. I'm out to dinner Wednesday night and want to look my best but the salon I use is booked up and I don't want to try somewhere new. Whereas you'd feel like more of a familiar option I can trust. Is there any way you could fit me in around five pm for a blow dry?'

Vi X

The book club was going out for a meal for Pauline's birthday. A new pub in town. Perhaps if I looked my smartest, the members wouldn't criticise my appearance. I sighed, not really looking forward to seeing them all again.

Hey, Vi,

Sure. You off to anywhere nice? I close at five but can make time for you.

Casey X

I push the laptop off my lap, let go of my phone and smile. I message back my thanks without answering his question and pick up the slipper I'd thrown. Knots in my stomach unfurling, I slip it back on my foot.

Chapter 19

I can hardly concentrate on work when Wednesday arrives.

'Violet?' says Irfan sharply as I zone out of a meeting with an author. Heat creeps up my neck. It's a debut and really important that I listen to the writer's ideas on how they'd like to be branded. After they've left, Irfan calls me back into the side room.

'What's up? You kept staring into space. And yesterday Felicity complained that you'd not replied to two of her emails, one of them marked urgent.' He offers me one of the biscuits but I decline. I had juice for lunch and apart from that, am managing on black coffee.

'Whilst Felicity apologised, we still have to do our damndest to prove our ability as editors.' His voice softens. 'You okay?'

'Yes. Sorry. I didn't sleep well last night. And I'm going to have to leave early.' I consult my watch. It's four. 'In half an hour. I hope that's okay. I'll check my inbox again before I go.'

Irfan stretches out and yawns. 'Fair enough. And Farah's coming in any minute – we're leaving early too as we're still catching up from the weekend.'

'The washing machine flooding?'

'It looks like we'll need new flooring in both the kitchen and living room.' He sits more upright. 'But I got in an hour early this morning. Perhaps you could do that tomorrow.'

I'm just about to leave my desk when Farah appears. She gives Irfan a kiss and then comes over to give me a hug. My arms hang by my sides as I allow hers to circle my shoulders. Eventually she pulls away.

'Everything okay?' she says.

'Shouldn't it be?' I reply and my stomach scrunches up, waiting for her to make a critical comment. I used to appreciate her maternal worries. Now I find they are just plain patronising.

She delves into her pocket and pulls out a chocolate bar. 'You should try this. It's my current favourite.'

'No thanks,' I say abruptly. I'm not going to defend myself and make up some excuse as to why I can't eat it. Why should I have to?

'Oh, go on – otherwise I'll only eat it.'

My forehead tightens and I glance around. A couple of employees are staring. I feel my cheeks blush. 'Farah. Please. No,' I say in a low voice.

'But—'

Suddenly I feel overwhelmed by tiredness and some-thing snaps inside me, like it had on Sunday with Kath. She and Kath never used to give me any advice when it really mattered, when I used to live my life with so little style.

'I know the changes I've made might make you ques-tion your own lifestyle, but that's your problem, not mine.'

'What do you mean?' She shoves the chocolate bar back into her pocket.

'Perhaps you think you could do with losing a few pounds, just like I needed to. There's nothing to feel ashamed of. You can change too. I'll help if you want.'

Farah looks down at herself and back up again. 'I've had children. I'm middle-aged. As long as the doctor is happy, so am I.' Her voice wavers. 'My life's got more in it than worrying about the size of my thighs – and yours used to as well.'

She can't see how successful people have to be the whole package.

'And good for you,' I say, exasperation sneaking into my voice. 'But please – respect my choices.' I turn and head for the toilets. I'm just about to go in when someone takes my arm.

'You've upset Farah. I know she can go overboard sometimes, but it's only because she cares.' Irfan shakes his head. 'What's going on? This last week or so you've had your mind elsewhere. This isn't like the Violet we know.'

'And that's a bad thing? She wasn't exactly the most popular member of the team.'

'What are you talking about?' His brow knots.

He's so naïve.

I push the Ladies' door open and go inside. I get changed in one of the cubicles and when I come out, one of the design team says they love my dress. Bella is a hard task master and lately has been making decisions for me. Sometimes I disagree, but she raises one of her finely threaded eyebrows. It's a look I don't like to argue with. So I've consumed nothing but juiced fruits and vegetables for two days. But my skin is translucent and my collar bones show as if I'm one of those influencers everyone loves on

Instagram. And tonight, I'm wearing one of Bella's animal print dresses.

I stare into the mirror. The door creaks closed and I'm left alone. My stomach pinches as I take in the sophisticated reflection and an unexpected sob escapes my lips. Any transformation will have its challenges. Just because I don't quite know who I am at the moment doesn't mean I won't soon. I'm not a bitch, am I, for the way I'm standing up for myself with Farah and Kath? *They* are in the wrong, not feeling happy for the way I'm turning my life around. I can't help it if it makes them uncomfortable.

I think back to my unhappy days at primary school, that Halloween, Alice and the spider. How I'd felt sorry for her when she cried and offered a tissue. What a schmuck. It's about time I stood up for myself and stopped worrying about the welfare of others so much.

I make some last adjustments to my hair, take a selfie and post it on Instagram. Thanks to the lighting in the Ladies', it doesn't need a filter. My shoulders relax as the likes start to arrive. Hugo dispels any further doubts as I walk past reception.

'Can you bottle what you are on and give some to me?' he says, coming around from his desk.

Hugo kisses my hand and I sashay out of the building.

Chapter 20

I walk into the hairdresser's and do everything I can to hide my surprise. For some reason, I assumed Casey's salon would look glossy and high-end, with chic staff and fizzy wine on tap. Instead I'm offered a coffee and digestive biscuit from a stylist comfortably dressed and old enough to be his mum. The chairs are tan leather and the units black. There's a distinct masculine feel softened by a tabby cat asleep on one of the hair-dryer chairs and the subtly brown and yellow floral wallpaper. I crouch down and it lifts its head for a scratch. The moss green eyes narrow and study me as if the animal knows my plans.

'Vi, meet Luna.'

'Lovely name.'

He strides over and he runs his hand down her back. She stretches and licks his fingers. 'I found her abandoned outside under a full moon. She was only about ten weeks old. With the vet's help, I brought her back to good health.'

'You should have called her Lucky.'

'I'm the lucky one. Some customers only come back because they know it means a couple of hours with her purring on their laps.' He looks at the woman who offered me coffee. 'Judy, you get off now.'

She gives him the thumbs–up and his eyes scan her grey waves. 'Have you decided yet about that pink tint?'

'No. Derek might divorce me. He contacted his solicitor last year when I mooted getting a tattoo.'

They both laugh. Judy looks my way. 'Casey's a terror for leading people astray, so just be careful. You might leave with a Mohican cut.'

'Excuse me, I'm very professional,' he says and brandishes a comb and scissors as if they are fighting off her insults.

'That he is,' says a young woman dressed in black with no make-up and shiny brunette hair. 'But I don't tell him that very often. There's no room in this salon for an ego the size of his.'

He waves to his two employees as they leave. The door rings as it closes behind them. Casey offers me a cupcake. I shake my head. 'Wise choice. One of my regulars, Eve, has just turned ninety. Such an inspirational woman. She still does pilates. However, she's never got over rationing during the war. These are austerity carrot cupcakes. Eve just uses that vegetable instead of sugar. I'm all for living on a budget, but this is a step too far.'

I stand up to sit in the chair he's pointing to by the wash basins. Casey can't stop staring. 'That dress. It's a knockout.'

As usual, Bella was right about me being able to pull off animal print. And just a slash of red lipstick must have brightened up my face without looking over the top. These are the sort of nuggets of information I'd have found boring a few months ago. But now, it was like finally trying the book of a popular author and understanding why they sold so well.

He ties a black cape around me and I lean back. Water runs and his fingers gently massage my hair. I cross my legs as electric sensations travel down my spine.

'I never knew your hair was curly. It looks amazing.'

'You wouldn't say that if it were yours.'

'Seriously, why do you straighten it?'

'It's just a mass of frizz if I leave it to dry on its own.'

We chat about products that could make the most of my natural wave. We discuss the warm May weather and the novels we are reading at the moment. Then he leads me over to a chair in front of a huge mirror. Our reflections smile at each other. I wait for him to ask me where I'm off to tonight – but he doesn't. Casey glances at his watch.

'It's okay. I'm not meeting my friends until seven.'

'Oh, sure. That's great, it's just I'm due to be seeing someone at half past six.'

Of course a man like Casey wouldn't be staying in. 'You should have said. I hope I won't make you late.'

'No problem. I'll have you looking tip-top in less than half an hour. So, you really want me to straighten it?'

'Please.'

'You out for dinner?'

At last he's curious. I talk about the book club and the new bistro pub my friends had wanted to try. I speak up as he turns on the hair dryer in his hand. Luna jumps onto my lap and Casey goes to shoo her off, saying something about my dress.

'It's okay.' I settle her down. 'So, what are you up to tonight? Food? Cinema? Another Chapter Battle?'

'None of those,' he says and stops for a moment. 'Drinks in a fancy bar. With Beatrix Bingham. She wants to meet me on her own.' He runs his fingers through my hair and they brush against the back of my neck. 'Is that normal? Shouldn't my agent be there? She hasn't even contacted him. She messaged me via Facebook.'

I stop stroking Luna.

'Vi? What do you reckon?'

I can hardly speak. 'Sorry Casey – could I bother you for a glass of water? Luna's like a hot water bottle.'

Gratefully I drink from the glass he brings over. 'It's… not unheard of. I guess I contacted you about *Alien Hearts*. Although I was never going to be your personal editor, and the submission process hadn't started then. Messaging you via Facebook does seem strange if she's a real contender to work on this book with you.'

Now there was no questioning the rumours about Beatrix – confirmation as well that those popular social memes were right about people needing to take risks to be successful in life.

'Maybe I should tell my agent.'

'Definitely,' I say and put down the glass. 'She's probably just keen, which is flattering, but you don't want to come across as unprofessional.'

We chat about holiday plans. Casey's always wanted to visit Cuba. This autumn I might visit Mum and Ryan in Spain. My mascara smudges as he makes me laugh. He asks more about Vintage Views and I talk about my friends and how recently I've felt as if we have less in common.

'You don't sound very excited about going out tonight,' he says.

'To be honest, I wish I could get out of it.'

Casey finishes the blow dry. 'You look beautiful. It would be a crime to waste this hair by staying here with me and Luna and eating pizza.'

I catch his eye and my chest flutters. Regardless of any book deal, I want to get to know this man better.

Being brave, I ask, 'Would it be bad of us to cancel our plans?'

'There's nothing wrong with being bad now and again.'

'Are you sure? Although I think there's something you need to know before we go up to your flat… my favourite pizza is ham and pineapple.' Lenny used to hate that. He said such toppings were supposed to show imagination but only showed the opposite.

'What do you know? Mine too. I blame my mum. She always drilled into us it was very important to hold onto your differences.'

'My Uncle Kevin believed the same.'

I take out my purse to pay for the cut and blow. He waves it away. 'Okay, then takeout is on me.'

He rings Beatrix. I hear him mutter something about feeling too tired.

He's turning down an evening with her to be with me.

I call Pauline. She can't hide the disappointment in her voice. But it's a night for me to put myself first – a concept the old Violet Lenny cheated on would have struggled to comprehend. We go upstairs shadowed by Luna who goes straight to her bowl by the fireplace. Casey lifts up a packet of biscuits next to it and shakes out some of the contents.

'This is lovely,' I say and study the full bookshelves. A carpet hangs above the mantelpiece. It's of an elephant and is covered with sequins. The light in the middle of the ceiling doubles as a fan and with sun rays invading the small living room and the African art pieces dotted across the room, I feel as if I'm abroad, somewhere exotic. Casey lights a joss stick and straightens the linen cushions on the compact burgundy sofa.

'It's home,' he says and goes into the kitchen. 'I've been lucky enough to travel widely and try to reflect that in the decor. It lends me a sense of freedom that is easy to lose in a city as busy as London.' The living area is open plan with two rooms leading off it, presumably the bedroom and bathroom. He pulls open the fridge door and takes out a bottle of wine. 'Chardonnay or would you prefer a cup of tea?'

'Wine would be great. Thanks.' I feel nervous. We're alone for the first time, not in a cocktail bar or park or salon. All I can think of is the way his hands massaged my head. Legs feeling shaky, I stand up and walk over to the kitchen. The words Shrinking Violet tease me in my head.

What would Bella do?

This isn't a difficult question to answer. She's the woman who stood up to her parents at eighteen and told them university wasn't for her. She's backpacked around Thailand – that trip widened her interest in wellbeing. Bella takes charge.

It's time I became more assertive in all areas of my life.

I take the bottle from him and place it on the work surface behind.

Is this a mistake? Should I sit and chat with him first?

No. The new me wastes no time in chasing her goals. She doesn't react, she acts.

And there's just something about his eyes, the curve of his mouth, the richness of his voice… there's a chemistry between us that makes me feel like I'm about to explode.

Our lips part. Casey's hands trail the zip down my back. He intoxicates me. Casey steps back and stares into my eyes. He curls his fingers around mine. I lead him into the living room. He looks towards a door – behind which is his bedroom, I presume – and back at me. I nod. We're in there within seconds and he pulls back the slate grey duvet. I smile as we kiss again and drape my arms around his neck. Clumsily I pull him downwards and we fall against the soft sheets.

With a building sense of urgency, I tug his shirt out of his jeans and undo the buttons. I inhale his smell. It's heady and masculine. It drives my hands over his bare chest. I imagine his doing the same to me.

But what if experienced Casey tears away the packaging and recognises that the real me is a frumpy misfit? What if I don't come across as worldly-wise as an attractive woman should?

Since when did sex become so angst-ridden? Now there are expectations to meet. I'd never really appreciated before how in some ways, it used to be easier just being me. What you saw was what you got. That left no room for disappointment.

I push him away instead of the negative thoughts.

'Vi?' He sits up. His breathing is laboured.

'I'm sorry, Casey. I can't… you see—'

He brushes dyed blonde locks out of my face. 'I guess we are rushing things.' He runs a finger over my lips. 'Perhaps we should have stuck to pizza instead.'

I wish the duvet would swallow me whole. It didn't take much to persuade him to stop. My fears are right. I don't turn him on.

'Ham and pineapple?' he says and tucks in his shirt.

I jump up and slip my shoes back on.

'No, no, sorry – actually I ought to go to Pauline's meal. I feel bad for letting her and the others down.'

Casey rubs the back of his head. 'Right. Okay. You're sure?'

I give him a quick kiss on the cheek without meeting his gaze. Feeling like an inexperienced teenager, I hurry outside and put my sunglasses on. Vision blurred, I almost collide with someone walking towards the salon. It's Beatrix, carrying takeout and a wine bottle.

It's Friday. Bonfire Night. The fun snaps are in my lunch box. I tried one out yesterday after school in the back garden just to be sure they were still working. I didn't notice poor Flossie. Her fur stood on end and she bolted. I called her back and said not to be frightened and snuck a handful of cat biscuits out of the kitchen, as biscuits always make me feel better.

Science goes on forever. It's the last lesson before we go into the dining hall. I grab my box and drinking bottle. A group of boys still make raspberry noises when I pass. As we queue up Alice sees me and talks in a really loud voice about the party she is going to tonight. That's what I don't get – I'm a nobody to her, so why does she bother trying to make me jealous?

It doesn't work anyway. I've got Flint now, and a couple of people I speak to in recorder group on a Wednesday after lunch. We file into the hall. Mrs Crawley the dinner lady is telling off a boy. We all strain to look. He's dropped something into one of the water jugs. It's white and swollen with a thread of string hanging out underneath like a firework.

'Do you know what a tampon is, Violet?' asks Alice and it's as if the whole class has stopped to hear my answer. I can tell from their faces that most of them don't but they're glad if I'm the one who's going to be made to look stupid. Luckily I know. I found a box of them once in Mum's bedroom and asked her.

'They are sweets for adults, made of really tough marshmallows. You can't eat them with baby teeth.'

Alice starts laughing. Everyone joins in, although they don't look as if they are sure why.

185

'You're a dumb fuck,' she whispers.

Sometimes Alice says really rude words. She reckons they are cool because her brother uses them.

Annoying tears spring to my eyes as everyone laughs and sits down to eat. Half the class queue up for hot dinners, including Alice.

I wait. Wait until she walks back towards the table. As she passes me, my fists uncurl and I reach into the fun snap box under the table on my lap. I have a quick look around and then throw three of them hard at her feet. Flint says one is too risky as it might not go off.

I needn't have worried about that.

Alice shrieks and tips her tray towards herself. I'm glad it's a messy meal. Gravy splats against her dress.

'It's hot!' she yells.

Mrs Crawley hurries over and in front of everyone quickly unbuttons her shirt. The boys laugh at her brown-stained bra and Georgie grabs a glass of water and throws it at Alice's chest. She howls and starts to cry. Mrs Warham appears and tells the boys to stop laughing. Mrs Crawley leads Alice away.

'Who did this?' she says in her sternest voice, which she normally keeps for children who copy each other during tests.

I stare at my apple. No one replies. If my heart thumps any louder, she'll surely hear and know it's my fault.

I almost sigh with relief as I hear Mrs Warham start to walk away.

'It was Violet.' I stare harder at my apple. Georgie's voice sounds defiant. 'I'm no snitch but Alice is my friend, she was really frightened and she might have got hurt.'

My knees start to shake.

'Violet?' asks Mrs Warham in a voice that doesn't believe what it's heard.

'It wasn't me. It wasn't,' I say.

'We'll discuss this in the classroom. Follow me immediately.'

I push down the lid onto my lunch box and stand up. I'd forgotten about the fun snaps box. It falls to the floor. Mrs Warham picks it up.

'It wasn't my fault. Flint told me to do it,' I say. I feel bad but Flint doesn't even go to this school so he won't get into trouble.

'Who's Flint? A nickname for someone here?'

'No. He's my friend.'

'Shrinking Violet doesn't have any friends,' says Georgie and the others laugh.

'Silence!' Mrs Warham looks my way with icy eyes. 'Come with me.'

I follow and wonder if I'll throw up my sandwich. We enter the classroom and she closes the door. She says she knows Alice can be difficult but that my actions were dangerous. Alice could be badly burnt. I don't know what to say. If she knows Alice is horrid, why doesn't she do something about it? But she's too cross for me to ask, as is Mum.

'I knew that Flint was trouble,' says Mum as we get in the house. When she picked me up, we had to go into the head mistress's office. I'm not allowed to go back into school until a vestigashun has been done. 'He's not coming around to tea anymore. You're to stop seeing him. I don't want to hear his name ever again.'

'He was only trying to help. Alice has been nasty since I started that stupid school, saying things about Uncle Kevin. She thought he was your boyfriend.'

Mum sits down at the kitchen table. She reaches out an arm and pulls me close.

'Don't you understand how serious this is? You are very lucky Alice's burns are superficial. You could have got into a lot of trouble if they were worse.'

'But she hurts me every day. Mrs Warham has given up doing anything. It's as if Alice and her friends being mean to me has just become part of school life like assembly or morning break. It's not fair. At least Flint is on my side.'

'So am I,' says Mum gently. 'Look, I'll have a word with the school; see if we can sort this out.' She gives me a hug. 'But I can't let this go unpunished. You can forget sparklers and bangers and mash tonight. I want you in bed early. I want you to think about how two wrongs don't make a right.'

'She says Uncle Kevin was a jumper. It's because of her I have those nightmares.'

Mum's face tightens. 'Just go to your room, Violet. I'll bring up beans on toast later on, but no cake or ice cream.'

'It's Friday!'

'Bad luck. I feel very disappointed.'

Legs feeling heavy, I snatch my bag off the floor and head upstairs.

I hate Alice.

I hate school.

I hate my life.

Flint is the only good thing apart from Flossie.

Whatever Mum says, there's no way I'm going to stop seeing him.

Chapter 21

I wake up the next morning at a quarter to seven. I turn off my alarm clock that is due to ring in fifteen minutes. I glance at my phone. There are no messages from Casey. He's probably still wrapped up with Beatrix. I shower, get changed and head out of the building. It's a beautiful sunny day.

The trouble is, I can't force myself onto the pavement and route into the office. My legs simply won't move that way. I sit down on the bench, next to the wooden bird table. I don't have many scraps for it lately. I often used to cover it, on the way to work, with a crushed stale scone or bread crusts. I lean back as the last blossom petals float down like hesitant confetti.

'Violet? Everything okay?' says Bella, looking super fit in her spa uniform and bouncy ponytail. She's out of breath. 'I forgot my purse. How are you feeling?'

'I can't believe what an idiot I was, running away just at the moment Casey and I were about to get really close. Thanks for listening to me last night. I didn't even ask how your date went.'

She sits down next to me and squeezes my shoulder. 'Violet… there's still over a week until the party. We aren't giving up yet.'

'What's the point of carrying on? I've been kidding myself.'

She insists I stand up, and marches me over to look in front of a window straight ahead. 'Compared to your average Joe that comes into the spa, you look great. But I promised that I'd make you look like an A-lister and there are still a couple of areas we could improve. Don't be weak like the old you. Get a grip, Violet, and stop feeling sorry for yourself. I haven't spent weeks getting you into shape for you to lose your nerve at the last minute.'

Harsh words. Perhaps I need to hear them. I look at her determined face and nod. Bella's not one to abandon a project.

'Let's combine the jogging with some fitness DVDs. And I watched an amazing show last night on top lingerie models. There was some serious ribcage bragging going on and they did look amazing. Taut. Slick. Not an ounce of flesh to spare. To me, that's perfection.'

Was it? I bit my lip. Hadn't I done enough already? Did I really need to go that far?

Bella must have sensed my hesitation and squeezed my arm. 'It represents someone who is ultra disciplined and prepared to do whatever it takes to get what they want in life. It's no different to Daniel Craig following his rigid regime to get in shape to play James Bond. Success is only achieved by working bloody hard. It won't be handed to you on a plate – certainly not a full one. My parents never supported my career ambitions. They said a degree was worth far more than a beauty qualification. But I've gritted my teeth and showed them I could make a success of my passion. We get on well now. They've even told me how proud they are of the direction my life's taking.'

She's right. I'm a fool for thinking otherwise.

We sit down again. A blue tit lands on the bird table and cocks its head before pecking at a lump of cake.

'You already fit my clothes, Violet. You've got used to wearing contacts and drink so much water you're almost under threat of being overhydrated. I'm so proud that you've come this far but please, don't disappoint me. I don't want to lose respect for the woman I've become so fond of.'

'Don't worry. And I'm grateful for how far you've got me.'

She stands up. 'Come on. Let's walk down the road together.'

'I just can't face going in today. Farah won't give up – she was trying to push chocolate on me yesterday. Irfan's cross at the way I spoke to her, but why should I be bullied into eating something I don't want?'

'You know what? Take the day off work, then.' Her voice becomes softer and she rubs my back. She always seems to know exactly what to say. 'Farah and Irfan don't understand you. Not like I do. Take a day to get your head together again. It's not as if you regularly ring in sick.'

'I never have. Not once.' What a mug. I bet Beatrix did if she'd still got a lover in bed or had been partying too hard.

'Whatever you think, it sounds to me as if Casey is really into you. Why don't you text and arrange another date?'

I don't meet her eye. She gives me a hug. Says she's proud of me for sticking with the programme.

Bella's a great friend. In fact… she's my best. No one understands me quite like her. We say goodbye and with a sigh I drag myself back indoors and am about to take the stairs up to my flat when the lift opens.

'Aren't you going in the wrong direction?' says Kath as she walks up to me.

I take out my keys. 'I'm not going in today. I wasn't well last night. It was optimistic getting up early and changed. In fact, I must ring Irfan. Have a good day.' I hurry up the stairs. A wave of relief washes over me as I close my flat door behind me and sink onto the sofa. I text Irfan.

> *Not well. Apologies. Hopefully in tomorrow. Violet.*

He replies.

> *Thank you for letting me know. I'll try to smooth things over with Felicity.*

Irfan didn't sign off with his name or ask what was wrong or wish me well getting better.

Shit. Of course. I was meant to attend a brainstorming meeting Felicity only holds twice a year where staff air their ideas on how to improve the company.

I sigh and change into my pyjamas and crawl back to bed. Is this what a duvet day is? I've never had one before.

I lay there, stomach gurgling. I placate it by drinking a glass of water. My phone bleeps. It's a text from Casey asking me how my pub meal went. I can't face replying at the moment. I just want to be on my own where no one can see me and put pressure on to eat or not eat. I fall into fitful sleep and am woken up several hours later when Flossie jumps onto the bed.

She reaches my neck and gently pats my mouth with her paw.

'I'm sorry, Flossie,' I whisper, 'if I've neglected you over recent weeks. I've just been busy, trying to move my life forwards. Do you miss Lenny?'

Flossie closes her eyes as I tickle behind her eyes.

'I don't. Not anymore, but I do miss the comfort of having someone in my bed. I miss being held in front of the telly. I miss holding hands as I walk along the street. But most of all, I miss feeling as if I am part of something that matters.' I stop scratching her head. 'I'm trying so hard to be the best possible version of myself – successful at work, be polished – but if I'm honest…' My voice breaks. 'It can be a lonely business. No one seems to get it apart from our new flatmate.'

The doorbell rings. I panic. Who is that? There was no way I can face seeing anyone. Not in this state. I get out of bed and wrap my dressing gown around me. I pad to the door. Perhaps they'll go away.

I don't want to see anyone.

I don't want anyone to see me.

I don't want to talk.

I don't want to laugh and joke.

Go away.

Leave me alone.

I'm safer on my own. I can't be judged. I can't be hurt.

And even though I miss having a partner, I don't need anyone.

'It's Kath. Open up, sweetheart.'

I stand statue still. However, at that moment, my phone rings. I grab it out of my dressing gown pocket and in a hurry drop it onto the floor. I bend over. It's Casey. I switch it off.

'Violet? I can hear you.'

I drag myself over to the door and open it. I stand back as Kath walks in, followed by Nora and Pauline carrying a wicker basket.

'What's all this?' I ask.

'We're staging an intervention,' says Nora.

Under any other circumstances, I would have laughed. Pauline puts the basket on the low coffee table and opens it.

'Look, thanks, whatever this is, but—'

Kath raises her palms. 'I'm sorry, Violet, but we're not prepared to simply stand by and watch you cut yourself off from people who care. You not coming last night was the last straw.'

'I'm fine; have never felt better.'

'You don't look it,' said Pauline bluntly.

I shake my head. 'All those months you let me go around looking like a scarecrow. I finally get my act together and that's when you decide to intervene? I don't get it.' I look at Nora. 'Especially you, who is such a big fan of so many fashion-conscious celebrities and love following them on social media. Why can't you at least recognise that I'm simply trying to improve myself like… like your favourite Kardashians?'

'But they've got curves, Violet. Boobs and bums, like you used to. And they're celebrities, a spectacle, not real people I care about. I hate to get personal, but you're wasting away.'

'And I'm sorry you've wasted a journey,' I say stiffly. 'But there is no cause for alarm.'

'Aren't you even going to ask us to stay for a cup of tea?' says Kath and sits down on the sofa. She calls over

Flossie, who looks happy that her day is turning out to be more exciting than of late.

'Look,' says Pauline and lifts up the lid of the basket. 'We do want to support you, Violet. There's only healthy stuff in here. Carrot sticks, wholemeal sandwiches, hummus dip and fruit. Let's have lunch together. Talk about that brilliant book *Vox*.'

'You should have rung. I appreciate it, honestly, but I'm not feeling well.' Bella warned me once that envious friends might lace food like sandwiches with full-fat butter.

'You won't even let us stay to talk for a few minutes?' said Kath. 'Even the women in that book are allowed one hundred words.'

'But what you've got to say won't be that concise, will it?'

'It could be,' says Pauline. 'I like a challenge.' She fishes in her handbag for a notebook and gives everyone a sheet of paper. The three of them squeeze onto the sofa with faces as perplexed as mine.

'Look – this is silly,' I say. 'Surely you're not suggesting – there's no need.'

'I think there is,' says Pauline. 'And where's the harm? We'll tell you our concerns in as few a words as we can manage.' She hands me a sheet. 'You can tell us why we're making a fuss over nothing.'

I shake my head. 'This is ridiculous. Please. Just leave.'

'We're bloggers now, Violet,' says Kath in a light tone. 'We work best writing things down.'

'And it sounds like fun,' interrupts Nora.

The room falls silent. With a sigh I pick up a pen and paper. I sit down on the floor and start writing.

'Me first,' says Nora twenty minutes later. She stands up and clears her throat. I admire the burgundy trousers and orange checked top that, against all the odds, go well with her red hair. She reads out from her piece of paper.

'Violet. I've always admired your unique sense of style. People laugh at my fur coat but I'm not bothered. And you used to be like that, dressing as you pleased without a care. At first I thought it was fun, your interest in fashion and hair – but now it's taken a serious turn. Your great figure used to go in and out. Now it's straight up and down. As for those gorgeous curls… Lenny has left the door open for a real man to stride in and win your heart. And he will. You don't need to change one iota.'

She sits down on the sofa. Ever the romantic, what Nora doesn't get is that my new image is to empower me as a woman. It's not all about trying to hook a man.

Kath puts on her glasses. 'What a difference you've made to my life, Violet. Helping me day-to-day. Laughing with me. Ferrying me around to appointments. You're an angel I miss sharing cake with. A truly genuine person. That rare beast is difficult to find these days. During my years of nursing I've seen the damage, caused through many illnesses, by a lack of weight. Anaemia. Weak bones. Infertility. That's where you are heading unless you realise this lifestyle is too extreme. The clothes, the hair, the make-up – that's all good fun. But please don't mess with your body.' She takes her glasses off.

I realise I've folded my arms. Kath is speaking to me as if I'm a reckless child. I'd bet my life savings on the fact that my juiced breakfasts are healthier than her toast.

Pauline clears her throat. 'Violet. The evidence is there that your makeover is damaging. You're off work, for a start. You've cancelled meeting up with us. Your change in image is becoming more than a physical revolution. Be careful, love. Bella sounds great but try to be objective. Don't be led astray. I know from my policing career that can so easily happen. Follow your own heart and the voice inside that tells you what is right and wrong.'

Pauline is suggesting Bella is some sort of criminal?

'How about you, Violet?' says Kath. 'You've written something too.'

Everything they've said confirms I've used the right words. My chest tightens as I look at my piece of paper and stand up. 'I know you don't mean to interfere but I'm an adult, not a child. Please don't take offence but I suggest you are out of touch. Look in any magazine. My size is not uncommon. Times have moved on. My cholesterol level must have drastically fallen. I can run up the stairs. Bella empowered me not to collapse in a heap when Lenny left. I wish you could be more supportive but you don't understand. Therefore I suggest we take a break. Nothing in life stays the same. That includes looks, relationships – and friendships.'

I fold up the note. Nora opens her mouth but after a look from Kath it shuts. The three of them stare for a moment as if willing me to take back what I said. Instead I lean forwards and close the lid on the basket.

'Thanks for caring,' I say. 'And I'll keep reading your blog. I'm really proud of how hard you've all worked. I've not missed a post and don't intend to. And any problems you have, just email me. I'm still happy to help online. But at this point, being in your company is doing more harm than good, and you are very capable of running the book club on your own.'

'Perhaps it's for the best,' says Nora flatly. 'That's the first time I've ever felt my age in your company.'

Kath pushes herself to her feet. The others follow. I open the door and they file out.

Chapter 22

It's Friday. I feel a massive sense of relief since speaking to the book club yesterday. I'm free now. Free to do what I want without inquisitive eyes. Hopefully Farah's got the message too. I wake up to a blue sky and jump out of bed. I drink a juice and feel an adrenaline high in the shower as I sing one of Bella's favourite pop songs, which she said I should learn because it's so uplifting.

After having my say with Kath and the others yesterday, the euphoria of having stood up for myself enabled me to get back to Casey. We didn't talk about Wednesday night. Instead he invited me to a friend's house party in Soho tonight. We'll meet at Tottenham Court Road underground station at eight.

I hurry out of the shower and get dressed for work. I'll need to go shopping again as I must have dropped almost another size. When I head into the lounge to look for my handbag, Bella is playing *Unapologetic Bitch* by Madonna.

'Here, catch!' She shoots me a mischievous smile and throws over a banana. She looks amazing, having had her hair tinted pink and wearing lipstick to match. We each use our fruit as a microphone. I know all the words. Bella always turns off my jazz and puts on her CDs. I don't mind.

I'm still whistling that tune as I stride into work. Hugo waves and asks if I'm okay. I give the thumbs up and say how much I like his cheerful yellow tie.

I walk into the office and nod at Irfan.

'Feeling better?' he says. A chill hangs in the air. I don't blame him. Farah is his wife. Loyalty's important. I wonder if Lenny will ever learn that.

'Yes. Sorry I couldn't come in yesterday. Anything I should know?' I pass him a takeaway coffee. I popped into a cafe on the way over. 'It's your favourite hazelnut latte.'

He doesn't reach for it. 'You know Farah doesn't like me drinking those now.'

'Okay. Have mine. A straight black with an extra shot. I've not drunk out of it yet.'

After hesitating, he accepts my cup. 'So yesterday…' Irfan takes a sip and puts down the drink. His brow smooths out. 'The meeting with Felicity went well. Lots of ideas thrown around. You can read the minutes. They should be emailed out to us all today. And *Me and Mr Jones*, the young adult novel by Kathy Freeman—'

'How's it doing? Did it make the Guardian review pages?'

'That happened last week,' says Felicity as she walks past and shoots me a quizzical look. Her gaze moves to Irfan and he shrugs.

'Of course, I mean…' What's their problem? I can't be expected to keep track of every fucking book.

'We've just found out it's also been shortlisted for a school library award,' says Felicity and heads into her office.

'That's fantastic,' I say to Irfan. 'But then Kathy deserves it, the way she's dealt with such a sensitive subject.' The story is about a schoolgirl who is groomed by her teacher. Irfan and I suspect it is based on personal experience.

'Violet, come into my office,' calls Felicity.

I follow her and perch on one of the chairs opposite her desk. I'm still holding the latte and put it down next to her phone. She hangs her light jacket on the back of her chair, sits down and leans back.

'Sorry about yesterday,' I say, 'I wasn't well and—'

She holds up her palm. 'It's okay. I'm more worried that you seem to have taken your eye off the ball recently. Irfan, he mentioned—' She cleared her throat. 'Everything all right?'

'Yes,' I reply brusquely. 'I've just been tired and…'

Felicity nods and stares for a moment. 'Okay. Well, perhaps get some earlier nights.' She gives a stiff smile. 'Too much reading into the early hours?'

'Something like that,' I say brightly.

'I hear you and am surprised *I'm* so chirpy today. I haven't had a single minute's sleep. I read *Alien Hearts* by Casey Wilde. I received the submission yesterday and couldn't put it down. Before I knew it, my clock said four am.'

'I've read it too.'

'Irfan mentioned that as he was leaving last night. That's why I want to chat.' She grabs the latte and takes a mouthful. 'How come you got an early look?'

'Lenny works for his agent. When we were still together, he was so excited and emailed it to me confidentially.'

'*His*?'

'Casey's a man.'

'Wow. This author gets more and more intriguing. My gut tells me *Alien Hearts* is going to be massive.' She takes another sip of the drink. 'We need to do everything we can to sign Wilde. What can you tell me about him?'

'He grew up in a female-dominated environment. He works as a hairdresser. He's popular with and loves the opposite sex. He's got nothing but respect for women and I think you'll agree that comes across in the manuscript.'

She nods.

'And, of course, it's not just a romance – it's science fiction. Casey's travelled widely and I think that's put him in a strong position to create an alien world that is very different to civilised western society.'

'And that alien world is so deep and intricate – dare I say his thoroughness reminds me of Terry Pratchett.'

'Are you going to put in an offer?'

'I need to think about my strategy. You sound as if you know him fairly well.'

'Our paths have crossed a couple of times and Lenny told me things…' I try to keep it light. 'You should know that Beatrix Bingham has approached him.'

Felicity's face darkens.

'We need to play clever, then.' She picks up a biro. 'Although it's questionable as to whether Alpaca or Thoth are going to be able to compete with the big advances I'm sure the larger publishers will offer.'

'Casey's a man of integrity. If he senses our passion, who knows? Perhaps invite him to next week's party.' This could work well. 'Say no pressure, it's just to give him a taste of how Thoth works. I could pass on the invitation tonight, as it happens – I think he's going to a do I'm attending.' I hope she doesn't press for details about the house party.

'Oh? A book launch?'

'Um… it's a poetry reading,' I say, knowing Felicity isn't a poetry fan. 'It's a monthly event I go to in—'

'Great, well that's an excellent idea. Otherwise he won't get it until next week and might have made plans. I'll slip in a personal note. Pass by my office this afternoon and it'll be ready.'

She opens her laptop, which is my cue to leave. When I get back to my desk, Irfan is on the phone with an over-anxious author, by the sounds of it, who wants to know what we are doing to improve their disappointing sales. I sift through my paperwork and consult the week's diary. This afternoon I'll be doing the structural edits on my favourite author's latest work-in-progress. Before I know it, lunch time is here. Bella can't meet me for shopping because the spa is too busy. But she's texted me a list of the kind of outfit she thinks I should wear.

I've come to rely on her opinion so much. Sometimes it feels suffocating, but then I remind myself of how low and directionless I was before I met her.

I buy an off-the-shoulder top for tonight and white jeans from the children's department, just to get that tight fit. Bella had told me to try the girls' section and said fitting those clothes proved that I had reached the ultimate size. Succeeding gives me a high like no other, as if I've achieved something that would be impossible for your average woman. I text Bella to tell her and she congratulates me with a suitable gif.

I manage to get back to Thoth with five minutes to spare.

'Out tonight?' Hugo says. 'Where's the old Violet? Won't Flossie miss you?' He digs my ribs in jest and I flinch. I wonder if his finger left a bruise. There's no flesh to protect me.

'How about you? A date?'

'Brace yourself. I've been seeing the same woman for a few weeks. This might get serious.' He fills me in on the gossip from yesterday. A reality celebrity turned up to discuss Thoth ghost-writing her life story. 'The camera really does put on ten pounds. There was nothing to her.'

That's what my book club friends didn't understand. Wallis Simpson really was right. You can never be too thin.

I spend the afternoon in edits. Half past four and I'm done. I don't have time for a coffee with Farah and Irfan tonight. Not that she asks. But I still get a hug. She asks if I'm feeling better. Then turns to go.

'I love your top,' I say. It's a beautiful silk.

'Thanks. It's comfy, if nothing else.'

'That shade of green really suits you.'

She doesn't reply. The couple depart. Inwardly I sigh. So Farah thinks she can tell me a few hard truths but won't accept them back? She feels she can comment on how slim she thinks I am, yet doesn't like it when I suggest that maybe she's carrying a few extra pounds? Well, I've done all I can. It's up to her now if she wants to continue this awkwardness. It's the same with my retirement home friends. They don't like to be made to feel old. I don't like to be made to feel like a child.

I've discussed it all with Bella and she's right.

'You don't need to justify yourself to anyone, Bae.'

Bae. Before all else. That word means a lot.

'In fact, why don't you delete those friends' numbers from your contacts list?' she continues. 'Because true friends wouldn't constantly throw negative vibes your way.'

I'm thinking about it.

I tidy my desk and clean the keyboard. I can't wait to get home and try on my outfit. I go by Felicity's office and pick up the party invitation. I only ate my microphone banana for lunch, but I don't need any more calories. I feel energised enough by how things seem to be falling into place.

Chapter 23

We meet at the tube station's ticket office and have one of those awkward embraces where neither of you is sure whether to kiss. Then we stroll past shops and bars and discuss what a beautiful June evening it is. I brought my denim jacket, but have it stuffed into my rucksack next to a bottle of vodka. I can't remember the last time I went to a house party. It was probably at university, when I'd been the only one not consuming mugfuls of randomly concocted punch and checking my watch to gauge when it was acceptable to go home. Unlike at school before that, it hadn't seemed to matter so much that I didn't fit in. Some university friends even expressed envy that I never missed a nine a.m. lecture. Their acceptance of my differences helped me embrace them.

As for this party, I wasn't sure whether to bring drink. Bella said of course I must. She also said clear spirits were the healthiest and made me take back the bottle of red wine. I breathed a sigh of relief when I saw Casey. He was carrying a four pack of beer. He wore a fashionably distressed suede jacket and a tentative smile.

'You okay?' he asked eventually as we swerve out of the way of a boy on a skateboard.

'Great, thanks. Yourself?'

'I wasn't sure if you'd come. Not after Wednesday night.'

We stop at a pedestrian crossing. I look up at the knotted brow and the eyes that were lacking their usual humour. My actions with Casey aren't conscious now. They just happen. Regardless of whether he might have let Beatrix into his flat to share that bottle of wine, to sign a contract, I reach up and hold his collar. I pull him towards me. My lips press against his.

I look back at the crossing and can still see an illuminated red man. Bella says it's best to lie to Casey about why I left the other night, but I think he'd understand the truth. She says I need to focus on him being my conduit to success and paying back Lenny and Beatrix for making a fool out of me. But I can't help the real feelings that feed my imagination with things I never even considered doing with Lenny. And a real passion for *Alien Hearts* has taken root. I want to see it taken up by a publisher who cares about every written syllable, every millimetre of the cover, every second of thought that goes into the marketing and pricing strategy.

As if they have a mind of their own, my fingers find his and our nearest hands entwine as the red man turns green. Words don't seem mandatory, despite us both belonging to an industry where sentences are king.

'I've not been here for a long time,' I say eventually and stare into a posh French restaurant.

'Melvin – that's whose party we're going to – lost his dad to cancer last year. He was left the flat. It's in a tower block but it looks a lot grander than you'd expect. Many of the residents bought their flats from the local authority in the eighties, Melvin's dad included.' He smiles. 'Bob was a great guy. I knew him well. It was like he automatically self-edited. He never spoke a superfluous word. But when he spoke, he spoke most about how the heart has been torn out of Soho.'

I study the chain stores and trendy coffee shops. 'I vaguely remember a trip to Liberty's with Mum – and Carnaby Street. It's certainly less seedy than in the old days. That's got to be a good thing, right?'

'Sure, the night life needed regulating, but Bob felt passionately that developers tore out the history instead of simply layering on a new façade. I mean, that's what you find in the best haunts – layers of past life put down and preserved like fossilised sediment. The rejuvenation of this area has literally ripped everything out. The sex shops and strip clubs have gone, and quite rightly in most cases, but that's affected the whole vibrant, bohemian vibe and the late night jazz club scene as well. Bob always said Soho was never perfect. It certainly had its flaws. But that's what makes character, not being like everything else – and now that uniqueness has gone.'

As we turn down a side street, a well of unease slops over its sides in my chest as I think about my transformation, about the changes I've put in place. Instead of adding a new layer of experience, have I simply ripped out what was there and tried to start over again? Does that mean I've lost my character and everything that shaped me to that point?

I don't know.

I try not to think about it.

But when I look in the mirror, I worry.

I worry that the woman staring back isn't me. She's a stranger and I can't find an instruction manual. I mentioned my concerns to Bella once.

'You're a better fit now. That's all that counts,' she'd said in a scornful voice.

Now and then Bella loses patience with me; says I need to forget the old Violet and that when I don't, I'm being ungrateful towards her after all the work she's put into my transformation.

What if Bella decides I'm wasting her time?

I rely on her. She's become my best friend, my cheer-leader, my confidante.

We arrive at the tower block and I gaze up at the red brick work and glossy black balcony rails. Melvin's flat is on the third floor. It's not big but this lends the minimalist walls a cosy feel. I hand over the vodka. He kisses me on the cheek. Everyone's pleased to see Casey and on the back of that pleased to see me. I'm passed a bowl of crisps and take a small handful. A few won't hurt. They are all I've eaten since lunch.

A curvy woman sucks in her dimpled cheeks. 'Aren't you lucky, being able to eat what you want?'

Don't say that.

Don't ever think that.

If you knew how tough my regime was, you wouldn't be envious.

Don't get me wrong, I am so grateful to Bella. I've gained endless knowledge about nutrition, cardio exercise, skin care and applying make-up, but over the last few months, I've also become aware of one thing: effortless glamour doesn't exist. Being the best you is bloody hard.

It upsets friends. It comes at a price you're not aware of until it's too late.

It's also addictive.

Sometimes it feels as if the road to perfection will never end, it'll just go on and on, passing less straight but more laidback avenues.

Casey comes back with two vodkas. He introduces me properly to Melvin, who's a graffiti artist, and wants to make it as big as Banksy. Inheriting this flat means he can get by as a barista in his spare time. I ask to see the albums of his work. He hesitates and doesn't want to bore me but I insist. Casey's face softens. Apparently I've made Melvin's night. He knows the crowd and half of his friends are too busy upselling their own artistic careers, whilst the others don't consider graffiti a true art form.

The room becomes increasingly hot as more bodies arrive after last orders. The lights are dimmed. People dance. The laughter and chat get louder, fuelled by the alcohol and the white powder I see traces of in the bathroom.

We find a spot on a sofa. Casey holds my hands. 'Wednesday, I was worried I'd scared you off, Vi.'

'No. I… it's just… I haven't had that many boyfriends and—'

Casey's laughter reminds me of Alice and her friends at primary school. He wipes his eyes. 'Very funny. Come on, what's the real reason? I can take it.'

I stare at the floor.

He lifts my chin. 'Shit. You were serious?'

I force a laugh. 'I'm just messing with you. Come on, idiot – less chat, I want to dance.'

I pull him up and lead us to the middle of the lounge where it will be far too noisy to talk. Casey tries nevertheless. I shrug off his unheard words. Maybe white lies are better than the truth.

Bodies move in unison as Michael Jackson sings about sunshine and moonlight. A woman with glossy black hair and eyebrows to match shimmies up to Casey and rubs herself up and down in the air in between them. My mouth feels parched. I need a drink. Casey's face blurs. I mumble something about going outside just before everything turns foggy and black.

When I wake, I'm stretched out on the floor. The music has stopped and the lights are on. I'm lying on my side.

'What happened?' I manage.

'You fainted.' Casey brushes my straightened blonde hair out of my face. 'How do you feel?'

Slowly I push myself up. The woman with black hair passes me a glass of water.

'Do you feel dizzy?' she asks.

I shake my head.

'Suze is a nurse,' says Casey, his fingers threaded through mine.

'Try to drink as much as possible,' she says. 'It's so hot in here and the alcohol will have dehydrated you. Have you eaten much today?'

'Not really. Busy day at work.'

'Should I take her to hospital for a check over?' asks Casey.

'No. No, honestly. No fuss. I'm feeling fine.'

Suze nudges me to take another glassful of water. 'I think you'll be okay but get yourself down to Accident and Emergency if you get a headache or feel sick, or if you get any pains or feel dizzy. You probably just need to sleep it off, rehydrate and have something decent to eat.'

Casey helps me to my feet. People shoot me sympathetic smiles. Melvin comes over.

'How are you, Vi?' His words slur slightly. The room is full of smoke and I feel sick.

'We're leaving. Cheers Melvin. See you soon, mate.' Casey slips an arm around my shoulders.

'No, honestly – you stay here. I'll get a taxi home,' I say.

'It's three in the morning already. I'm ready to leave and you aren't going anywhere on your own. In fact, come back to mine, Vi. Let me look after you. And my breakfasts are legendary. We're talking pancakes with cherries and Greek yogurt with—'

Too tired to argue, I nod. We don't speak in the taxi. I sit next to Casey, my head against his shoulder, my eyes closed. I don't object when he helps me off with my jeans and settles me under the duvet in his double bed. He turns the lights off and sits in a nearby chair. He yawns.

I hold out one hand. 'Don't be silly, Casey. Sleep in here with me.'

'It's okay. I'm fine here.'

Tears prick my eyes. Am I really that much of a freak? A sob escapes my lips. I try to disguise it as some sort of cough but within seconds Casey is crouched on the floor, by my side.

'Vi?'

I pull him nearer. Our mouths meet. He's so gentle. I unbutton his shirt.

'Vi? Are you sure?'

Perhaps it's my collapse. Perhaps it's being here in the dead of night. Or maybe it's the alcohol, but this time I don't think about my own body. All I can think about is his.

It's near the end of November. Mrs Warham is still cross. I can't remember the last time she asked me to take the register to the office. I used to do that often. It's a very important job. At least Mum is giving me ice cream on a Friday again. Every day, she asks me what's been going on with Alice. She came in to see Mrs Warham a few days after Bonfire Night. Mum was very red in the face afterwards but gave me the thumbs up.

But I still dread school. My tummy hurts every morning. Since spilling the gravy, Alice has kept her distance. She just sticks her tongue out and turns her back on me. I pretend that it isn't happening. Sometimes I hang out with the boys. Since the fun snaps, they've started asking if I want to play football. But not every day. My books help me to not feel quite so lonely. They don't stick their leg out for me to trip over. They don't pinch my arm or laugh at my glasses and hair. They aren't mean like Alice's group. Always there offering me escape from a life I hate, they are my best friends in the world – apart from Flint.

It's Saturday and Mum's boss, Ryan, is here. They are going to watch box sets. It turns out they like the same shows. She asked if I wanted them to take me to the cinema. I shook my head. Now I hate the weekends too.

Mum did ask if I minded Ryan coming around to the house. What could I say? *Yes. I hate having another man here doing Uncle Kevin's things like making you laugh and helping you unblock the sink. And it's not fair. You have a good friend. So should I. I hate you for making me stop seeing Flint. And he's much more fun than stupid Ryan.*

However, Mum doesn't know that I have a secret.

A big one.

I haven't stopped seeing Flint after all.

I usually catch him on the way back from school. After Mum's gone in, he appears outside and we chat. I even managed to smuggle him inside yesterday. Mum ran a bath when I got home so I waited a while before me and Flint headed up to my bedroom with drinks, trying to keep in our giggles. Mum came in to ask what I wanted for tea and he hid under the bed. Flint stayed until my burger was ready. We agreed to meet in the treehouse today.

Mum lets me eat cheese and pickle sandwiches in my room for lunch. Afterwards I creep downstairs. I peek into the lounge. Mum and Ryan are on the sofa. His arm is around her. They are watching a programme with women in pretty dresses and men in suits. I go into the garden and quietly shut the back door. Mum has drawn the curtains so the telly is easier to watch. Good. She can't see me squash through the fence and into Applegrove Wood.

I head to the tree house, my face turned downwards as I study pine cones and twisted roots. Perhaps I should find the woods scary but I don't. All the fallen leaves are dead, and the sun can't get through, but I've felt so sad lately it matches my mood.

I reach the treehouse. Flint is waiting at the bottom of the ladder. Instantly I feel better.

'*Ryan*, Mum's boss is around,' I say and pull a face.

Flint puts his fingers into his mouth and pretends to make himself sick. He climbs up the ladder first and goes in. I almost fall backwards when I reach the top.

'Don't be scared,' says a man with a straggly beard and dirty coat. He has a rucksack and shoes with holes in. He looks a lot younger than Mum. I hover, not sure what to do. I look at Flint who shrugs and sits down.

'I must look a sight,' says the man. 'I haven't washed for a week.'

Flint grins. It is kind of funny. Lucky man. I get bored of my nightly bath.

I wonder why he's so dirty. Most adults are obsessed with soap. Slowly I go in.

'You must smell,' I say and sit down.

'You don't notice after a while. Is this your treehouse?'

'It's ours,' says Flint.

'It's a great place to read,' I say.

'Do you mind if I stay for a while? It's cold outside today.'

'Haven't you got a home?' asks Flint.

'Where do you live?'

The man looks at us both. 'I don't have a home at the moment. My name's Tim.'

'I'm Violet.' I jerk my head towards my best friend. 'This is Flint. You mean you haven't got anywhere to go? How did that happen?'

Tim looks from me to Flint and then back again. 'You're lucky to have each other. Friends are important. I've lost all of mine. I've been living on the streets for a year. I used to read a lot. Romances. My dad said I was soft.'

His bottom lip trembles. That told me his dad wasn't a very nice person. I feel sorry for Tim despite all the dirt.

'Would you ever go back home?' I say.

Tim snorts. 'Never. I'm happier on my own. Dad… he did things he shouldn't have done. So I left as soon as I could.'

'But you haven't got any money. How do you buy food?' I ask.

'I manage. Anything's better than going back to live with that bully.'

That's how I feel about school. Alice's friends have just taken up where she left off. I'd do anything not to have to go back on Monday.

'You must be hungry. How about me and Flint get you some food?' I look at Flint and he nods. 'I don't live far. Wait here?'

'Really? That would be great. I haven't eaten for two days.'

My tummy rumbles if I miss one meal. Me and Flint hurry down the ladder and run to my back garden. I go inside whilst Flint waits by the door. Mum hears me and I force myself into the lounge so that she doesn't wonder what I'm doing. She says to zip up my coat if I'm going into the back garden. Says that in an hour we'll go out for cake. I force myself to smile at Ryan.

Then I go into the kitchen and grab a packet of biscuits. Mum only buys two cans of coke a week – we have one each, on Saturday night, as a treat. Tim needs mine more than I do. I stuff it into my coat pocket. I also take a banana. Five fruits a day is important. I don't understand why. It's not as if bodies can count. Sometimes the things teachers tell us to do are stupid.

I go outside and Flint and I hurry back. Tim is still there, blowing on his hands. He doesn't say much. I've never seen anyone eat a whole packet of biscuits. Even though he's starving, he offers me and Flint one each. Flint says no so I take two for myself. Tim finds that funny.

He says my purple glasses are pretty. No one has ever said that before. Tim tells us about a pet dog he once had. I tell him about Tinker. Tim is easy to talk to. He likes my coat. He says I'm a kind person and he'd like to be friends with me and Flint.

I don't have many friends. This is good.

We have things in common. We don't fit in. Most importantly, we both like reading. He tells me about his favourite childhood books. Tim also likes the woods. And animals. He likes biscuits. But most of all, Tim used to hate his life, just like me. But he did something about it and now he's happy.

We agree to come back tomorrow morning with more food. On the way back to my house, Flint says that Tim is brave. That maybe running away from home isn't so scary. His eyes shine as he says a life on the road, with someone like Tim, would be such an adventure.

We look at each other. The sign of a great friend is that you can read their mind and I know exactly what he is thinking.

The same as me.

Chapter 24

Bella would have been impressed if she'd been home an hour ago when I got back. She must have spent the night sleeping over at her new boyfriend's, whereas I left Casey to wake up alone. I wasn't going to. I wanted to stay in bed and relish every second I spent in his arms. But I'd finally woken up, bleary eyed, around nine o'clock and gone to the bathroom. Fate did me a favour. The dirty linen basket was in there. A pair of Casey's socks lay scrunched on the floor. Without even thinking, I bent over to tidy them away. But when I lifted the basket's lid, all I saw in the bottom was a pair of pink lace knickers.

I lifted them out. The label said Victoria's Secret. I thought back to the Facebook message I'd read between Lenny and Beatrix.

Quickly I got dressed and called a taxi. I left Casey's invitation from Felicity on my side of the bed and scrawled a note on the envelope saying I forgot to give it to him last night. I thanked him for a great evening.

I thought we'd had something special. I was wrong. Thank goodness I hadn't let on to him about what I was starting to feel.

I curl my fists, fighting the tears. I won't ever put myself in a position to be made a fool of again. I sit on the sofa and hold my head in my hands. Just one week to go to the party. I can't back away from Casey right now. I still want him to sign with Thoth for the book and Felicity's sakes. Even though things are going to be awkward now between us.

I drag my hands away from my eyes and notice a piece of paper on the coffee table. Someone else has been leaving notes. I lean forward and pick it up.

> *Dear Violet,*
>
> *I had to use the spare key to come in last night. I hope you don't mind, but a neighbour was complaining that Flossie was caterwauling. If you remember last time that happened, she'd got locked in your bedroom. I assumed Bella was out. I think Flossie was upset because the litter tray wasn't in its usual place. I found it on the kitchen unit, empty and next to a bag of litter. I filled it and put it on the floor. She was bursting.*
>
> *Love from*
> *Kath x*

Poor Flossie. I'd just cleaned out the litter tray and meant to put it down before I left. I look around. Eventually I find her curled up on Bella's bed. I crouch down and tickle her ears.

'Sorry girl. Really sorry. It won't happen again.'

She stretches and pats my arm with one paw. That's her signal that I'm allowed to give her belly a rub. I run my hand across her stomach and her purr intensifies.

Eventually I pad back into the lounge and study the note again – and the scrawled kiss. I toss it back down and decide to curl up and go back to sleep when I notice a piece of white material on the floor. I bend over and scoop it up. It's a handkerchief with a K embroidered into the corner surrounded by flowers.

Kath used to embroider before her hands became stiff. She's often talked of night shifts where instead of going to the canteen, she'd sit with patients in intensive care and talk to them even when they couldn't hear. Her embroidery filled in the gaps that should have been full of their words. She'd work on handkerchiefs with the initial of their first name in the corner. When they recovered, it provided the perfect personal gift.

I sigh. If I don't return it, Kath will only come back, probably at a most inopportune moment when I'm in the middle of a facial or waxing. And I should really say thank you for sorting the cat. I don't need to discard my manners just because we aren't seeing as much of each other. Reluctantly, I get to my feet and tie my hair back. I slip into my trainers without bothering to wash or apply make-up – or rather, remove last night's. Normally I'm scrupulous about that. At least I'm wearing my new jogging suit, the one just like Bella's. I put on a fleece as well. My body misses the natural insulation I used to carry around.

I think back to how warm I felt last night, snuggled up to Casey before it all went wrong. I try not to think about Beatrix and what I found in his bathroom.

Trying not to think of them together, I take the stairs up to Kath's floor even though I'm shattered. I can't remember the last time I used a lift at work. That's one of Bella's tips on how to fit extra exercise into your day without putting in too much effort.

I knock at Kath's door and wait. She always takes time to answer. Eventually it opens.

'Here's your handkerchief. I found it on the floor.'

Kath doesn't act surprised and for a second I wonder if she left it there on purpose.

'Thanks,' I say and give a tentative smile. 'I don't know how Flossie would have coped without you.'

Sometimes I miss the chats we used to have. The coffee and cake sessions that have petered out. I wonder how she's managing to apply her shoulder cream.

Kath opens her mouth but then shuts it and stares. Her arms stretch out and she leans forward. They slip around my neck. What's this about? She squeezes tightly before stepping back.

Kath's crying? Why? I've never seen her do that. Not even when her nephew threatened to evict her or when her arthritis was particularly bad last winter. She motions for me to come in and we sit down on her compact green sofa.

'Sorry. I don't know what's come over me,' she says and blows her nose into the handkerchief.

'What's the matter? Is it Norm? Has he tried to up your rent again?'

She shakes her head.

'Is… is everyone at Sunflower okay?' What if it's one of the friends I made feel old and unnecessary? Nora is getting on in years. Perhaps I really upset her. My chest tightens.

'It's just… I'm always here, you know – to talk to. I won't judge. I can help. When you're ready, Violet. I'm so sorry. I didn't realise things had gone so far. I knew something was up. I shouldn't have just stood by and let it get worse.'

What is she talking about?

Kath takes a deep breath. 'I know about Bella.'

Heat floods into my face. 'Know what? Have you been snooping around my flat?'

'No, of course not. But I couldn't find Flossie after she'd done her business. I wanted to double check that she was nicely settled before I left. I found her in Bella's room. I couldn't help but see—'

'See what? Bella's got nothing to hide.'

'All this time you've kept it secret. I can't imagine how much you've suffered.'

'I don't know what you mean.' My hands feel sweaty. She can't know the truth. 'Me and Bella get on fine.'

Kath touches my arm but I pull away.

'You need to get rid of her, sweetheart,' she said. 'It's the only way. You must know that. She's bad for you. Let me help. I'll—'

No. No. This was Mum and Flint all over again. Someone else thinking they knew best when all they're doing is looking in from the outside. Mum didn't really know Flint and Kath doesn't know Bella. How she's the reason I get through each day. Without her, I'd still be wading through the swamp of self-pity I ended up in after I found out about Lenny and Beatrix.

'It's none of your business,' I say in a raised voice and get to my feet. 'There is no need for you to worry. Just leave me and Bella alone. She's a good friend and I won't have anyone tell me otherwise.'

'She's a friend? Really?' Kath stands up and stares me straight in the face. 'Because I don't agree. I can see her exactly for what she is. Her room and its contents told me everything I need to know. And I know that's hard for you to hear, but she's *dangerous*. Enough is enough, Violet. Can't you see how she's running and ruining your life? Let go of this parasite before it ends in the worst possible way.'

'That's not true. I don't want to hear any more of your false accusations. You don't know her like I do.'

I hurry out of the flat, ignoring Kath's calls. I descend the stairs two at a time and rush out into the garden. I start running, slowly at first. I cross roads and swerve around bins and people. My pace becomes quicker. It starts to rain. I hardly feel it.

Chapter 25

It's Sunday lunch time. I sit in the Canterbury Tales. The landlord I met at the Chapter Battle recognises me and jokes about why a woman of my class would waste her time with a scoundrel like Casey. I take out my phone and look at Vintage Views. The latest review is one by Nora about a gay romance. Pauline's before that focuses on a top ten thriller. They are gaining followers, some influential, and by the looks of it, quickly learning how to best use hashtags.

Gay romance. See, your friends aren't outdated or old.

I ignore the voice in my head that dares to disagree with Bella and I sip my sparkling water. Casey texted and suggested meeting for lunch. He's the kind of man who appreciates transparency, so I've decided to ask him outright about Beatrix's underwear. I start to read Nora's review when the table rocks. Casey steadies the scratched surface and puts down his pint.

'Sorry I'm a bit late. I overslept,' he explains and sits down.

Was he with Beatrix again?

'Vi?'

'What? Oh, no problem. I haven't been here long.'

'Everything okay? Why did you rush off yesterday despite my irresistible offer of pancakes and cherries?' His hand covers mine. 'After fainting like that, I was worried when you didn't reply to my texts until late last night.'

'Sorry. I was still recovering. It must have been the heat and too much drink.' Keeping my tone light, I raise my glass. 'I'm still rehydrating.'

Casey studies my face. 'What's wrong?'

'Nothing. Look, let's order and—'

He puts the menu on the table next to ours. 'I'm serious. Friday night… it was…' He shook his head. 'There's no other words. Vi, it was fucking fantastic. I can't stop thinking about it.'

I almost cry. Lenny shredded our love story and left it in bits. Yet here I am now, feeling like this, part of something new that feels as if it could really be worth something.

But I can't let my emotions interfere with the plan that's almost fully executed.

'It was a difficult day. I fell out with my neighbour.'

'How so?'

'Oh, this and that…'

Casey takes a mouthful from his pint. He knows I'm holding back. I can't bear to see him hurt.

'She doesn't approve of my flatmate, Bella.'

'Why?'

'Since she's moved in, I've kind of overhauled my lifestyle.'

'In what way?'

'I got fit. Bought a new wardrobe. Just had a refresh but Kath doesn't like change. She misunderstands things that she thinks she knows about Bella. It's complicated. She even called her a parasite.'

A shiver runs down my spine as I recall how angry Bella was this morning when she came home, and I let slip that

Kath had been in her room. It all came tumbling out of my mouth – what Kath had discovered in there. How she didn't approve of my new flatmate. I'd never heard Bella shout before.

'Don't you ever forget what a pathetic creature you were before being friends with me.' Bella's chest heaved and her ponytail cut through the air violently. 'Don't you remember? You let Lenny walk all over your self-esteem. What happened was no surprise. You were hardly competition for someone like Beatrix.'

I curled myself into a ball on the sofa. 'Bella. Please,' I said in a small voice. 'I'm sorry. I hate to see you upset. I stuck up for you. You've got to believe me.'

She pursed her lips. 'I've made you what you are today. And how do you repay me? By talking about me to other people?'

'It wasn't like that.' My voice wavered. 'You must know how much I respect you.'

Finally her frown disappeared. She sat down next to me. We'd hugged and once more my world felt all right.

Bella was right to remind me that before meeting her, I was a nobody.

She's turned my life around.

I mustn't ever forget that.

'What did you used to look like?' Casey pushes his pint away and leans forwards.

I give a nervous laugh. 'Let's just say not quite as on trend.'

'Is that so important?'

'Clearly you follow fashions, so you don't need to ask me.'

He looked genuinely puzzled and gazes down at his Hawaiian T-shirt, which somehow looks cool with his leather jacket. 'No I don't. I just buy what I like.'

'Then you must be blessed with an innate sense of style. Anyway, enough about Kath. Have you thought about Felicity's invitation?'

'Yes, and I'd love to. I've heard about the Anubis and it's supposed to be an eye-popping venue. But until I've signed a deal, I don't think it's appropriate. It sends out the wrong message to the other publishers. I'll email Felicity on Monday.' He reaches for the menu and passes it to me. 'I don't need to look. Roast with all the trimmings for me.'

Keep your head. I look at my watch in the way men have sometimes done whilst talking to me in the past.

'Somewhere else to be?' he says and smiles.

And that's why I like Casey. Straight to the point. He deserves the same in return.

'I could ask you the same. What happened with Beatrix the other night?' I tell him that I almost bumped into her after leaving. I mention the underwear. Make up a story about how I'd seen her once shopping in Victoria's Secret.

'You think I've slept with her?'

'I'm just protecting my feelings. You can understand that.'

'You've been hurt in the past?'

'Haven't we all?'

'Nothing happened, Vi. Oh, she tried it on.' He covers his face with one hand and shakes his head.

'What?'

'I'm a gentleman. I shouldn't really say.'

I don't reply and finish my drink, acting as if I'm about to get to my feet.

'We're not teenagers, Casey. I'm not interested in playing games.'

He removes his fingers. 'Look, okay. She asked to use the bathroom and when she came out had stripped to her underwear. It was like something out of a B movie. She's got guts, I'll give her that. I didn't know where to look. I told her to stop but she slipped out of those pants and threw them behind her. For once I was speechless.'

Me too.

'Don't get me wrong. I find lots to admire in naked women. But it felt downright sleazy. Ambition can take people to strange places. I was good friends with a male hairdresser once. Or so I thought. He'd pop into the salon for a chat. Over time I worked out he had been trying to poach my customers. My feelings had been worth nothing. His goals had made him so blinkered.'

I grimaced.

'And as people, Beatrix and I have nothing in common. When she first arrived she made a point of saying that my lounge was only slightly bigger than her shoe closet and a deal with Alpaca would mean I could buy a proper place to live. Beatrix is all about labels and one-upmanship, which couldn't be further from where I'm at.' He kisses my fingers. 'It's the emotional connection that interests me.'

I truly believe that after reading *Alien Hearts*.

'Why did her pants end up in the dirty linen bin?'

'She left them behind and I didn't know what to do with them.' He grimaces. 'Out of sight out of mind.'

They didn't sleep together. Mostly, it's a relief for my heart, but also for my head.

Casey is curious about my flatmate. I tell him about her spa job and her exercise and juicing tips. Briefly we fight over the bill. I win so he insists on taking me to the cinema during the week.

I hesitate because I can tell he is keen. It's hard, trying to manipulate. It's not something I'm used to – partly because I've never had the necessary tools before.

I stand up. 'Lunch has been great. Thanks for the cinema invitation, but I'll have to say no. I've got a full-on week ahead at the office with preparations for next Saturday. I've got goody bags to fill and Irfan and I are working on a presentation. In fact, that reminds me to check the projector. I also need to check in with the interns who are decorating the room side by side with the hotel. Most nights I'm going to have to work late.'

We head outside.

'So when will I see you again?'

Tonight. Please. Us skin to skin.

'Perhaps next week. I'll be too tired Sunday after the celebrations. It's going to be champagne on tap and a jazz band has been hired. We'll be dancing until midnight.' I reach up to kiss him on the cheek but Casey turns and my eyes close as our mouths meet. Despite all my resolutions, it's impossible to resist.

Eventually his lips brush my neck. Sultry air warms my ear as he speaks in a husky voice.

'Then I guess the only way I'm going to see enough of you is to come to this party – as your very own personal guest. I guess it can't harm. No promises on the book front, though…'

A heady sense of power infuses me.
Holding hands, we hurry back to his flat.
Bella says I don't need anyone.
But it's lonely trying to be perfect.

Flint meets me out back at ten o'clock in the morning. It's two weeks after we first met Tim. Even though it's nearly the end of November, the sun is out so Mum doesn't mind me playing in the garden. Her Sunday mornings are always spent in the lounge listening to church music on the radio and ironing. We argue a lot these days. I don't see the point in bothering much in school. Mrs Warham hardly talks to me and lessons are boring without friends.

I secretly make a peanut butter sandwich for Tim and I take one of the little orange juice boxes that go in my lunch box.

Flint meets me by the fence and we hurry to the tree-house. It smells musty inside. Tim must have slept in there again.

He's huddled in the corner, blowing on his fingers, and doesn't talk until he's eaten the sandwich.

Flint looks at me. I nod and clear my throat.

'Flint and me have got something to ask you.'

Tim wipes his mouth and puts down the squashed orange carton. 'How long have you two known each other?'

'A couple of months,' says Flint.

'Since my Uncle Kevin died.'

Tim doesn't say anything for several minutes. 'That must have been tough. I loved my Auntie Sue. She always stuck up for me in front of Dad. But then she got married and moved to Wales and…'

We've talked a lot this week. Mum's had to work a couple of hours late every night because someone is ill. She's paid Zoe next door to babysit me. She's only sixteen and we've come to what she calls an arrangement. Zoe lets me play in the woods for a while and I don't tell Mum her boyfriend visits. I've seen them kissing on the sofa. It's disgusting.

I really like Tim. Even though he smells. He's started to give me a hug when I leave. It didn't feel comfortable at first. But after the first time, he noticed the bruises on my legs. He asked me to lift up my school skirt to show him as he wanted to know how bad they were. He got very angry when I told him about Alice and said if he was at my school, he'd protect me. I felt closer to him after that.

'So, what did you and Flint want to ask me?' he says.

'It's all planned,' says Flint.

'We're running away tonight. We want to live with you, Tim.'

Tim blinked for a few seconds. 'No, that's a bad idea. You can't hang out with me. People wouldn't like it.'

'But they wouldn't know.' I fold my arms. 'We're doing it anyway. Flint and me have decided.'

Flint nods. 'I want an adventure. It sounds so cool, sleeping under the stars.'

'And I hate my life,' I say. 'Just like you did, Tim.' I'll miss Tinker. And my bed. I'm a little scared of the dark. I don't like the cold. And I do like cake. But my life can't go on as it is.

'But it's winter and fucking freezing out here. Wouldn't you miss your mum?'

'She wouldn't miss me.'

'I'm sure she would.'

'Do you think your dad wishes you were back?'

'No, but that's different. He used to hit me and… much worse.'

Perhaps he confiscated his phone. Zoe gets really angry when her mum does that.

'Tell him your mum hits you too,' whispers Flint.

'Violet… the streets aren't a place for kids.'

My voice wavers. 'My mum hits me too.'

That's what Zoe would call a little white lie. She says they aren't really bad. I'm not sure why. It's not like white makes things better. I hate milk. And egg white. There's nothing worse than a blank white page at the end of a school test. And Alice, with her holidays abroad, is always saying my white skin is horrid compared to hers, which is tanned.

He frowns and it makes him look older for a moment. 'You've never said.'

Alice's group cornered me the other day and punched me. They heard me telling the boys about putting the spider in her bag.

'Don't you believe me? My ribs are covered in bruises.'

'Show me, Violet. Show me where you're hurt.'

Flint nods so I take off my gloves, my coat and jumper. That leaves my vest. I hesitate as goosebumps appear on my skin.

Tim leans forward as I lift it up.

'You said we were friends. And you said you'd protect me. There's nothing for me at home. Mum has Ryan. Mrs Warham hates me. Alice and her lot are never going to stop being mean. Uncle Kevin is never coming back. You and Flint…' A sob darts out of my throat. 'You are the only people who care.'

I get cross with myself as tears run down my face. No one says anything for a few moments.

'Okay.' Tim rubs his forehead. 'You and me, facing the world together.'

'And Flint.'

'Sure. That's what I meant.'

I smile. Tim smiles back. We agree to meet at the tree-house at eight o'clock. Mum will be watching her Sunday night detective programme. I'll pretend to be asleep in bed.

Tim gives me a much longer hug than usual when we say goodbye. Tells me I'm his special little girl. That he'll always do right by me.

Tim makes me feel important. Grown up. Pretty.

Me and Flint and Tim. My own little group at last. We'll all look out for each other.

It's going to be ace.

Chapter 26

Every evening this week I've spent in the office. Every night I've been out jogging, apart from Wednesday when I stayed at Casey's. A toothbrush of mine now resides in his bathroom. I've discovered it's true that his pancakes are second-to-none. I could tell that even though I only ate a few mouthfuls.

I didn't like leaving Flossie on her own again. Bella slept over at her boyfriend's too. I nipped back after work to check the litter tray and left food down and headed back after an early breakfast with Casey to change clothes and see her once more.

Do I feel guilty? Bella insists my life can't revolve around a mere animal. Sometimes it used to. Once when Flossie was ill, I booked two days off work. But things have changed. They've had to.

Tonight – in precisely an hour – I'll be meeting Casey outside the Anubis hotel. The canapés have been ordered. The jazz band's song list has been approved. Yesterday I helped the interns fill the last of the goody bags. Each contains a gold pen in the shape of an Egyptian obelisk, a tote bag bearing the Thoth logo, an Egyptian musk fragranced candle and two of our latest paperback releases.

I finally finish applying my gold nail varnish and blow on it to dry.

'Patience,' says Bella and smiles. She shakes her head. 'I can't believe how well that airbrush tan sets off the white dress. You look untouchable. I'm so proud of how you've stuck to the plan.'

I glance at my golden arms and remember Alice, a girl from school, who used to say I was whiter than glue – and stuck around just as bad.

'I couldn't have done it without you,' I say.

Bella takes my elbow and leads me from my bedroom to the lounge. We stand in front of the mirror. This final week of juicing has paid off. I'm now sporting celebrity cheeks and collar bones. Bella helped me find a suitable dress online that's Egyptian-themed, but in a subtle way. The pleated material clings to my body, its upper edge cutting under the chest. Rising up from that were two shoulder straps that neatly covered my breasts and produced a low cleavage.

I wear a beaded gold necklace with a matching bracelet we found in Camden market. Bella chose them. She also decides on my make-up and applies it for me, the black kohl eyeliner being slightly thicker than normal.

I stare at myself in the mirror. Are those tears in Bella's eyes?

'You did it,' she says. 'Tonight you'll show that loser Lenny just what he's missing. And I hope Beatrix chokes on her canapés. Talk about having to eat their words. Later I want to hear every single detail.'

'Thanks Bella. Now it's all down to me.'

'Just remember what we've talked about these last few months – how Lenny only used you to get cheap accommodation. He always bought you the same old presents for birthdays and Christmas.' Her top lip curled. 'How his comment to his brother that "looks aren't everything" meant that he'd never really fancied you at all. How him getting together with Beatrix proves that he's shallower than you could ever have imagined.'

I've needed Bella to spell all this out to me. I'm still not sure why I couldn't have seen these things for myself. For the hundredth time, I feel so grateful she came into my life. Even though, just sometimes, it feels as if she's got too much control and I'm scared of what will happen if I try to back off.

Yet deep down, I'm also scared of managing life on my own without her.

I shake myself and glance at my watch. The taxi will be here any minute.

'This is your moment,' she says. 'You're a strong, empowered woman who's achieved every goal we set. Casey will be the final accessory for your outfit.' Bella rubs her hands together. 'I'll timetable a more demanding exercise plan for the next month. Just to keep you in tip top shape.'

'We could just carry on as we—'

Bella held up her hand. 'I know best.'

I've given up trying to argue. She winks.

I head downstairs, her words in my ears. I don't like thinking of Casey as an accessory. He has become so much more than that. I walk into the downstairs entrance area and stop dead. Kath stands there. And Nora. Pauline too. The middle of June. Of course. Kath's birthday comes soon after Pauline's. She talked about it a few weeks ago whilst we were still on friendly terms. She didn't get the chance to cook for people anymore and had felt excited about laying on a small buffet. She used to do that at work when someone was leaving, or if a longstanding patient had finally become well enough to go home.

'What a lovely outfit,' says Nora, tentatively. 'You look like an understated Elizabeth Taylor in Cleopatra.'

The others nod and give small smiles but look at each other as if they are unsure what to do.

'Happy Birthday, Kath,' I say, surprised by an ache in my chest. She hadn't invited me tonight.

Who could blame her, says a gentle voice in my head that I haven't heard in a while.

'Enjoy every minute of your party, sweetheart. You deserve it.'

I go outside, relieved to see the taxi. Bella ordered it so that I'll arrive a little late. She thinks of every last detail. Firstly, she said it won't do Casey any harm to be kept waiting a short while. But, more importantly, it means Lenny and Beatrix will probably be there already and I can make the grand entrance she and I have dreamed of for so long.

I feel like a princess going to a ball. Perhaps I should have outgrown such outdated fantasies. But the thing is, I never really grew into them. No Prince Charming was ever going to marry Violet Vaughan. I never had a date for the prom. I didn't mind. Uncle Kevin told me heroes came in many different guises. I didn't need a dictionary to explain that word. I just understood what he meant and agreed. At nights I didn't dream of being swept off my feet by a handsome man in armour. I wanted to be friends with brave Dorothy out of *The Wonderful Wizard of Oz* or run through the jungle with Mowgli. I wanted to share the wit of Matilda or become part of the mystery-solving Famous Five.

Lenny was the first person to make me seriously consider the appeal of those romantic fairy tales.

'That'll be twenty quid, love,' says the driver.

We pull up. I pay him and get out.

The dress code is formal and Casey doesn't disappoint in his ability to stand out. His black jacket is gothic style, emblazoned with red outlines of roses. He wears a black shirt and red bow tie. The cut accentuates his broad shoulders.

'You look stunning, Vi.'

'You too. I love that jacket. It's so you.'

I kiss him on the cheek and heat instantly flames between my legs. We go inside and both stop to drink in the luxurious lobby. Two statues of the Egyptian dog god Anubis stand on either side of the reception, the top halves of their bodies resembling black jackals. Framed prints of hieroglyphic writing are dotted across the sunny blonde walls. The floor is ornate tiling. Glossy-leaved tropical plants accentuate the heatwave feel. In a bigger hotel, it would shout tacky, but in Anubis it looks exotic and sensual.

A woman introduces herself. She's an old intern from Thoth who decided that being an agent was more for her. We haven't seen each other for about six months. It takes her a few minutes to realise who I am. The look on her face feels like a shot of adrenalin. Casey shoots me a sideways glance.

'It must be the airbrush tan,' I say and we walk up a flight of stairs. I take a deep breath as we enter the hotel's biggest conference room. I must buy the current interns a thank you present. In conjunction with the hotel manager, they've done a top-notch job of preparing the venue. It's simple and classy, with just a few gold balloons featuring the number twenty. There's a chocolate fountain in the corner run by a waitress who is also serving small cupcakes bearing the Thoth logo. On the way in, the interns wearing badges hand out drinks and personally welcome each guest. The projector is set up on a table at the front draped with a gold tablecloth, underneath which the interns have stashed the goody bags. Vases of terracotta lilies with sprayed gold leaves stand in the middle of each table and add to the dusty Egyptian ambiance. The band members, dressed in tuxedos, play smooth jazz from the back. We're twenty minutes late and already the room is two-thirds full.

Casey and I each take a glass of champagne. I nod across the room to Felicity who grimaces and points to her watch. She'll be giving her presentation at nine. A blogger comes over and thanks me for a book bundle I recently sent her. Irfan appears with Farah by his side. He'll give a short talk about our children's fiction department and he runs the key points of it past me again after Casey has shaken both their hands.

'What a beautiful dress, Farah,' I say about her turquoise silk saree with sequins and a leaf print.

She doesn't meet my eye. One of the mini scones is in her hand.

Felicity and I had discussed the menu at length.

'Nothing worse than fussy food. Keep it British. Simple. I don't want Sushi or polenta chips.' Felicity had pulled a face.

We'd decided on mini jacket potatoes oozing with chives and sour cream. There were tiny cornets of fish and chips. Beef-filled Yorkshire puddings. Mini cheesecakes and colourful fruit tartlets.

I fantasized a lot about food these days. Perhaps I'd treat myself to a few mouthfuls tonight.

'And good evening to the most stunning woman in the room,' says Hugo. 'May I?' He grins at Casey and leans forward to kiss me. He shakes Casey's hand and points out several guests. Hugo's never needed name badges. I don't see Lenny and Beatrix.

'Do you recognise anyone here?' I ask Casey as Hugo disappears to mingle.

He scours the room. 'Yes. An author from a Chapter Battle session last year. They finally signed a deal.'

'You don't mind if I leave you for a few seconds? I really ought to just check in with Felicity and—'

'Hey! Lenny!' Casey says in a loud voice.

Shit.

This is for real.

My heart beats. Our paths haven't crossed since the launch of Gary's Smith's *Bubbles*.

This is everything I've worked towards. Proving to Lenny, and Beatrix, that I am good enough. That I matter. That people can't just toss me aside like yesterday's paper or an empty takeaway cup.

He comes over. I feel sick. Not elated.

'Casey, mate,' they shake hands.

He turns to me.

Chapter 27

'Violet?' He steps back.

A woman standing behind Lenny turns her head. It's Beatrix. Full of confidence, I smile in her direction. Her jaw drops, then tightens as her eyes run over my body that's slimmer than hers. More golden. More slick. It's been worth every minute of juicing, jogging and learning about cosmetics just to watch her cheeks turn a fiery red.

'You?' she says. 'But… how… I mean…' She stops speaking and scowls.

'Good evening, Beatrix,' I reply coolly. 'How brave of you to wear that A line dress. It's very department store.' I look up at Casey and pull him closer. Meaningfully, I look back at her and by the way she swallows, I can tell she knows I've got closer to him than she did.

Despite the black stilettos, for a second she looks small. Whereas I feel like the fifty-foot woman.

Or do I? This is everything I've wanted. Yet Beatrix actually looks great. Professional. Like she always does. Mouth open, she stares my way.

'Vi?' Casey looks confused. 'Is there something I should know?'

His words snap Beatrix out of her stupor and she rummages for her phone. Presses on an icon. For the first time I notice the distance between her and Lenny. They have no eye contact and she makes a particular effort not to get close to him. She holds up her phone and the smile drips off my face as if gravity is pulling it onto the dance floor.

It's a photo of the old me from my out-of-date Thoth editorial profile. My hair is curly. I'm wearing no make-up and my face is framed by my old purple glasses.

'I hadn't realised this was a fancy dress party, Casey,' says Beatrix in a steady voice. 'Violet has certainly disguised herself – although I'm not sure what she's done with all those excess pounds.'

I squeeze his hand. 'I simply fancied a change,' I say, keeping my tone bright. 'I mean anyone can make themselves slim and blonde. It's not as if it's anything special.' Bella's words sounded so good when I practised them but now they just seem bitter.

Her perfectly threaded eyebrows knit together and she shrugs. 'I wouldn't know about that. I was born this way. This is me. It doesn't require any work.'

Her words puncture my lungs and with them my self-esteem.

'Please don't tell me you've signed with Thoth, Casey,' she continues. 'Did Violet tell you that she used to date Lenny – before he left her for me?'

Casey's arm feels slack against mine.

'I thought not. She's used you to get her own back. Hats off to you, Vaughan. I didn't know you had it in you. It's quite flattering, really, that—'

'It's not true,' I stutter.

'And if her boss put her up to it, well, everyone knows I stole the *Earth Gazer* series from under Thoth's nose.'

Casey looks at me. 'I didn't.'

'I guess Felicity would see signing you as the perfect payback,' she says and smirks. 'What's more—'

'Christ, just shut up,' Lenny says to her in a low voice. 'Can't you tell that something isn't quite right here?'

What does he mean by that?

I wait for Beatrix's retort but she simply looks puzzled for a moment, looks at me again and then backs off. Lenny is just about to speak when a senior agent he works for collars him. With a backwards glance, he walks off.

No.

No, I internally scream.

That did *not* just happen.

Not after months and months of hard work.

I feel sick. Dizzy. Beatrix can't crush my plans. That stupid bitch can't be allowed the last word.

And then there's Casey. Not the author or tool for payback, but the man who's stolen my heart; a heart that will spontaneously combust if he gives it back.

I grab Casey's hand and drag him out of the party room. After a quick word with a member of staff, we're allowed to use the manager's office. I shut the door behind us and pull Casey down onto the chestnut leather, studded chaise longue. I reassure him that I'll explain everything. That things are not what they seem.

Does that include me?

'What's going on?' he says.

I can do this. I can save our relationship. Yet I have to turn away for a moment, too ashamed to let him look at me.

Am I ashamed of the old version on the phone – or ashamed of the woman I've become?

'Vi. Is it true? What Beatrix said? That Lenny left you for her? About the *Earth Gazer* series? That all I've been is a player in some sort of revenge plan?'

'No. I mean, maybe at first.' I can't lie anymore. I just can't. The words fall out in between painful gulps. 'Beatrix was so desperate to sign you. I knew that turning up at this party with you on my arm would—'

Casey's head drops into his hands. 'I thought we were good together. I can't believe that you've just used me.'

I pull his hands away. 'We *are* good, Casey. My feelings changed. Can't you tell how much I like you?'

He looks up. 'I don't know. I don't know you. You've seemed like such a sweet person – and intelligent, with ambitious goals and integrity. Have I been dating a real person or has it all been an act? I don't get it. And why change your appearance so much?'

'Please don't do that.'

'What?'

'Patronise me. You saw the photo.'

'You looked great.'

'Oh come on – just be honest.' My voice trembles. 'A man like you wouldn't have looked twice at the old Violet.'

'A man like me? And now I'm a liar? Talk about judging a book by its cover.' His voice is hard-edged now.

Casey pulls out his phone. Enters Instagram. Presses on a photo and shows it to me. It's a woman with very short black hair. She's a little bigger than I used to be. Not a scrap of make-up. A fun-filled smile.

'That's my last girlfriend. We were together for almost a year.' He puts his phone away. 'You assumed things about me that aren't true. You judged me by my appearance just as you seem to think people used to judge you. I'd say that makes you a hypocrite of the highest order and not the person I've… I've… Do I know you at all?'

I blink rapidly.

It's as if I've gone to the cinema and ended up watching the wrong movie.

'But… but Lenny would never have looked at Beatrix if she'd looked like me.'

'Who or what has made you believe that?'

I think for a moment. Only one name came to mind.

I'd hung onto her every word. I needed a friend and she provided the answers I couldn't find.

Bella.

'Please. This is just a misunderstanding. What we've got… I've never felt like this about anyone.' My eyes feel wet. 'You've got to believe me.'

'How can I believe a single word that comes out of your mouth?' He shakes his head. 'You know the crazy part? Something that all fell into place when Beatrix showed me that photo? Something that's been niggling at me?'

'What?'

'It started when I washed your hair at the salon and realised it was curly. This jolted a memory but I haven't been able to pin it down before this moment. I remember because it was Valentine's Day. We were on the underground. You had your jumper on inside out. I loved your style. And your hair. I thought that was a woman I'd like to ask out.'

The tall man in the cap who'd worn sunglasses even though it was winter? He'd flirted with me. How striking he was.

That was Casey?

He'd liked me, the old me that Lenny had dumped?

But that would mean… everything Bella's said…

Could she have been wrong?

'You'd really have manipulated my career, regardless of what was best?' Casey wrinkles his nose. 'And here I am thinking you truly loved *Alien Hearts*.'

'I did. Do. Casey, at least believe this.' I kneel on the floor and take his hands.

Please don't let me lose him.

'Books have always been what it's about for me. Not the authors. I couldn't have encouraged you to sign with Thoth if I didn't passionately and utterly believe it was the best editorial home for your story.'

He removes his hands from mine and stands up. I get to my feet too. My knees feel as if they might buckle.

'I've been so confused these last few months – about myself,' I say. 'My friends. My life. Everything, apart from you. You're the one thing I'm sure about.'

Casey straightens his jacket.

'Don't go,' I whisper.

Chapter 28

I sit slumped by the bar and nod for another top up. A waiter fills my glass with prosecco. I hardly notice his flirtatious smile. Felicity's presentation went well, I think. I'm not really listening when she comes over to talk.

'I've just been speaking to Casey Wilde,' she says in an abrupt voice.

'That's nice.'

'I had no idea you knew him so well. He politely told me that he's withdrawing his submission. That you tried to acquire his book using underhand means. What's wrong with you lately? Have you any idea what a bad stain this is on Thoth's reputation?'

She shakes her head. Tells me to meet her first thing Monday morning in her office. I take another mouthful of my drink. Gary approaches me, still sailing high on the crest of his debut success. *Bubbles* is in the last selection of this year's Young Adult Book Prize. He doesn't stop chatting, which suits me. I just grunt in the right places. The jazz band play more loudly now. Irfan and Farah dance alongside Hugo and one of the interns.

For once ignoring the sugar content, I order cocktails and after a while begin to feel queasy. A man sits next to me. I see his grey suit from the corner of my eye. It's Lenny.

The man who's caused so much hurt.

I slip off the stool that almost falls over as my feet touch the floor and hurry towards the front table. Behind that in the corner of the room is a door for staff that I noticed earlier. The manager said it offers a backstage route to the kitchen and outside for staff cigarette breaks. I don't engage with the familiar faces saying hello as I stumble that way. I yank the door open and hurry down the corridor. A Fire Exit sign at the end catches my attention. Grateful for the anonymity, I rush outside. The air smells of stale tobacco but no one is there. It's a small backyard with recycling bins and a metal bench. I sit down and stare at a pile of dustbin bags. One of them is torn and spewing out rubbish.

The door creaks. The grey suit sits down next to me again. I move further towards my end of the bench.

'Are you okay? Where's Casey?'

'Where do you think?' I give a hollow laugh. 'He left. Thanks to you and your stupid girlfriend.'

'We've split up.'

'So that's why you are showing concern? My God, you really are a complete prick. She's thrown you out so you're trying to get back into my flat?' The volume of my voice increases. 'Well forget it. Someone else has your room now. And as if—'

'I finished with her. And I've finally got my partnership at the agency so I've found a bedsit to tide me over until my pay rise comes in and I can get my own place.'

'Congratulations,' I say with a sneer. 'What swung it? Did Beatrix somehow exert her influence? Did she shag one of the partners?'

'Beatrix has got nothing to do with it. It's just all the hours I've put in and a windfall at work financially. There's going to be an auction next week for *Alien Hearts*. I think it'll go to six figures.'

'Poor Beatrix, after all the effort she put into snagging you.'

'It wasn't like that.'

'Oh, please.' I hope my face reflects utter disgust.

Lenny stares at me. 'I'm worried, Violet. What's happened to you?'

'Nothing,' I snap. 'Although a bit of honesty from you would make the evening a great deal better. So, tell me – what *was* it like, then?'

Lenny loosens his tie and his eyes ran over my frame. 'I guess I at least owe you the truth. It was never about Beatrix chasing me in order to get to Casey. Not in the beginning, anyway. We just fancied each other, that's all, after meeting at a book launch. She didn't even know I worked at an agency.'

Everything went into slow motion for a second as I looked at him. '*What*?'

'She flirted with me. I found that flattering. I guess I was a little in awe. And,' His cheeks flushed, 'I'd be lying if I didn't admit that I thought she could be useful to know, with her reputation and contacts.'

'Yeah, well what's not to like about her.'

He shrugged. 'I wouldn't say Beatrix was my usual type, but when I was with her, I don't know, somehow, I felt important and more connected to where I wanted to be in the publishing world. I didn't fall for her like I fell for you.'

I blink several times.

His words replay in my head and our surroundings sway for a second.

Surely I must have misheard?

'Why… why did you leave then?'

'We'd grown apart. You must have noticed.'

We had been talking less. But I still loved him.

'Our relationship, it was the best I've ever had, Violet. It was. But I just didn't feel the same anymore. That made it easy for me to cheat. I'm not proud, but that's the truth.'

'But I logged into your Facebook account to get Casey's contact details. I saw your messages. You told Beatrix sex with her was the best you'd ever known.' I realise Lenny is holding my hand and take it away, even though I feel like I'm drowning in confusion.

'Oh Christ. You should never have seen that. Violet, I'm sorry. I just got carried away. Looking back, our relationship was pretty shallow. I said things like that which I never really meant.'

'What about the messages with your brother after he first met me? You told him looks aren't everything.'

Lenny looks puzzled. 'So? I meant it. My brother's only just turned twenty and, well, let's just say he's yet to realise there is more to beauty than the supposed perfect hourglass figure. I said that because you're a real woman. A real woman I always loved for being different, unique, gorgeous. You must have realised that.'

I screwed up my forehead. He's right. I did. Until listening to Bella gave rise to doubts.

'What about birthday and Christmas gifts? You always just grabbed the same vouchers and chocolates.'

'Vouchers? Chocolates?' Lenny rubbed his forehead. 'But you always seemed so happy with those and said they made the perfect gift.'

And they had. It was Bella who made me think otherwise – that Lenny was lazy when it came to me, and thoughtless.

Bella.

'But you never used to introduce me to your friends.' Not like Casey did.

Lenny shrugs. 'You aren't – weren't – the most social animal. And there's nothing wrong with that. I thought you'd prefer things that way.'

I stare into my lap. My hands shake and suddenly my wrists look really small.

'But why, Lenny? Why didn't you tell me all this when we split up? I asked for more of an explanation, but you kept brushing me off.'

'I admit, I was a coward. I couldn't face breaking up with you before Valentine's Day. I was going to do it straight afterwards. But talking it all through… I just couldn't face it. I'm sorry. It was the least you deserved.'

I don't know what to say.

'But we had fun, didn't we? Moving in together? Cooking? Those Sunday mornings in bed? I'll always have fond memories.' His voice wavers. 'You were my first love, you know?'

You were mine too.

'You didn't just move in with me to get cheap rent?'

'You really believe that?' Lenny stands up and paces the yard. 'I know I've been a shit about the way I left you, but have you always had so many doubts about the way we were?'

No. Not until my new flatmate moved in. Not until she explained how things were and made me realise how people have walked over me. So, I've followed her plan to the letter to regain my self-esteem. But it hasn't worked. Most of the time I feel like crap. I recall Kath's words. She called Bella a parasite.

I've lost friends.

I've lost me.

I've lost sense of what me and Lenny meant.

'Remember that holiday you paid for, when I was skint?'

Numbly I nod.

'We got a cheap week in Barcelona and you had a go at me over my male pride. You insisted on paying and I didn't like it. But we talked it out and you made me realise that if it was the other way around, I'd do the same – that it was just due to financial circumstances and nothing to do with me failing as a man.'

'So what?'

'I couldn't afford the rent when you bought the flat. We both knew that. I didn't want to be a dick like I was over Barcelona – so I thought I'd be the one to suggest me paying less and make it easier for you. And I was also mad keen to live with you, for us to share a bed together every night.' He sits down again and shakes his head. 'What's happened? What's got your thinking so screwed?' His eyes run over my body. 'You look so… I'm really concerned.'

'You aren't supposed to be concerned,' I say angrily. 'You're supposed to be widely jealous. Enthralled. That's how Bella said things would turn out.'

'Who's Bella?'

'She… she's…' I gasp for a moment as if I'm about to have a panic attack. Lenny. Casey. Kath and Farah. The Book Club. I can't take it anymore.

'Why have you and Beatrix broken up?' I croaked.

He broke eye contact. 'You were right all along. I should have listened. At first, we got together because of a powerful, mutual attraction, but when that started to wear off, I sensed that Beatrix felt that waning of passion too. But by then she knew about my job and was only staying with me to try and sign Casey. I had it out with her. After a long argument, she confessed as much.' He held me close. I felt his hand brush over my spine. 'Christ, I'm so sorry, Violet. For everything. I had no idea—'

Half-heartedly I push him away.

'You were my best friend for so long. My lover. You deserved better. What can I do to help? You name it.'

Am I in some parallel universe where Lenny is full of affection and respect for me?

His voice wavers. 'I'll do anything to make it right.'

Hot, emotional tears that have percolated for months trickle down my cheeks. My shoulders start to shudder. A lump rises in my throat and ejects the words I've held back for so long. They come out as a wail.

'I want Uncle Kevin. I want him back. I still do. Get rid of the nightmares, Lenny. I can't stop him jumping. He looks so sad and there's nothing I can do.'

Quickly Lenny takes off his jacket and wraps it around my shoulders. I wipe my eyes and black kohl streaks across the back of my hand.

Lenny's face has gone white. 'He's always sounded like such a great guy.'

'He was my hero. And then he disappeared. There was nothing I could do about it. Nor could the police. Or the firemen. And Uncle Kevin couldn't save himself. You were my hero too, Lenny. I didn't know I needed saving until we met. But you opened up a part of my heart that for so many years felt safer to keep closed.'

Lenny takes a handkerchief out of his trouser pocket and passes it to me.

'At least I had Flint to see me though when I was at school. And now my flatmate Bella.' Even though I've developed doubts about her, she's all I've got.

'Who's Flint? You've never talked about him before. And this Bella. Would it help if I call her? At least let me do that.'

'No!'

I give Lenny back his jacket. It feels scary to let down the guard Bella has helped me build. What if I get hurt again? I let in Casey and now I'm paying the price.

But I won't let Lenny ring Bella. Her secret is mine.

Flint had a secret, too, that I kept – just like I've kept Bella's. And Mum killed him when she found out.

Killed him with no regrets.

Ended the existence of a boy who was nothing but loyal and funny and sweet, who thought I was good enough and the perfect fit.

I won't let the same thing happen to Bella.

Despite the things my flatmate might have got wrong, without her I'm nothing.

Me and Flint arrive at the foot of the treehouse. My stomach feels screwed up like an empty crisp bag. As expected, it has been easy to slip out of the house. Mum came upstairs and read me a story before turning out the lights. Even though I hate her at the moment for trying to stop me seeing Flint, I gave her a really big hug. I wanted to tell her I loved her but couldn't quite manage that. When my watch said it was fifteen minutes later, I got dressed, grabbed my coat and rucksack and crept out the back door. Flint was waiting. I knew he would be. He's always there when I need him.

It's cold. My breath is white as if I'm breathing out smoke. That usually makes me feel grown up but right at this moment I feel like a very little girl. An owl hoots. Owls are clever. Am I? Is this the right thing to do?

'Are you scared?' I whisper.

Flint shakes his head and his ponytail flicks from side to side like a horse's tail. 'Nah. Tim is cool. This is going to be SO much fun. I'll be a real man after this adventure. My brothers won't be able to boss me around anymore.'

It is so dark. Not even the moon shines through the treetops. I already miss my warm bed.

'Don't be a wuss, Violet. You're doing the right thing. This way you won't have to ever see Alice again. And your Uncle Kevin would be so proud. He travelled the whole world. The least you can do is see a bit more of England.'

He's right. Flint always makes me feel better. He climbs up the rickety steps first, turns around at the top and violently jerks his head for me to follow. I do as I'm told.

Tim is waiting, rubbing his hands together. He clears his throat. 'Hi guys.'

Why does he sound nervous? And he's a bit out of breath. I hand him a sandwich and he smiles before wolfing it down.

'You're decent to me, Violet,' he says. 'And I hope one day you'll realise that I've only ever wanted to be decent to you.'

What does that mean? I shiver – and it's not from the cold.

Voices appear from the bottom of the stairs.

Voices I don't know. Adult ones. Strangers' ones.

My heartbeat sounds really loud in my ears. 'Who's that?' I whisper.

'Nice people,' says Tim. 'Nothing to worry about.' He bites his nails.

My hands feel clammy in my gloves. I look around but Flint isn't there. Where has he gone?

What's happening? Footsteps sound on the wooden ladder. I suddenly need the toilet.

'Tim? I don't want to stay here anymore.' My voice sounds all wobbly.

He smiles. 'It's okay, Violet. Everything's going to be all right.'

For the first time in a while, I think good things about Mum. Her arms around me. Her warmth. Her closeness that smells of cooking and laundry.

Tim reaches out and takes my hand. He squeezes it. A woman's face appears. She's got crooked teeth and smells of cigarettes.

She looks scary.

'May I come in?' Without waiting, she ducks her head and crawls next to me. She sits down.

I feel as if I've done something really, really stupid. I try to run but my legs won't move.

'I want to go, I don't like this treehouse anymore, don't try to stop me,' I shout.

Chapter 29

I'm lying in a bed. It feels softer than my own. I open my eyes. A crack in the curtains lends the room enough light for me to distinguish the detail. Books, make-up, joss sticks, posters of Shawn Mendes.

I'm in Irfan's house. This room must belong to his eldest daughter. Farah went to a Mendes concert with her last year. I glance at the digital clock on the small pine table by my side. It is already ten o'clock.

I stare at the ceiling. It's coming back to me now. Lenny leaving me in the backyard as I tried to stop crying. Farah appearing. Her arms around me. Her and Irfan bundling me into their car. A cup of tea before bed. Me being grateful for no questions. I look under the covers. Farah lent me one of Irfan's shirts.

Someone knocks at the door and I sit up. Farah comes in. I shuffle up into a sitting position and another mug of tea finds its way into my hands.

'How do you feel?' she says.

'I'm okay. Sorry about last night. I must have had too much to drink. I'll go when I've finished this and—'

'No,' she says firmly. 'You relax here for as long as you like. If you want anything to eat just let me know. I'll be downstairs if you need anything.' She turns to go.

I reach out my hand and tug on the bottom hem of her blouse. I recall doing that to Mum when she used to leave my room at night. I'd always beg for just one more story.

She sits on the bed.

'Can you ever forgive me?' I say. 'Last night – Casey, Lenny, it's made me realise – I'm so sorry if I've upset you.'

'And I'm sorry for not realising just how hard it hit you – about Lenny and Beatrix. Whilst I was worried about this new regime of yours, I don't think I fully understood just how much… how much you've been struggling.'

'I've messed everything up,' I whisper. 'I don't even know who I am anymore. I thought I was so empowered, taking charge of my life and turning it around, but now I'm not so sure.'

Farah takes my hand. 'I've never talked to you much about my life before meeting Irfan.'

'You grew up in Leicester, didn't you?'

'Yes – although, as you know, I was born in Pakistan. We moved here when I was six. I loved growing up in Leicester. It's home to the widest number of religions of all the cities in this country. I really felt at one with the diversity. I got a job in a coffee shop in the sixth form and went clubbing with colleagues. My parents were great. They understood that I needed to embrace English culture in order to be happy and make friends. Yet I knew it was always part of their plan that one day I would have an arranged marriage. As I got older, we would have trips back to Pakistan. Very sociable ones where I met extended family and respected locals. My parents did their best to compromise and let me go to university. I moved back home for a while afterwards. My idea was to save and become financially independent.'

I nod.

'I loved – do love – my parents very much and had managed to swerve the subject of an arranged marriage for years. However, the pressure really started when my older sister got married. Everyone kept saying I was next, but I wasn't interested. At the same time I didn't want to disappoint my parents. I saw the joy my sister's union had brought them and they were so thrilled when the family of a successful businessman, Adeeb, showed an interest. I just couldn't bear to let Mum and Dad down and somehow found myself pretending to go along with it.'

'But you didn't love him?'

'No. He was a kind man, but not my type. He didn't even read novels.'

We exchanged looks and both managed a smile. I took a mouthful of the strong tea.

'The pretence started to take its toll – the weeks of acting as if I was this perfect daughter, happy to do things the traditional way. I'd stopped eating all the Western junk food and drinking alcohol. My dress style became more modest. I was only a size ten back then.'

Heat flushes into my cheeks. 'Farah, I never meant—'

She pats my arm. 'All I'm saying is, I modelled myself to be the perfect obedient, pretty-little-wife material. Over time, I became fond of the man Adeeb, but just as friends, and the deceit started to eat away at me even more. We didn't meet often. He still lived in Pakistan, but when we did, I play-acted with him too. Things had gone so far I didn't know how to call things off. I didn't know how to tell him or my parents that I wanted a career and my own flat – that I wasn't ready to settle down yet and when I did, that I wanted to choose my own partner. I just wanted to be myself.'

'What happened?'

Farah smooths down the duvet. 'I had a breakdown. Ended up in hospital. I didn't know who I was anymore… just like you now. Mum and Dad were horrified.' She swallowed. 'I'm so lucky that all they wanted was for me to get better – even if that meant the marriage being called off. That was a massive thing for them and I'll never forget it. And Adeeb was very understanding. I think he felt the same way too. He works in Dubai now and is married.' She pauses. 'The thing is, Violet – all the time I was pretending, I thought of myself as doing the right thing and being so strong and such the role model daughter. But I was living a lie. It nearly killed me.'

'How come you've never talked about this before?'

'Because it's a part of my life I don't care to remember. And it's so long ago. I can't relate to being that person anymore. These days, it sounds corny, but I just follow my heart. I eat too much. I'm not always smartly dressed. I enjoy a glass – or three – of wine. I have my own bank account. I'm not perfect, by any means, but my head's straight because I'm being true to myself.'

She takes my tea and puts it on the table next to the digital clock. She leans forward and embraces me.

'That's all that matters, Violet, that your conscience is happy. It'll tell you if it's not. Anyone else's opinion of what you should look like or how you should behave is irrelevant. That includes this Bella, even if she is trying to help. Perhaps if I met her and—'

I shake my head violently.

The doorbell rings. Farah backs off about meeting my friend and instead we chat about the party. Someone knocks at the door. Irfan.

'Everything okay in here?'

Farah and I nod.

'Violet, you've got a visitor. Apparently Lenny went to your flat to find her.'

'Violet, please don't be scared, I'm here to help.'

I stop shouting and my breathing slows a little. At least the woman sounds friendlier than she looks. I clasp my hands together. Must be brave. Must be my own hero.

She loosens her collar. The uniform doesn't look very comfortable. 'In fact, we can take you home right now.'

'*Home*?' I stare at Tim. 'You said you were my friend. Now I'll get into trouble.'

'Tim did the right thing,' says the police officer. 'It's very dangerous out here at night. And your mum would have been so panicked, finding out that you'd gone.'

'No she wouldn't,' I mumble. 'She's got Ryan.'

'Violet. I'm sorry,' says Tim. 'You're a great little girl, but this is for the best. I thought about it all day. I was just going to do a runner. But I'd have been worried knowing that you were here, on your own, waiting for me. I went down to the police station and then ran all the way back here so that you weren't on your own if you got here early and the police or your mum hadn't arrived. One day, you'll understand – I promise.'

'Adults' promises don't mean much. Uncle Kevin promised he'd be home at Christmas.'

The police officer jerks her head. 'Come on. My colleague, Paul, he's waiting for you down on the ground. He's just spoken to your mum who can't wait to see you. She's really worried.'

'I'm going to get told off.' Tears slide down my face.

'No, you aren't,' she says softly. 'Your mum will just be really pleased to have you back safely.'

The police officer tells me her name is Clare and takes my rucksack whilst I climb down the ladder. The man called Paul helps me down the last few steps. Flint's not around. I'll have to wait until I see him tomorrow and ask where he went.

Clare says something to Tim about him going to the station with one of her friends and making a statement. The police would then find him a hostel. I wonder if that's something Tim's lost.

Tim gives me a quick hug. As usual he smells. I don't mind. Never have. I thought he was my friend, but I'm on my own again. Apart from Flint.

'Take care,' he says. 'Things will get better. Your life won't always be like this.'

Clare and Paul take me home. Mum must have rung Ryan. He's waiting in the hallway when I walk in. I stare at the floor, waiting for angry words. I say it was Flint's fault. That he persuaded me to do it. I feel bad but I bet his mum's so cool she won't be cross.

Instead of telling me off, Mum's crying and I can hardly understand what she's saying. She gives me the tightest hug and tells me how much she loves me. She asks Ryan to make hot chocolate.

Ryan crouches on his knees and stares me straight in the face.

He's been crying too.

I don't know what to say.

He pulls off my woolly hat and says what a sensible girl I was to dress up warmly. He asks if I want a biscuit with my drink as a special treat. I nod.

Clare and I go into the lounge. There's another woman there from something called Social Services. I have to sit with her on my own for a minute. She asks me about the bruises. About Mum hitting me.

Apparently Tim thought I was making it up. Over the last two weeks, I've talked to him about Alice and he worked out it was her and her friends.

But for some reason the woman has to hear me say that it wasn't Mum.

I do. She believes me. Not long after that, she leaves but we might have to meet again.

Secretly I'm glad to be home again. Mum ran me a bath using her fancy bubbles. I'm glad until she tucks me up in bed and says tomorrow we need to talk about Flint. And that she'll be making an appointment with someone next week who will make me realise that Flint isn't really a good friend at all.

Chapter 30

There is a chair in front of the dressing table. Farah pulls it over to my bedside. She and Irfan leave. Kath sits down. She takes off her summer rain jacket and puts her handbag on the floor.

'Lenny actually came to get you?'

'He was looking for Bella. He came up and asked if I knew where she was. He thought she might be able to help you.' Kath moves to get comfortable. 'Lenny seems very worried, and determined to help sort things out. On the way over, he told me how much he'd valued your relationship and that he was mortified at how badly he'd behaved back in February. He didn't look well. I don't think he could have slept much last night.'

I couldn't cope with the idea of Lenny actually caring about me. Not at the moment. It was all too much to take in.

'Last night, did you enjoy your birthday buffet? I know you were looking forward to having everyone around.'

'Yes. We missed you though. I believe your big bash last night – things didn't go to plan.'

I shrug.

'What went wrong?'

I start slowly, but soon, word by word it all pours out. How Beatrix hadn't chased Lenny from the start. How

Casey thought I was only using him. How both Thoth *and* Alpaca had lost the chance to publish *Alien Hearts*.

'Is there any chance with Casey? What if you—'

'I don't think so and I just can't face seeing him again. Not now.'

I'd forgotten what a great listener Kath is.

'Thanks for coming by,' I say. 'But I'd better get back. Bella will be wondering—'

'No.' Kath raises her voice. 'Violet. Stop that.'

My eyes tingle.

'I know her secret.'

'I don't know what you mean.' I lift the tea mug to my lips, hoping it hides my face. I feel sick. My pulse quickens.

'You want me to say it?'

'No!' I slam the mug down on the bedside table. Tea spills over the sides.

'That time I went in because Flossie was caterwauling—' Kath carries on as if she didn't hear me.

'Speaking of which, I'd really better go.' I twist the duvet between my fingers. 'Flossie might be upset again.'

'All the clothes in Bella's room,' continues Kath. 'They've still got the labels on. The shoes haven't been worn. The make-up is still sealed. The bedsheets looked fresh.'

'Stop. I'm not listening. You don't know what you are talking about.' I pull the duvet up high and bury my face in it. A sense of dread fills my chest. The same dread that engulfed me when Mum used to take me to see someone to talk about Flint.

'Violet, you've got to face this. Bella isn't your flatmate. She doesn't work at a spa.'

I pull the duvet away. My hands curl into fists. 'Shut up! Yes she does!'

'Bella isn't real,' said Kath, quietly. 'She doesn't exist.'

'Don't be ridiculous! Of course she does. What a thing to say. We've gone to the cinema together. Drunk coffee. Shopped. Laughed. She's taught me how to cook healthy food and shown me all sorts of websites for my new lifestyle.'

'Is that where you first heard about Bella? On a website?' she asks gently.

I open my mouth to remonstrate but something catches in my throat.

'Tell me, darling. Tell me the truth. Don't carry this alone any longer.' Kath's eyes glisten.

I realise my hands are covering my face.

It's the secret. Bella's secret, which I've kept for months.

'Was she originally called Ana?'

I part my fingers so that I can see Kath through the gaps.

'You know I used to work in mental health. For six months, I worked in the eating disorders wing. We didn't let the patients go on the internet. The anorexics used to log onto websites that revered their illness and called it Ana, as if she were a best friend.'

I hear a whimper and realise it came from me.

'It's okay, Violet. I… I understand. I only want to help. Why call her Bella?'

My hands drop. I gag. Quickly Kath passes her hand-kerchief. I hold it to my mouth. Bile shoots into it.

I wipe my lips and we sit in silence, the secret hanging between us, between our friendship.

The secret that I realise made me sick.

'Ana… it sounded too abrupt and ugly,' I whisper. 'So I thought Anabella was more fitting – and then that give me the idea of Bella, meaning beautiful. It was perfect.'

I stare at Kath, bottom lip trembling.

Her forehead relaxes. 'Well done, love.'

'What for?'

'Admitting that. Facing up to the fact that Bella, she… she isn't real.'

I rock to and fro. 'I want her to be. I need her. I can't manage on my own.'

'Oh, darling, she's not good – you must know you've lost too much weight.'

'It gives me a high and I thought looking this way would make me happy.'

'Has it?'

At first, yes. But eventually? No. Quite the opposite.

'I want you to think about going to the doctor. I'll go with you, love. I can even make the appointment if—'

'No. No, I won't go through that again.'

'This has happened before?'

We don't speak for a while. Not until tears clear and I utter the F word.

'Flint. After my Uncle Kevin died – he helped me stand up to the bullies at school. I didn't feel so alone with him.'

Kath nods.

'Mum played along at first. I'd invite him to tea. She'd make an extra meal. I think she was glad to see me happy. I made him up after watching a programme about children who didn't go to school and whose parents let them do what they wanted. He was a free spirit and just what I needed.'

Another grown-up had pretended as well. Tim, the rough sleeper. Years later, Mum told me that he'd seen all sorts of mental health problems on the streets and didn't find it difficult to play along.

'How did it all end?'

'With Flint's help, I almost ran away. The police got called. Mum decided enough was enough and took me to a psychiatrist who specialised in treating children with imaginary friends.'

Kath nods again.

'I hated it. The psychiatrist was okay at first. He said pretend friends weren't unusual for someone of my age. But because Flint had encouraged me to stand up for myself in a way that was sometimes unpredictable and dangerous, I suppose, he agreed with Mum that more should be done to get rid of him. I was so angry. I didn't want to let go. I know it sounds mad, but I still miss him, you know?'

'We should never underestimate the power of the mind. It can convince us of almost anything.'

'Mum and the psychiatrist said I was taking refuge in the friendship with Flint and that this was holding me back socially. And looking back, that was true. But he helped me deal with my grief. I was only seven. I didn't know how to deal with losing my uncle. It felt as if Mum and the doctor had killed Flint.'

'I remember an article written a few years after 9/11. Several children who were related to those who died in the towers suffered with mental health problems. You haven't been alone in this.'

'School eventually got better. In juniors, I was put in a different class. I was less conspicuous in high school and I formed a small group of friends and learned to like myself. University consolidated this with laid-back friends who liked me for me and not what I wore or how much I drank. Then Lenny. But when he left, I wanted Flint back. I know it sounds childish, but he'd been the one constant all those years ago, when I also suffered an upheaval. Bella became the next best thing.'

We talk for more than an hour. Kath tells me about her work in the unit. How the people she helped care for felt more invincible the thinner they became. As if they didn't need anyone else. As if they were the best version of themselves. That if they were the slimmest in the room at least no one could beat them at that. All of this meant they could never be hurt again.

It's as if I'm listening to Bella.

'But then they crossed a line,' Kath says, 'and started to feel powerless.'

Farah pops her head around to ask if we'd like a sandwich. Kath leaves to help her in the kitchen. I get dressed and say I'll be down in a minute.

I look down at my wrist and see the friendship bracelet. I take it off. I kiss it hard and slip it into my handbag and know exactly where I'll put it. In the cardboard box under my bed that has the silver book pendant from Uncle Kevin and the two conkers from the prickly case Flint helped me open that first time in Applegrove Wood.

Bella's been such a support, but she was supposed to make me an even stronger, independent woman. Whereas looking back, in the last few months, it's as if it's been mostly about men.

I head down for lunch. Everyone looks pleased when I manage a sandwich and a half a packet of crisps.

Irfan drops me and Kath back home. She says she'll call around tomorrow. I can't hug them both tight enough.

I let myself into the flat. Flossie is waiting, but seems okay, even though she is alone. I sit down on the sofa and she jumps onto my lap. Uncle Kevin's cuckoo clock chimes and reminds me of something he said a long time ago, in a park.

'You can identify a true friend by one thing: a true friend accepts you for who you are.'

I glance down at Flossie whose paws massage my concave stomach. I think about acceptance. I was always good enough for Kath, Pauline and Nora, for Irfan and Farah, for Felicity, for Hugo before his wolf whistles, for Casey on the bus with my jumper inside out. And, as it turns out, in a way, even for Lenny.

But Bella. I swallow and glance towards the spare room. A realisation hits me.

She was the one for whom I was never good enough.

Author's Note

Dear Readers,

Thank you so much for buying this book. You are the reason I collapse into my chair every morning, after my bicycle ride, and turn on the computer. It's an exciting time for me at the moment in my career, moving from lighter to darker women's fiction. It means everything to know my stories are finding their way into the hands of old and new readers.

When I was younger I had a friend like Bella. Sometimes she still gets in touch and tries to influence the life I have now. So this story comes from a very personal place. If you've enjoyed it an Amazon review would be fantastic, without revealing Bella's secret. Those reviews really help books become more visible and I appreciate feedback so much.

I hope none of you have friends similar to Bella but if you do, please, don't be afraid to tell someone about them.

Take care.
Samantha

Acknowledgements

Knowing You is a story close to my heart. It's about finding your tribe that doesn't care what you look like or what clothes you wear. For them it's the in-side that matters, not the out. So it's only right that first and foremost I thank the three people who accept me completely for who I am. Martin, Immy and Jay I love you so much. Thank you for your unwavering and continued support.

I'd like to thank my exceptionally talented agent Clare Wallace, from the Darley Anderson Literary Agency. I've gone through a tough couple of years, on the personal front, and she's been there, helping me take my career in a different direction and face new challenges. She's a steady rudder on an impetuous boat that sometimes considers heading way off course!

Thanks to my brilliant publisher, Canelo, and the team who've worked so hard to give this story the very best chance – Michael Bhaskar, Kit Nevile and Ellie Pilcher.

Bloggers, especially Rachel Gilbey, thanks for all the support. I hope you've enjoyed this novel, set in the publishing world. As Violet might say, you are all super-stars. I never stop appreciating how generously you give your time to this industry.

And lastly but certainly not least, I'd like to thank Helen Bardsley for helping me keep myself safe from friends like Bella.

Lightning Source UK Ltd.
Milton Keynes UK
UKHW010645190220
358976UK00003B/107

9 781788 635158